KT-441-777

Lucy FitzGerald was born of an Irish mother and an English father. She spent much of her childhood in Ireland, and has travelled extensively in Europe, the Middle East and India. She is married to a musician and now lives in Wiltshire.

LIAR BIRDS

Lucy FitzGerald

BLACK SWAN

LIAR BIRDS
A BLACK SWAN BOOK : 0 552 99795 1

First publication in Great Britain

PRINTING HISTORY
Black Swan edition published 1998
Reprinted 1999

Set in 11pt Melior by
County Typesetters, Margate, Kent

Black Swan Books are published by Transworld Publishers Ltd,
61–63 Uxbridge Road, London W5 5SA,
in Australia by Transworld Publishers (Australia) Pty Ltd,
15–25 Helles Avenue, Moorebank, NSW 2170,
and in New Zealand by Transworld Publishers (NZ) Ltd,
3 William Pickering Drive, Albany, Auckland.

Reproduced, printed and bound in Great Britain by
Clays Ltd, St Ives plc

For my mother

For Muncle and May

and all my cousins

LIAR BIRDS

ONE

Everyone in Ballycanty knows Mary Alice O'Shea is a superstitious old busybody. She's been superstitious and a busybody for most of this century, and now, with the millennium so close, there's little hope of her changing.

My grandmother Foley went to school with Mary Alice back in the Dark Ages of black woollen stockings and big bows brooding over your tortured ringlets, and she can vouch for both aspects of her character. It was Mary Alice O'Shea who said that no rain in Ireland meant the beginning of God's terrible judgement on the land. Well, as everyone in the world now knows, there was no rain that summer. And as for the beginning of God's judgement, it'll be up to you to decide.

Of course, we've had our moving statue and our dancing sun in Ballycanty just like everywhere else. Our statue is in the Lourdes grotto right by Dooley's bar, and this proximity accounts for the fact that no-one was inclined to believe Niall Murphy when, late one night, he said he saw the Virgin move her hands and her veil ripple in the breeze.

Our Virgin is a masterpiece of Italianate piety, her smooth face and joined hands painted too pink to be true and her blue eyes – the same enamel as her sash – raised to heaven. It's the shine on her I particularly dislike, and it's generally agreed she'd be more convincing looking down at Bernadette instead of upwards, and with dark eyes like an Israeli. Her rosary is free-hanging from her wrists. It's her third. The other two disappeared over the years, but miraculous intervention wasn't suspected in those days. About the time of Niall's story, moving statues were the stuff of every newspaper article, so despite their scepticism plenty of people went along to look at the Lourdes statue and stared so long their eyes began to spin like in the cartoons. Then they saw the lights coming out of her.

One thing leads to another, and before you could say Mary Robinson there was a rival crowd with a dancing sun, down by the Druid's Spring on the Wexford road the other side of town. The Wexford road doesn't lead to Wexford unless you take a few turns out of your way, and nobody knows who the Druid was, but that's Ireland for you.

As luck would have it, the Druid's Spring is on Mick Dooley's land, and Mick is a brother of John Dooley of the Grotto, and another publican. They say the Guinness runs in the family: they've all black blood. Anyway, the rumour was that Mick was going to charge ten pence a shot for water from the spring, whether you had it in a whiskey at the bar or scooped it up in a chained mug from rocks outside, because after the sun had spun over it, it was Holy Water. Sanctified or not, it was nearly the ruin of Mick. The regulars stopped going to him and traipsed all the way to John's instead; John wasn't charging extra for water with bits of moss in it. Mick was forced to take away the chained mug and cut his prices on all drinks for a week to entice the customers back again. They enjoyed themselves tormenting him every night with how the crack was better at John's and they were thinking of going back there for good, until he took another penny off a pint and put a bowl of free nuts on the bar. There was no more talk of holy springs after that.

Mary Alice, for once, wasn't having anything to do with the signs and wonders. Mary Alice is a woman with good quality knitwear and hair set in concrete at Bernie's every week, so she has a vein of worldliness despite the piety. She saw the photographs someone had taken of the Miracles of the Sun, and pushed them aside with contempt.

'Any fool can take a fotergraph like that if they pint the camera into the light. What'd Our Lady have to do with an old pagan Druid? There's a lot of eejits in this town that'd believe *annything*.'

My Nana Foley was contemptuous too, though not in front of Mary Alice. 'There's none more sceptical about other people's miracles than a superstitious old woman beaten at her own game,' Nana told us in the privacy of her own home. She pointed out that as Mary has her own holy well in her back garden, with statues of saints in little concrete niches all round it, if we'd only waited a bit instead of rushing off after the false lights at Mick's we'd have seen the sun spinning at No. 36 Dunmore Road. Mick Dooley's sun pre-empted Mary Alice's, as you might say, and stirred up a bit of professional jealousy.

All this was the year before the dry summer. The wonders withered away over the winter, though somebody did start up a prayer group. The people who went to it were the people who would join it anyway. It kept going, just, but didn't attract any more members. In the words of my Great Uncle Danny the Priest, 'Praying is dull work without a few little miracles on the way to keep up your interest.' By the following summer we were all of us – prayers and heathen alike – going mouldy for the lack of some action.

Ballycanty's a small town still, in spite of the housing estates they've built stretching up the slopes of the fields in the last ten years or so – long rows of light-weight Georgian front doors and *en suite* garages to give you the illusion you're living in Dublin or London or somewhere really smart. There's not much of a garden to any of them, but the webs of tarmac running between draw in all the middle-aged and affluent married youth of the community, lured by the fashionable novelty. Meanwhile down in the old town, among the grey pebble-dash housefronts and brown-painted window-frames, though there are two supermarkets

11

now and a pedestrianized shopping mall, the mind of old Ballycanty still lingers in the days when the farmers came in from the country to gossip and smoke and buy trousers and horses, and spend most of the day 'talking business' over the pints. They wore terrible old jackets with sagging pockets and dusty white along the shoulders where they'd leaned against somebody's wall. I can only just remember going along to look at the horses with my sister Josie.

The markets have long gone, but some things about Ballycanty will never change, and the way everyone knows who everyone else is related to, in the minutest detail, is one of them – 'The history of Adam's father' as Nana Foley calls it. But it isn't just a total recall game of 'Family Trees'. Every name has a little tag attached to it, like a plant in a nursery. 'Oh yes, Tommy – he was the one who went to England and lost his foot on a building site', or 'Shelagh – she was Annie's third daughter and it was her who had the handicapped baby'. The disasters are the important bits of the Latin names, the ones that identify the individual species.

Another thing that didn't look as though it was going to change – although that dry summer caused more than a drought – was the way that everyone thinks they know everyone else's affairs, inside out and outside in, and is entitled to pass judgement on them. I suppose villages and small towns the world over are like that, but our particular brand of gossip has a lot to do with the tribal mentality of the Celts: a passion for secrecy coupled with a thirst for public drama. We've grown men coming into the solicitors where I work who'll hardly tell you their name, in case you get to find out they're the ones having the boundary dispute – though the whole town is commentating on the fight and cheering on the contestants behind their backs. Then they'll pay their legal bills in notes from under the mattress rather than let the bank manager into their fiscal affairs. But those very same champions of privacy will be making a grand tragedy out of their neighbour's marital difficulties down at John Dooley's on a Saturday night.

We read a description of Gossip at school, translated from a Roman poet. Gossip was a woman of course, and a man writing the story. She spread everything, true and false; starting small, she swelled into a huge bird-monster, an eye under each feather, tongues and mouths all over and ears forever pricked for news. The only thing that struck me as really remarkable was that she was flying round ancient Carthage, when I'd have sworn she was born and breathed in Ballycanty.

In this town you need only *one* beady eye and *one* flapping ear, and with the usual oral equipment you can do more mischief than any old Roman poet could dream.

TWO

It was Oonagh Hennessy who first told me, in episodes like a TV soap you catch up on from friends.

Oonagh and I both work for McCormick's Solicitors. We're nothing so grand as solicitors ourselves, only glorified typists and earning accordingly. Oonagh has been there longer than I have, because she was the year ahead of me at school. She now calls herself secretary to Mr Joe McCormick, the old man of the firm. Joe has eyebrows on him like lichen, and even his bifocals have a frosty glaze, but Oonagh isn't wasted on him altogether. She's got one of those figures with the curves that spell SEX at you in banner headlines, and she wears tight clothes. My Grandmother Foley always described her as 'bold' and thought she'd come to a bad end, but that was only because she could speak up for herself at school and argue with the nuns. Now she's reduced to teasing Joe.

McCormick's is a big old private house converted into offices. It has draughty sash windows and a porch with pillars, and the offices themselves are far from streamlined and ultra-efficient, with occupants to match. The partners often have lunch-breaks that last all the afternoon while they meet their friends and make a bit of extra cash on the horses. I can't pretend that in the meantime the rest of us are crushed entirely under the weighty correspondence of our litigious clients. There are days when I've typed fewer than half a dozen letters.

Oonagh and I were in the ladies' cloakroom – a converted box – going through the morning's opening rituals. There's no room at all in there: the toilet cubicle is like a coffin on its end – you have to let your body sink down at a peculiar angle towards the seat with your knees and your head against the door, and if anyone opened it you'd topple out. The toilet cubicle takes up half the space.

'You'll never guess what I've heard – an amazing story!' Oonagh couldn't even wait to struggle out of her coat. 'The whole town's going wild with it!'

'Can't be,' I said crossly.

I hadn't had time to finish painting my nails, and I was late because I couldn't find the skirt I wanted to wear, and suspected my older sister Josie had taken it. I've two other older sisters besides Josie, but she's the one you'll hear most about. I didn't feel charitable towards her, as I'd been late arriving for work the day before. It's all very well for Oonagh to take an elastic view of time; she has the Venerable Joe McCormick the Boss in her hands (metaphorically speaking) like a child's catapult – stretching him, and letting him sag back, and then pinging him against random targets to distract him. It's different if you work for a woman; there's no chance of my pinging Mary Brennan, Wills and Estates, against anything of my own choosing.

'I haven't heard of it,' I said. 'Whatever it is.'

I had the pot of varnish on the edge of the basin, and I was trying to work round Oonagh who still had one arm in a sleeve.

'Just because Treesa Carmody's behind with the news, it doesn't mean everyone else is. All right then, I'll admit it – this one's exclusive!' She made a show of craning her neck round the coffin lid, and lowered her voice with the sheer exclusivity of it. 'There's at least one man in this town for certain has got an *unmentionable disease*!'

I finished my nail.

'Which unmentionable disease?'

There are so many unmentionable diseases now. They're all of them referred to by capital letters in hushed tones like Oonagh's. *He's got ME, she's got MS*

15

– *the Big C.* It's ironical how people openly allude to the Old Disgracefuls like syphilis and gonorrhoea, when they won't mention cancer. So as it surely wasn't one of the venereal afflictions, I couldn't think what Oonagh was talking about.

'Give you three guesses!'

That was destined to be the cliff-hanger until the next instalment. We were on our way down the corridor by then, and I'd got almost to Mary's office door.

'You'll have to tell me later,' I said. 'Or I'll be writing my own last will and testament.'

So that was the gist of Episode One.

Oonagh Hennessy, Rose Walsh and I used to think such a lot of ourselves when we were at school. We were an Unholy and Unoriginal Trinity, upsetting the nuns, what was left of them, by sticking up for abortion, homosexuals and Sinead O'Connor. We wore our school skirts too short, or too long, for the regulations, and make-up that it was only just possible to deny if you were brazen enough. With Oonagh as our leader, we clung on childishly to that primitive gang mentality – all for one and one for all – even into the Afterlife beyond the school gates.

At the time of the events I'm telling you about, we still thought a lot of ourselves: so worldly-wise, so cynical and polished we were positively dazzled by our own conceit. Determined that nothing could surprise us, we didn't allow ourselves to care about anything very much. The way we looked at it was this: it was a bad old world our parents brought us into, and short of suing them for abusing our right not to be born, which is not yet legal in Ireland, the solution was to take only one thing seriously – having fun.

As a lifestyle, hedonism is irresistible to a generation like ours. We were brought up on the right to freezer foods rather than humble thanks for bread and potatoes, and we can see no reason to take in anything that looks grey and starchy. Since it stands to reason that Life is wonderful while you're enjoying yourself, you owe it to yourself to pursue the enjoyment. You dance along to your own headphones, despising the silent plodders in your heart, and everything's grand – unless you trip. Then you discover there are pits mining this funworld, deep pits you don't even like to dream of, ready and waiting to swallow you in. You trip, and all of a sudden the music stops.

At the time Oonagh was amusing us both with the recounting of Ballycanty's own soap, I don't think I was aware that there were any pits at all.

Episode Two was relayed in Whelan's, in our lunch-hour. Whelan's is the only decent place for a cup of coffee in town. Once you're in there, you can stretch your imagination as far as a café in Paris or Milan – as they appear on the films anyway: smoked-glass table tops, metal-tube table legs shiny as platinum, and the lighting set like bulging eyes into the ceiling. Whelan's only opened a couple of years ago. At first everyone criticized it because it didn't fit in with the town's image, and then went to it out of curiosity. Now it's packed, and the tourists like it in the summer because of the colonial-style fans that stir the hot air about, and look as though they're doing some good. Oonagh and I went there nearly every day. Apart from the fans, we enjoyed the international ambience.

Oonagh smoked and I drank coffee, and we both ignored the pastries under the glass counter for the sake of our figures. We liked to think we talked in a sophisticated way about fashion, and the latest films, and perhaps planning a trip to Dublin for a bit of LIFE, as well as discussing men. In our own minds we were well-informed, incisive, witty – in short, two liberated Irishwomen.

The reality of our verbal exchanges wasn't quite up to the above. I'd started going out with Declan O'Connor that spring, and Oonagh was between boyfriends and fancying anybody with a good haircut. Usually, by the time we'd compared notes about the males in our lives, there wasn't a minute left for other topics.

'This mystery disease – what is it?'

I wasn't thinking when I asked – not anticipating the answer, if you know what I mean, so I was taken off guard. I'd been calculating how much time there was before starting back to the office; Ms Brennan, my own peculiar boss, had been filing her tongue.

'Aids,' Oonagh said, without any preliminary deep breaths or silences to warn me.

I stared at her. Her eyes were very blue, and excited. 'Say that again?'

'Aids!' she said again. 'You know, Acquired Immune Deficiency Syndrome.' Everyone thinks they know what the disease is, though it's harder to remember what the letters stand for.

'In *Ballycanty*?'

'In Ballycanty.'

It was a bit of a stupid conversation, but it shows you how stunned I felt. Ballycanty – *Ballycan'tbe*, as we say – the World's Backwater! Though we've been using the postage stamps for quite a while, and we've even got cable TV, they still measure out twine by the yard along the floor in Mooney's hardware store.

I'm ashamed to admit it now, but when Oonagh told me I couldn't take the news seriously. It was no more than an echo from a wider world outside where people *really* took drugs and murdered each other. In Ballycanty such an unlikely rumour would masquerade as hot gossip because there was nothing else going on. After a while it would be doomed to die away in the usual confusion, though its brief existence wouldn't be entirely forgotten. The Irish have long long memories, and years later the Ballycanteens would still be saying, 'Do you remember the time when . . . ?' and there it would be, blazing up again with the coals for the duration of a fireside tale.

Perhaps that's why we're all so fond of gossip: we're still a storytelling nation at heart.

'Who? How? Where?' I demanded.

'Isn't that what we all want to know?'

'You've no names then?'

Oonagh shook her black hair. 'I heard it last night from Joe Duffy. He said Dermot Reagan had told him, and he knew who one of them was but he's not saying.'

'You mean there's more than one?'

'Joe said Dermot told him it *might* be two. That was all. It's a deadly secret. No-one knows yet.'

'Except Dermot, Joe, you, me . . .'

Oonagh said, 'We shouldn't be laughing. Whoever has it is going to die. That's for sure.'

'We're all going to die,' I said. It was so glib. I was twenty-one that summer, and Death seemed so very far away. 'These two – how do they know for sure they've got it?'

'Dermot told Joe they'd been to England for a test.'

'We might be able to work out who they are then.'

'Don't be an eejit, girl. Everyone goes to England in the summer, all the time! Will we have another coffee?'

So that was Episode Two.

THREE

None of us expected to see Josie on the doorstep the Thursday afternoon of the first week of June. We had the arrival story after the event from my mother. Unlike Josie, I had been at work, slaving away in Mary Brennan's office, and it all burst over me like a firework when I got home that evening.

What I'm telling you now happened a whole month or so before Oonagh passed on the Aids rumour. The hot summer was just beginning, and you expect fine days in June – blue skies and the first real warmth in the air though the sea is still as cold as spring water.

Well, there was Josie on the doorstep large as life and twice as troublesome (Mam's words) – tight white trousers, gold shoes and matching handbag, wrap-around sunglasses that were the *sine qua non* of the fashionable that year. The only thing she lacked was the Cannes tan.

'Josie!' my mother said, when she'd recovered from the shock. 'We thought you were in England! Aren't you at the school?'

'No, Mother. I'm here!' said Josie, taking advantage of her confusion. She knew perfectly well that Mam's question was code for 'What's happened to your job?'

Mam peered past her down the front path. She hadn't missed the smart new suitcase on wheels, and the keys of a car jingling in Josie's hand. There in the gutter, with the Corporation dust and the chewing-gum wrappers dropped by the Kennedy children as they run over pedestrians on their mountain bikes, was a gleaming silver Citroën. 'Is that *yours*, Josie?'

'I borrowed it from a friend who doesn't need it.'

SOME FRIEND! as Mam said later, even though Josie had sounded almost bored about it. I've never been sure how much Mam sees through, especially with Josie. She long ago adopted a pose of amused tolerance when dealing with her offspring, and most of the time I suspect she'd just rather not know what we get up to. She's abandoned the idea she might have any real influence over us.

'I only want to stay for a couple of nights,' Josie said, 'until I can get the keys to Aggie's cottage. She's renting it from her aunt again this holiday, and we thought we'd take it for the whole summer. Aren't you going to ask me in?'

To use a phrase favoured by my sister Denise who lives in England, we were all gobsmacked that evening when we heard about it – Dad, Brendan and I. And Grace when the news got to her. Grace is married in Ballycanty, but sometimes there is a time-lag when it comes to hearing the immediate family gossip, unless she happens to be visiting.

Josie on our doorstep, with a smart brand-new car announcing she'd come to stay for the summer! To see why it was so surprising, you have to know a bit about her.

Josie's been difficult from the day I was born. Everyone in the family agrees on that. My mother says she never got over the shock of not being the youngest any more. Denise, our eldest sister, was four when she appeared, and thinking Mother had been away specially to buy her a doll, made a pet of her. Grace was only two, but Grace has a loving nature and never had time to be spoilt, so she just copied whatever Denise did, and for nearly five years Josie had the star position in the family all to herself. Then, after two miscarriages, my mother had me.

My two oldest sisters were delighted, and everyone assumed Josie would in her turn lavish attention and admiration on the newest baby. But Josie wasn't having any of it. From the moment I was brought home, she meditated murder. First she pushed me off a bed, in the hopes I'd be dashed to pieces on the carpet. When this failed she tried poison, and fed me slugs and berries from the garden. It wasn't until she was taken off to school that my mother thought it safe to leave me on my own for the odd five minutes. Then Brendan came along, and after that I didn't have much scope for being ruined by indulgence.

There are as much as four years between him and me, and Brendan was the boy my father had been waiting for. Now you might think he would be the most spoilt of the lot of us, with four sisters and a father thinking he'd fallen out of heaven (my mother knew different — after twenty years, the sex-for-pleasure message was just filtering through to Ireland from the rest of Europe and she didn't have any more after him). But he's clever and independent, and doesn't care whether other people pay any attention to him or not.

Josie's reaction to him was interesting. He wasn't a rival in the way that a younger sister had been, and she was fascinated by him. She 'adopted' him as her own. Denise said years later that this touching devotion to her little brother had been an early manifestation of Josie's consuming interest in adult life: the male sex.

From the time she was eighteen, Josie has spent every summer out of Ireland. When she gave up nursing she went off to Israel to work on a kibbutz, and that gave her a taste for foreign countries. Then she went to stay with Denise who's married in England, and got a job with a travel company; she was a ski rep in the winter and did courier work in the summer, and took her own holidays in France, Greece, Turkey — wherever she wanted. She stuck that for three years, then she announced she was tired of living out of a suitcase, and the next we heard she was working in a smart prep school in England as a matron.

'Josie a *matron*!' Brendan hooted when he heard. He has no illusions about the sister who used to indulge

22

him as a child. 'She'll last about five minutes!'

It was Denise who explained the attraction: the school was in Oxford, a fine big city full of men – students, tutors and tourists. Josie had free accommodation at the school, and was working with a lot of other very young 'matrons', all of whom were avid for a good social life. Then there were the long holidays.

She'd done three terms, starting the previous summer, and after her flying visit in the Easter holidays we'd all thought she was going to make it to the end of the school year. Now two huge questions flashed up on the family autocue when she unexpectedly appeared at home: WHAT'S HAPPENED TO YOUR JOB? and: WHO LENT YOU THE CAR? It didn't escape any of us that the Citroën had an English number-plate.

But it's a brave soul, as Mam said, who'll ask Josie for the information she doesn't want to give.

We used to live in a high terrace house, built in the bad old days before the Republic, and grander in consequence than the boxes they put up now. We had three floors, and high ceilings and a garden full of dark green shrubs that dropped brown cardboard leaves over the beds and stopped anything else growing. I liked that house, but Mam always complained the plumbing had been ruined in the time of Noah, and the house was cold. By the time Denise and Grace were married, we had moved.

Now we live in a detached Eighties dream. Our garden is full of builders' rubble and still nothing grows. The house isn't cold, though – the walls can act like radiators, and that summer we had to open the patio doors permanently and live in the dining area.

'They break up early over in England, don't they?' my father remarked at tea, the evening of Josie's arrival.

Josie leaned back in her chair, and stared out of the patio doors. They were open, and the cool of the June evening lay over the pots of miniature roses Mam had put out there. It was all very Mediterranean for the time of year; we'd already had a good spring.

'Oh, they don't do public exams at prep school age, Da. What's the point of keeping them on in lessons when they've done all their work for the year?'

'No boy at that age has ever done all his work for the year. No wonder the education's in such a poor state over there.'

There was an uneaten pile of salad on Josie's plate, and she was pushing it around with her fork. Da gave her a look under his eyebrows that meant *You're not telling me the whole story, young lady*. When we were children those were the words he used. Now he just gives the look.

'You're too pale, Josie,' Mam said. 'What are you doing to yourself in Oxford? You need feeding up.'

'I'm fine, Mam. Don't fuss!' Then Josie the actress couldn't resist a gesture that demanded sympathy for her lonely and overworked exile in England, and swept a languid hand across an alabaster brow in a manner that would have graced the Abbey stage.

Mam and Da exchanged looks.

'So to what do we owe the honour of this second visit within the year?' Father asked, with the usual ponderous humour. 'We weren't expecting you back until Christmas.'

'They said it was going to be a good summer. What's the point of paying all that money for sea and sand when you can have it here for next to nothing?' For the benefit of the rest of us, she explained again her plan for the next few months.

'Aggie's aunt's lending us her cottage out on the cove road. I thought I might stay out there until September.'

'I'd have thought she'd be letting it to tourists,' my mother said.

'It's too early for the full rates. Anyway, Aggie and I are paying her. At least she knows we won't wreck the place. I'm moving in on Monday. You'll have to come over and visit when I'm settled.' She included us all in an expansive sweep of the arm.

24

'And when's Aggie moving in?'

'Oh, as soon as work finishes.'

Agnes Riordan is an old schoolfriend of hers. She too has a job in a school, but she has university qualifications and teaches English.

Josie was sleeping in the spare bed in my room for the few nights she was staying. We'd once had to share, but it has been my space for a good five years now, and I resented the way the room was suddenly full of her things – her clothes crammed into my cupboards, half a dozen suitcases conjured from the car spilling over the floor. Even the dressing-table had her make-up on it, and a pool of her nail varnish.

'Do you have to make such a sty of it?' I asked, with as much good humour in my voice as I could muster.

Absence is supposed to make the heart fonder, but it doesn't change the familiar resentments and irritations at all. It's depressing how quickly you fall back into the old patterns with members of your family.

'Don't make such a fuss, Terry! You'll be rid of me after Sunday. Where else am I supposed to put all this?'

She had hung up some very expensive clothes on the floor, that's all I can say.

In bed that night we chatted as we used to. She propped herself on one elbow, hand under cheek and hair sweeping the pillow like a model in a bedding advert, while she watched me fiddle with a pair of eyebrow tweezers. 'Who are you going out with now? I don't remember who it was at Easter.'

'Well . . .' I wasn't sure I wanted to discuss my amorous progress with Josie. She couldn't be trusted not to use the information against me if it suited her. 'I've seen quite a bit of Declan O'Connor lately.'

'And what about Oonagh?'

'She and Dan broke up. She's off serious men.'

'So who's this Declan? What does he look like – is he Katie O'Connor's younger brother?'

'Tall, quite dark, grey eyes. Yes, he is.' There's no way you can keep a man hidden in Ballycanty; every available boyfriend has a sister, and every sister has a girlfriend who is your sister. 'What about you? There must be loads of men to choose from in Oxford!' I was feeling my way through the protective fog of non-information with which she surrounded herself, towards a question about the owner of the car. We were all certain she'd borrowed the Citroën from a man. For Josie, she sounded suspiciously uninterested. 'Oh, I've been out with a few since Easter. No-one to write home about.'

I tried another route, and asked her straight out, 'Have you given up your job as matron?'

'Well, I have,' she said. 'But you're not to tell. You know what a fuss everyone makes.'

'But how can you afford the car?'

'Oh, it isn't mine. I'm only borrowing it.'

'Who from?'

'A friend.' Very final.

'He must be very kind if he'll lend you such a new one!'

'Who said it was a man?'

'And what about the petrol if you're not earning any money?'

She punched her pillow and threw herself back on it. 'What *is* this – the Inquisition?'

'I only asked,' I said, and turned out the light. Still the old Josie, and no mistake.

Her voice said out of the darkness, careless again and sort of brushing it off, 'I've enough money. I saved a bit while I was at the school. Before I run out I'll look for another job. Work like that – it's easy enough to get in England.'

Perhaps it was. But, knowing Josie, the story wasn't half as simple as she was making out.

On the Sunday evening, when she'd gone off to have a preliminary check of the cottage with Aggie's aunt Mrs Riordan, Mam cornered me. She had her worried frown on.

'Do you think she's anorexic? She's hardly eaten a thing since she's been home.'

I'd not noticed anything out of the ordinary, and I certainly didn't think she was ill. She was different every time we saw her. Sometimes it was the hair – shoulder-length and a purple prune colour, then chopped off to the ears and dyed chestnut with eyebrows to match. She was fat, she was thin; one day a junk-foodie, the next a health-fadder, with her hemline going up and down according to her spiritual beliefs. I was just relieved Mam wasn't grilling me about her job, and tried to laugh it off.

'Who, Josie? I thought alcoholism was the problem among school staff these days. You haven't found a bottle of Bushmills under her bed yet?'

Mam was amused in spite of herself. 'Get away with you! You're a real Job's comforter. We've never had any alcoholics in the family.'

Still, I'd swear I heard her going upstairs to have a look.

Grace once said of Josie, 'She was born a generation too late. She'd have loved the Sixties. All that dope and irresponsibility, and it being so easy then to shock people.'

And Dad had said, 'She's a born actress. It'll always be the limelight she's after – and the applause.'

· FOUR

It was a priest who told me dancing is all about sex. I was sixteen at the time.

'It is *not*!' I argued with him. 'We go to the disco to see our friends, chat, work off a bit of energy.'

'Chat!' he said. 'How can you chat when you can't hear yourselves scream?'

'We go outside if we want to talk seriously. And we can talk at the bar – anyway, we see each other nearly every day. We don't need to chat.'

'So you *don't* go to chat, then? You go to see your friends and work off the energy on a dance floor. So they did in the nineteenth century. You know they banned the waltz? At least the old Victorians saw the appeal of it for what it was. All we do is lie about it, with immorality eating into the very fabric of our lives!'

'It isn't like that!' I protested. 'It isn't!' And the more I protested, the more vehement I became. I thought that was just typical of a priest (the one in question happens to be my Great Uncle Danny), disapproving of the fun he wasn't having himself. In the end I stalked off, indignant, and wouldn't speak to him for weeks.

Although I didn't agree with his views, I remembered the conversation.

Years ago, somebody bought an old warehouse on the coast road and did it up. Now there's a disco out of town on Saturday night. To begin with it wasn't much of a place: whitewashed breeze-blocks and a few flashing lights you could scarcely see in the summer nights for the remains of the sun flushed through the sky. Once they had put up proper blackouts and built a decent bar, a disco could hardly fail. There's nowhere else to go locally. 'Reds' it was named in the days when that might have meant something smart and political.

I first got on more than speaking terms with Declan O'Connor at the disco. It was just after Easter. I'd noticed Declan lots of times, and I knew who he was, and he'd noticed me – he told me afterwards. That night he came up to me not long after Oonagh and I arrived. Oonagh was waiting for her boyfriend Dan, and we were warming up a bit on the dance floor.

The music was loud. It was still early, but there was already quite a crowd.

Declan stood in front of me and yelled, 'Dance?'

I yelled back, 'OK.'

By the end of the evening the place was packed: smoke, darkness, flashing lights and the kind of hard rock that bulges from the walls in a steady pulse. Nobody could care what anybody else was doing, and I was wrapped round Declan and he round me. Even our feet had stopped shuffling. Only our hips moved, and Declan's tongue in my mouth. The noise of the bass amplifiers filled my head. I couldn't think, only feel. It seemed like heaven.

If it hadn't been so cold that night, I think we'd have gone outside and ended up having sex. I couldn't sleep for hours when I finally got home. By the next morning I'd sobered up a bit. I'd already learned that sex with someone puts a kind of obligation on you. No-one ever tells you that before you start, of course, and you wouldn't believe it even if they did, but it's a variety of emotional blackmail. If you've done it once, you can't refuse it again without hurting their feelings, so you go along with it. Acquiescence is easier than the scene you're going to have to go through if you refuse.

Because Declan was studying in Cork and only came back for the weekends, I couldn't see him every night after that, and perhaps it was just as well. The week apart put a kind of strangeness on us every Friday.

I knew from friends that Declan had another girl-friend at university. He didn't deny it when I asked him about her, but he said it wasn't serious. I used to spend the week thinking about them, wondering if it was getting *more* serious during the five days until the Friday night than it had been the week before, or *less*. Oonagh was bored with all the speculation.

'If you're not going to drive down there and march in at midnight to find out what company he's keeping, will you give it a rest, Terry? You'll drive yourself mad with the guessing.'

He said he didn't sleep with her, but I was old enough to know that men can have different versions of the same truth depending on whom they're speaking to. *Sleep*, for instance, could be taken in its literal sense.

I began to wonder what qualifications you needed to apply to university – and that, from someone who'd spent her school career resisting all encouragement in that direction, shows you how serious it was. I thought that if I got a place to study at Cork, I'd *know*.

'So what subject are you going to study – men?'

That was Oonagh, of course, but it was Declan him-self who had started me thinking about university, even though it turned into a bit of a joke. The very first time we'd had a real conversation – and we did have a few to begin with – he'd said to me, 'You know Terry, you're wasting your time in a third-rate job. Why didn't you go on with your studies?'

I'd been considered lazy at school, and of course I'd not much to show for all the education. Bright enough, but lazy. Now I thought that Declan was either teasing or trying to flatter me.

'I mean it,' he said. 'You read a lot – you've got a clever way of putting over your ideas – why didn't you study English?'

I thought of the way Oonagh and I wasted our

lunch-hours. 'If gossip and reading a few paperbacks is all you need, the whole of Ireland should be calling themselves professors. Anyway, Brendan is the brains of our family.'

'That doesn't mean to say he has the monopoly.'

'No, but you see the way it works. Denise and Josie are the beauties – well, no – Denise is the beauty, Josie's the actress, Grace is the saint, Brendan's the brains.'

'So what's Terry?'

'Oh, Terry – she's *herself*.'

That's what we say in Ireland when we can't find one of those Latin labels.

Declan and I used to end up on Friday nights at Miracle Mick Dooley's, with Oonagh and Dan, before she broke up with him, and a crowd of others. On Saturday nights we'd go to Reds and that was the real high point – because by Sunday evening Declan would be going back to Cork, until the term ended and the long holidays came.

As the weather grew warmer, and the danger of going outside grew greater, it all seemed like part of one long seduction with an inevitable, orgasmic (that's another word nobody's afraid to say these days except in front of Nana Foley) conclusion. But not yet. There was one thing I'd made up my mind about: I wasn't going to have serious sex with Declan while there was still that other girl in Cork, whatever the temptation. I believed in serial monogamy, and it was her or me, as they say in the soaps.

Mrs Riordan's cottage is hidden in the folds of the cliffs, where they begin to dip towards the sea. There's a track that leads towards it from the coast road, between the gorse bushes and the tufty grass. It passes quite close to the cottage before it winds down more steeply to the cove. A narrow curving path to the cottage itself branches off the track to the right, and beyond the little yard at the housefront cuts its separate way down to the shore.

The first time I ever had a friend I called a boyfriend we used to go there. Birdwatching. It's a grand place for linnets and little chirpy things called stonechats that flit from bush to bush. On fine days the sea in the cove is shades of green and turquoise and purple, and you can look down on the gulls' grey backs as they plane along between you and the water. We were both fourteen at the time, and he wasn't a proper boyfriend. He was more interested in the wildlife than in me, and though I was very curious to know what it was like to be kissed – I didn't want to be branded as last in my class to have that experience – I wasn't sure what it would lead to and I was afraid someone might see me and tell my mother.

Now, none of us *ever* believed you were in danger of hell-fire if you let a man touch more than your hand. Some of us like to pretend so because it makes a better story; but we just borrowed the idea from my mother's generation, and possibly the truth of it lies in my grandmother's time. Our nuns wore short skirts, and one of the postulants had even been seen on the beach at Jamestown in a bikini. In our days, they were well into emptying the convents, according to my Uncle Danny.

The cottage is a typical old Irish one: a front door and a window either side, whitewashed walls, slate roof, and a crooked chimney-stack. Originally there had been only one large room downstairs, and a ladder to the loft. Aggie's aunt had divided the one room for letting purposes into a living-room and a bedroom. A second bedroom and a small bathroom had been built on behind the house, and the loft upstairs converted into a third bedroom. You had to walk round up there like the hunchback of Notre Dame or you knocked your head on the rafters.

Josie came to the door yawning when I hit it loud enough. It was half six on a Wednesday evening, a week and three days after she'd moved in. She was fully dressed, but she looked as though she'd been sleeping in her clothes. I'd visited three or four times already, and she always appeared like a gypsy who'd spent the night under a hedge. I was relieved to see the skirt and top didn't belong to me.

'Mam sent me down with a pie,' I said. 'You're to heat it. And there's fruit cake in this but you're to put it in a tin. And here are some apples. And here's a message from me and Oonagh – we'll be at Mick Dooley's again tonight if you'd like to join us and a few others.'

Apart from worrying about Josie's diet, Mam couldn't think how she spent the time all day.

'There's none of her friends around at the moment, Terry. You and Oonagh ask her out. She hasn't even Aggie for company yet. She must be lonely down there.'

'It's where she wants to be, Mam,' I said. 'But I'll try. She won't want to come. She thinks Oonagh and me are terrible silly.'

'So you are. But ask her.'

I just had. And she didn't want to join us. I thought about the loneliness, and although I didn't believe it and wanted to get straight back home, I tried.

'Can I come in for a minute, or are you busy?'

She did grin at that. 'I was just turning out the presses and dusting the china,' she said. 'Mind how you step in the silver.'

'What silver?' The place was already a tip. Two meat pies and a lasagne were lined up by the sink. I recognized the ovenware bowls under them from home, and one of Mam's pies had mould blooming on it.

Now when Josie really laughs, you see the person looking out through her eyes – dark brown eyes like a Spaniard's – who can captivate almost any mortal on earth. I say 'almost' because there are exceptions: the members of her family. We've all heard how kind, caring, beautiful Josie is, what a lovely nature she has, etc, and felt irritated.

'Will I take these dishes back if you've no use for them?'

She shrugged, so I scraped the two old pies into a bucket that had milk cartons and a baked-bean can in it. 'You could still eat the lasagne,' I suggested. 'It's only the day-before-yesterday's. Don't you have a fridge?'

'Oh. Yes.'

I opened the door and shut it again. The grey tentacles nearly dragged me in. I couldn't live like that, but Josie doesn't seem to notice.

'Are you going to tidy up before Aggie moves in?' I asked, braving an outburst. She shrugged again, very apathetic.

'I might. Did you walk over?'

It's four miles.

'I've a loan of the car. Talking of cars, what have you done with the one *you* borrowed?'

She pushed her fingers back through her hair. It was long and dark – her natural colour. Josie *is* beautiful. 'It's down at the cove,' she said. 'The ground's too uneven here.'

The track to the cove opens out onto shingle at the foot of the cliff. There is a small concrete jetty built out round one arm of the rocks. It's not ideal as a car park.

'You're not worried about something happening to it?'

'Ah, no-one's going to break into it down there. We're in Ireland, Terry, not London.'

'They'd break into it here soon as anywhere,' I said cynically. I've always been irritated by the sophistication Josie assumes because she had spent so much time in England. England always has to be faster, smarter, wickeder than poor idiotic old Ireland, still away with the fairies. And by association of course, Josie herself has to be faster, smarter and wickeder than the rest of us.

'I wasn't thinking of break-ins,' I said. 'More of a freak storm. The waves wash in there very strongly on

34

a high tide. You know the sea wall was broken down by a storm a couple of years ago at Tramore? Great blocks of stone just tossed about by the water!'

'The weather's grand,' she said. 'And the forecast is for a fine summer. It's perfectly safe. D'you want a cup of coffee?'

I said yes to be companionable, and she wandered aimlessly, and then she said, 'There's no milk. We'll have to have it black.'

I boiled the kettle on the gas ring and washed the mugs. The water was cold. I assumed she hadn't put any money in the electricity meter, and I had no change. She sat by the table, one foot stretched out resting on it while she concentrated on the ends of her hair, thick as paintbrushes in her hands.

'Aren't you bored here, Josie? Isn't it a bit dull after Oxford?' I was going to say 'A bit of a come-down' but thought better of it in time. 'What do you do with yourself all day? Not sunbathing by the look of it.'

'Ultraviolet ages you.'

I put a black coffee mug by her elbow. She ignored it, but then I wouldn't expect any thanks from Josie in the usual course of events.

'So what do you do?'

'Oh, I get up late. Read. Things like that. I need a rest. Oxford is hectic.' She spoke of it in the tone of a college student, worn out by the intellectual and social effort. Again the languid hand passed across the brow.

'Many Arab sheikhs?' I still hadn't found out anything about the boyfriend scene, and was beginning to wonder if she had been protesting too much about the availability of men.

She raised her eyebrows in a silent question.

'You remember, you used to tell me how you wanted to run off with an Arab sheikh and have a wild affair in the desert?'

'Not much desert in Oxfordshire.'

'Oh come on Josie – what about the wild affairs?'

She made an impatient sound like 'Uhgg!' and moved abruptly, stretching her hands behind her head and tipping her chair backwards so that she was balanced on it with both feet crossed on the table. 'Wild affairs!' she said with contempt. 'That sounds so *dated*, so *naive*! Who has "wild affairs" these days? They sound so safe and conventional.'

This was a thrust at backward Ireland again, and perhaps a glimpse of her latest pose: The Beauty Jaded with Life, Josie Weary of the World. What was she going to try now? She's already been a Buddhist, and the rigorous and celibate life of a Christian hermit certainly wasn't up her street. Perhaps she was thinking of joining some evangelical cult in mid-America. Whatever it was, there would have to be a dramatic run-up to it.

I was irritated, as usual. 'Would you deign to tell me what's *safe* about a wild affair?' I asked, as cutting as I could sound. 'This is the Age of Aids, in case you hadn't heard.'

She gave me a sharp look and then shrugged again with impatience. 'No-one has to catch it. You talk so childishly, Terry. What does anyone really know about Aids, or wild affairs for that matter, in a backwater like this where the only hang-up is losing your virginity? You're all just out of the ark.'

She sounded really contemptuous, almost angry. I got up, leaving my coffee.

'OK,' I said. 'Be unpleasant if you want to. I don't have to stay and listen to you.'

I was at the door when she said, 'Don't let's quarrel, Terry! It is boring here just now.' She got up quickly and opened a door under the sink. 'Let's have a glass of wine.'

There were two dirty glasses on the table. This time she washed them.

'I've got to drive Father's car back.'

'One glass won't do you any harm. Have something to eat with it – some of that stuff you've just brought, otherwise I'll have to go to the shop.'

The shop is a further mile along the coast road. I ate some of Mam's pie, but didn't bother to heat it up; the day itself was hot enough. I couldn't face washing congealed plates in cold water, so I ate it with a fork straight out of Mam's dish. Josie had a few mouthfuls from the opposite side. I was glad that Aggie's aunt didn't think to pay us a visit and catch us through the open door: Study for Two Slatterns at a Table. A week's washing-up had hedged us into one corner.

She began to communicate a bit during her second glass of wine.

'I thought I might go abroad again after this summer.'

'I thought you said you'd be looking for a job.' Could this be the path that would lead to the New Age cult?

'I could work abroad. I thought of going to Africa – or the Far East. Life's getting too complicated here.'

I'm sure my eyes must have narrowed suspiciously. 'What do you mean? Now *you're* sounding naïve – like a Sixties hippie. "It's all so simple out there – space, man. Peace." You *can't* believe all that rubbish!'

She was impatient again, and I'd spoilt my chances of finding out anything more. 'Of course I don't! I'd just like to disappear for a while, that's all.'

'Then why not take the Citroën and drive round the wilds of Ireland? Plenty of space to get lost.'

I expected another snappy reply, but she almost sounded as though she took it seriously. 'I'm not sure how much petrol there is in it. I was driving it round for quite a while with "empty" on the gauge. I don't want to be completely stranded.'

'Then why don't we drive in Da's car to fetch a can of petrol? A gallon would easily get you to the nearest garage.'

She waved one hand in a dismissive gesture. 'I haven't any money until I get to a bank.' There was a pause. 'Can you lend me some – about twenty pounds? I'll give it back as soon as I get into town.'

Josie asking for a loan is full of the conviction of repayment. If you've never lent her money before, you believe her, but I said goodbye to the ten-pound note that was all I had with me, and of course I don't remember that she ever paid it back.

FIVE

It was the second week in July when the Aids rumour started. That was when I heard it from Oonagh who heard it from Joe Duffy who heard it from Dermot Reagan.

It was Dermot Reagan who knew the name of one of the victims, if you remember.

For a whole week we discussed it strictly between ourselves, especially who might have it and how they'd got it, but inevitably the circle widened. I told Declan cross-his-heart-and-hope-to-die not to whisper a word of it. He'd finished at Cork for the year, there was no word of The Other Woman, and he was working in a bar for part of the summer. It meant we couldn't meet as often as we'd hoped. As far as I was concerned, the Saturday disco nights that July were dead when he couldn't get someone to sub for him. It wouldn't be until August that Reds opened two nights a week, because with the holidays and the tourists there would be enough demand for it. Anyway, Declan hadn't heard any rumours, but said he'd keep his ears open. That of course gave the lie to Oonagh's claim a whole week earlier that the town was buzzing with it, and it did cross my mind that Dermot Reagan might have made the whole thing up.

I'm not sure if Oonagh told a schoolfriend or two or whether they knew already, but we were like a secret society – a little knot of Freemasons with our hidden knowledge, our nods and winks and funny handshakes. Josie had accused me of talking childishly about affairs and such, but *that* was childish: hugging such a gleeful secret to ourselves when it was a terrible thing if it was true.

Then it turned out we weren't the only ones who knew. Half Ballycanty was muttering in secret, and speculating, and blaming, and prophesying, though it took an outsider to blow the lid off it.

Even my mother came up to me before the week was out.

'Did you hear anything about an Aids scare, Terry?'

I was ironing a skirt for Saturday and I didn't want to make a mess of it; it was a good excuse to keep my attention on the board.

'Who told you that then, Mam?'

'Mary Alice O'Shea. It's here, in Ballycanty.'

'Well, I did hear something. What did you hear?'

'That there's at least three boys in this town has got it, and there might be more. They think there's a woman spreading it.'

'Well, they would say that, wouldn't they? Any other more likely way of getting it would be too shocking for Ballycan'tbe. Homosexuals? Drug abusers? The curse of God would strike us all for sure – brimstone on the Hyper and an earthquake under the shopping mall. I bet old Mary Alice is down the garden at 36 Dunmore Road this very minute, consulting the statues and asking God for a nice normal convenient whore who'll give them all a bad fright and let them see the error of their ways.'

Mam put on her expression which meant she thought she ought to disapprove. She's not really shocked by remarks like mine. She's capable of saying just the same sort of things herself.

'Don't talk that way, Teresa. It's no laughing matter. It's a tragedy for the families if it's true.'

'I wasn't laughing, Mam. I was just offering pertinent social comment. Will I do Father's shirts for you while the iron's hot?'

'I suppose you might as well. I'll be glad to sit down for five minutes. You're a good girl – sometimes.'

It's an old joke, and it makes me feel guilty these days. I'm not such a good girl even by her definitions, and I'm definitely a bold bad one by Nana Foley's. My mother's generation was only just out of its teens in the Sixties, when Women's Lib struck America and England. Feminism didn't strike Ireland then – more tapped her enticingly on the shoulder, and got fought off by the Church. My mother was married when she was just twenty-one, and that froze her attitudes for a few years while she played at housekeeping and swapped baby stories with her friends over the pushchairs, but she's become more and more liberalized as each of her daughters has grown up. We found her out long ago: she doesn't really disapprove – her pretence is her way of keeping the peace with her own mother and the older generation.

The strident Irish feminists always make me laugh. Oonagh says that's because I'm too physically lazy to struggle for a worthwhile cause, and too mentally lazy in the first place to think through the necessity of doing so. I say it's because Ireland is the one country that doesn't need today's brand of feminism. Just look at the average Irish mother – the most fearsome woman on earth! I read somewhere that back in the days of the Romans, it wasn't the Celtic warriors that scared the Roman legions rattle-kneed, but their wives. The women ran screaming up and down the battle-lines, nagging at their husbands, and frightened off an invasion of Anglesey.

The females of the race have calmed down a bit since then, perhaps, but they've the same blood in their veins. Look at my sisters: Denise, married to a rich Englishman, giving all the orders in a life of idleness; Josie, who has the upper hand with just about everybody on account of her uncertain temper; Grace, quiet, but built into the house timbers so that her husband's scared to disturb her in case the roof falls in. Then there's Mam, poor underprivileged Sixties Mam, soft-voiced like Grace, but when did she ever fail to get what she wanted?

Mam wouldn't exactly approve of the way her unmarried daughters behave, did she but know about it, but she wouldn't be making the Novenas like Nana Foley either – she hasn't much time for the Church these days. None of us but Grace would meet Nana's requirements, because out of all the brides I've seen in this town, and that includes family ones, only Grace was a virgin on her wedding day.

In fact, to my certain knowledge, there's now a grand total of ONE virgin over the age of eighteen in the whole of Ballycanty.

But her story comes later.

I went along to Miracle Mick's where Oonagh and I were meeting for a drink. I arrived early.

Mick has done out the bar like the inside of a stable – wooden stalls for the customers with iron railings along the top, that sort of thing. The walls are dark green and the carpet's dark green, and if you can see the ceiling through the smoke, that's dark green too. I've been into pubs with Denise in England, on my two visits there. It strikes you at once how much more comfortable they are than the Irish ones – more like going into private living-rooms with chintz curtains and bowls of flowers and fireplaces full of logs. But there's not a lot of conversation going on in them; it's as though everyone's struck dumb admiring the furniture. Irish bars are the opposite. You could go deaf in one evening.

My brother Brendan calls Mick Dooley's 'The Jockey's Concussion' – the whole world turfed over, even the sky is grass. I prefer something a bit more open, where you can see everyone, and the groups expand as your friends come in, but Mick's is the most convenient to us.

It was hot in there, and it was hot outside. Mick has a poor ghost of a garden at the back, with tables and benches, but even the Holy Water had dried to a damp green patch, and I'd had enough of the sun. The place was empty, and I had my pick of the stalls. I told Johnny, Mick's son who was behind the bar, I'd wait for Oonagh. I could have stayed and talked to him, but he's always angling to ask me out and I'm not interested. He laughs at remarks with no humour in them to show what a good sort he is, so I told him I was going to write a letter, waited for the delighted applause, and sat at a distance with the paper in front of me, fanning myself with a beer mat.

I wanted to talk to Denise about Josie. It's expensive to call England, and I couldn't do it from home. In a public telephone booth I'd have been pouring in the pound coins until the box fell off the wall. Perhaps Denise might ring me if I wrote. She's very lazy about letters.

With every other stall in the bar to choose from, a man came up to mine. He was quite young, about thirty I'd say, and good-looking. I'd not seen him before. He had a pint in his hand, with some of the thick froth creaming down over his fingers.

'Hello there. Do you mind if I sit with you? It's dead in here. Will it liven up later, d'you think?'

I looked up from my letter, and told him I was waiting for my friend. If he hadn't been so good-looking I'd have frozen him off completely. Instead I told him he was welcome to sit there if he wanted – I couldn't stop him.

He grinned. 'Can I get you a drink?'

I told him I'd wait.

'Do you live in Ballycanty?'

I mentally said goodbye to Denise's letter; it wasn't too painful being chatted up by a good-looking stranger. I hoped a few friends besides Oonagh might come in and see us. It would do Declan O'Connor good to know he wasn't the only pike in the Ballycanty pond as far as I was concerned, and it might push him to a definite decision about Miss Cork University.

I looked at the man straight in those zap-you-into-bed blue eyes. 'I take it *you* don't – live here, that is.'

'Just visiting. I'm from Dublin. So you *are* from Ballycanty?'

'I am.' He had a friendly way, and a nice smile. And he had the dark Continental sort of looks you see in men's clothing ads, and eyelashes that are only born on boys. Then I wondered if I should suggest we moved on to another bar with more life in it before Oonagh got to us. I can't compete with her, and I knew she'd like him.

'D'you work here?'

'I do.' I found myself telling him about McCormick's and Mary Brennan and the old Wills and Testaments, and about everybody else who worked there. I left out Oonagh. He'd find out about her soon enough.

'What do you do, when you're not just visiting Ballycanty?' I asked him. 'After all, we know it rivals New York for excitement, but I'd have thought Dublin has just a few more things to offer?'

'I work in the paper industry.'

I knew somehow he meant me to think he had a job in paper production – its manufacture or distribution and sales. I don't know why – perhaps it was one of those revelations from God that Mary Alice is always talking about – but I felt certain he was a journalist. I had nothing to go on, and he didn't let me follow it up, but asked about the local swimming; he was staying in a guest-house down on the coast road. Was the beach any good?

I told him about Josie's cove, which is one of the safest for a swim, and then regretted it because my sister would want to eat handsome Mr Paper Industry for breakfast. I had discovered him first, and I felt proprietorial in a childish way. No doubt he could look after himself.

We talked about Angela Phelan's where he was staying. I asked him if she still put plastic over the stair-carpet to save it, and locked up the soap.

'What's your name?' he asked suddenly.

'Teresa Carmody. Terry,' I said.

'I'm Sean Butler.'

The name didn't mean anything to me, but I made a mental note to check on him afterwards.

Then he said out of the blue, 'It must be too early in the season still – there's not a lot seems to be going on round here yet. Except I hear there's an Aids scare in the town. Is that true?'

It didn't have to be a journalist's question. You'd only have to be around Ballycanty a day or two, and staying somewhere like Phelan's, and you'd know everything there was to know about the rumour.

I was wondering whether to fob him off, or to make up a little story to keep him happy while I looked at his eyelashes, when Oonagh breezed in. She saw us at once.

I introduced them, regretting I hadn't suggested a move to John of the Grotto before she'd caught up with us; I could have pretended afterwards I'd misunderstood and got the wrong Dooley.

'This is Sean Butler. Oonagh Hennessy. Sean works in a paper mill, and Oonagh works with me.'

He got up and shook hands with her. I could see from the acquisitive blue in her eyes she thought he was a find, and she was all but swooning under the smile and the good manners, and I could have kicked her. I noticed he didn't rush to correct the 'paper mill'.

'Hello Oonagh. I've heard all about McCormick's and you and Terry keeping the place on its feet. Would you like a drink? And will you have that drink now, Terry?'

We sent him off to the bar for gin and martinis and Oonagh said straight off, '*Where* did you find him! He's *gorgeous*!'

He'd been so quick with the flattery, I felt even more annoyed with myself for not transferring to John Dooley's. I said quickly, 'He's a journalist!'

'But you said—'

'It's sort of what he told me, but I'm sure he works

for a paper. He was just asking about Aids.'

She rolled her eyes towards his back, and flicked her hair behind her shoulder.

'Oh, he was, was he? Then why don't we tell him?'

She's a terrible tease, and she was laughing.

I finished my letter to Denise that night. There wasn't much to relay in the way of general news. She already knew about the Aids rumours – from me. Everyone was well, apart from Josie, but that was the point of the letter, and I never told Denise much about my current boyfriends. She's no opinion of Irish men anyway, which is why, I suppose, she married a Gloucestershire accountant.

I covered three pages about Josie, and then tore them up. I had such strange little things to say about her, put down in a list they sounded like nothing. In the end I wrote, 'Is there anything the matter with Josie? She's very odd, even for her, and looks terribly thin and pale in spite of the glamour. Should we be dragging her to hospital, the ante-natal clinic or the psychiatrist? Please answer soonest, as Da says they used to write on telegrams.'

'Did you hear that Tommy Power's been tested HIV positive?' Oonagh said in Whelan's one lunch-time. Rosie Walsh was with us that day. Rose has worked in the Bank of Ireland since leaving school. 'They say he's been looking awful pale lately. You hardly ever see him around now.'

A name at last! A *frisson* went round the table – half chilling in case the rumour were true, half delicious because we didn't really believe it. I knew Tommy well. He was the one I used to go out with on the cliffs when we were still at school, and I thought him the least likely to lead the sort of life would get you Aids of anyone I knew.

'Go on. He's got flu or something.'

'In the middle of summer?'

'Well then, a cold. Tommy'd never go off with a whore. He must be chaste as the driven snow.'

'After all those months he spent with you, Treesa Carmody! Don't tell me he's still a virgin. I'm surprised at you.'

Rosie's blue eyes were big and mock-innocent. It was the sort of talk – let alone any of the implications of it – for which the older nuns might have had us into the confessional as being detrimental to the pursuit of purity. They might just as well have saved their breath over such matters; no-one took the slightest notice. We used to swap detailed notes about how far we'd got with the boys we went out with, until there was something real to tell, and then it was just like confession: you'd dredge up any number of tiny sins to fill in a respectable time in the box if you had to, but say not one word of those that are supposed to have you tripping merrily down to hell.

'Yes, well. He's been out with a member of *your* family since then, Rose. All the Walshes are fast workers.'

'Are you implying my sister Joan's a loose woman?' says Rose, mild as milk. 'Because if you are, I might agree with you. You've heard this "Angel of Death" theory?'

'No,' said Oonagh. 'Go on – enlighten us.'

Rose's eyes brightened at the thought of being first with the news. 'They think it's maybe one woman who's spread it—'

'Didn't I tell Mam they'd be blaming some poor whore?'

'And here's me suspecting Joanie of bringing ruin on all those fine young men. But if it was her we'd know by now. She can't keep a secret for the life of her.'

'So what about this Angel woman?' Oonagh asked. 'Doesn't she know she's got it, or is she a revenge syndrome?'

'They think it's revenge. She caught it from someone, she knows she's dying and wants to get her own back.'

It was a nice little drama, but some things didn't quite add up.

'Wait a minute—' I said. 'Slow down. Why couldn't all this have been caused by drugs? We're constantly being told by the medical experts that unless you're into pumping yourself with infected syringes it's not that easy to catch Aids. Now if you believe the favoured rumour, there could be dozens of men in this town supposed to be HIV positive, all infected by *one* woman. That means either she's been at it for years – in which case why are they all showing up positive at the same time? – or it happened in a matter of months and you're telling me this vendetta or whatever it is has gone on unremarked under our very noses. Either way, we'd all of us know who she was by now.'

'Not necessarily. Maybe it isn't revenge – maybe she doesn't know she's got it, and she just likes casual sleeping around.'

'Don't we all?' said Rose.

Oonagh waved her hand impatiently, and raised her voice above the noise of the Italian coffee machine. 'Shut up, Rosie Walsh. We're trying to be serious in case you hadn't noticed – how long before you find out you've got Aids after you've had sex with an infected person?'

'Why ask me?' said Rose, indignant. 'I just *said* that about sleeping around – the chance of it'd be a fine thing.'

'I still think drugs would be the quickest way to spread it, if we're talking epidemics,' I said.

'Where'd the likes of Tom Power get drugs round here and nobody knowing?' Oonagh sounded scornful.

'All right – I admit that here in Ballycanty it's unlikely, but Tom's been studying in England for a while. Though there's drugs everywhere if you know where to ask.'

'Well Terry, I'll have a half pound of the heroin and a couple of the sacks of coke, please. And that'll be all for today.'

Rose can't take anything seriously for long, and we began fooling for a while and forgot what it had all been about.

But the thought of Tommy nagged away at me underneath all the joking. Quiet, gentle Tom. The rumour had to have been put about by someone with a bit of a sense of humour – it was so *unlikely*.

I asked Oonagh before we left, 'Where did you hear about Tommy? It's just gossip, surely. I can't believe it.'

Rose chipped in. 'Mam says that when they start lighting candles and knocking on the door of the presbytery it's a sure sign – especially in this godless age.'

'Well wouldn't you, and Death staring you in the face? Think about it – suppose there *is* no reincarnation – or suppose you *don't* just fizzle out! Wouldn't you be wise to be taking out a bit of insurance with the Church?'

Oonagh said it half joking, but – Death. Suddenly I was thinking about it. We all were. I saw her put her cigarette towards her lips, and stop, and look at it, hesitating. I knew exactly what was going through her mind – the words on the posters, on the cigarette packets, the cinema advertising: Smoking can Damage your Health. I saw her think: you can get cancer from this. Then you, Oonagh Hennessy, die. Death – the end of the film. The credits roll up – and the debits . . . all the things I have *not* done, Lord . . . All the things I *have* done, badly. All my sins, confessed and unconfessed . . . Then: The End. Blank screen. Nothing. Ah, if only you could be *sure* that was the end!

Hamlet put it better in a lesson at school.

Oonagh's thoughts and my thoughts were the same. I recognized them in the way her fingers shook a little, the way she blinked a couple of times, quickly, as though trying to clear her inner eyes of that blankness. I didn't look at her directly, and she didn't look at me but stared down at the smoky dark glass of the table. Even Rose was quiet.

Then Oonagh looked up, deliberately breathing in a

long breath, the cigarette between her lips, drawing in the smoke. Her eyes said: Low Tar, High Poison, You Die Anyway. She blew the smoke towards the two of us in a long sigh, the gesture of a sex goddess of the old silver screen, and laughed. The reel was flickering again, the images coming back, bright and distracting.

'We live too long these days,' she said. 'I'd rather be wasting the taxpayers' money on cancer treatments than fighting off involuntary euthanasia in the geriatric wards when I'm past some arbitrarily chosen politically correct age, and they're tired of fetching me my teeth in the mornings.'

Rose and I looked at Oonagh. She was a vibrant gypsy that summer with her black hair and her tanned arms, and her curves filling her scarlet silk teeshirt. She was smiling; strong white real teeth in her red mouth. We said in our heads: not for us, Death. Not yet. The blank screen's a long way off. For us, and for all our friends and Tom too, the film's only just started, and who knows? By the time it's half through, they might have found us a way to be young for ever . . .

'Why couldn't he be a man, this Angel of Death?' I said, as we were leaving. 'Do we reject a homosexual theory simply because nobody can work out what the necessary relationships might be – and we don't know how many victims we might be dealing with here?'

'Aaah, well now . . .' Rose said in her Father-Jim-Lafferty-in-a-catechism-class voice. 'They're all terrible bad at sums in this town.'

Oonagh said, 'It does seem there's *one* victim, whichever way you look at it.'

Again, I didn't want to believe it was Tommy. 'We don't know that. It might all be nothing but a rumour—'

'Wait a minute though,' Oonagh interrupted. 'Are we talking about *our* rumour, or the real one?'

'Is there any difference any longer?'

*   *   *

We dawdled back to work, the sun bleaching through to our bones as we trailed along the pavement.

'What does all this amount to?' Oonagh asked. 'Is any of this Aids stuff true, or none of it? Perhaps all this national obsession is just the Dail trying to distract our attention from something worse—'

We were outside Rose's bank now. 'You mean they're trying to distract us from a dastardly plot of the English to sabotage the health of the nation, by shipping rabid moles and snakes back to Ireland before you can say St Patrick?'

Rose has such a wild imagination, I forgot Tom. 'And there was I worrying about Ireland's hideous debt to the EC, and international monetary collapse and all! But I'm taking my gold sovereigns out of *your* bank, any road, Rosie Walsh. Mary O'Shea told my Nana Foley the best place for real money these days is in a sock under the bed.'

'The only gold sovereigns I've ever had are chocolate ones from Christmas,' said Oonagh. 'But I'll pay them into Rose's bank – over the counter to Kieran O'Reilly. He won't know where to look . . .'

We left Rose, and laughed all the way back to McCormick's picturing Kieran's confusion. Oonagh's a good actress. She's a star in the town amateur dramatic society. And Kieran (God grant him some day the sense of humour He left out) fancies her.

SIX

It was two hot weeks before Denise rang. Ten working days of melting in the office with the wretched sash windows wide open, and not a breath of a draught when we needed it; fourteen endless evenings of not knowing whether it was better to be inside or outside when it was like an oven whichever way you chose. There's not one building in the whole of Ballycanty with proper air-conditioning, and there was a run on electric fans that summer.

When Declan and I went down to the cove at weekends, the sea lay before us like a glassy blue floor, and there was not a sigh stirring across it. The sand and stones burned our feet, and the water was warm. There was a disco twice a week now, but it was too hot to dance even the slow smoochy numbers we liked.

Denise rang the second Sunday evening, when Da had gone up to the golf club, Mam was visiting with Nana one of her old ladies for the St Vincent de Paul Society, and Brendan was out.

I picked up the phone, and she said at once, 'What's all this about Josie?' It's easy to recognize Denise's voice. Irish with all the T's chiselled away to a sharp stutter and the vowels split and polished with ten years of living in England. She'd be flattered by that observation about her accent. There's the right sort of Irish to be and the wrong sort. The right sort means that when the potato chips are down, old boy, in spite of boasting about Irish attitudes to life, Irish poverty and Irish friends, your blood runs not hot red Celt but cold blue Saxon. Denise is the wrong sort, and has done her best to obliterate the bog-peasant origins of

52

the Carmodys completely. Her true allegiance only comes out in a crisis.

'I don't know about Josie,' I said. 'You see her more often than we do over here, living the kind of life in England we can only dream about—'

Sarcasm always creeps into my voice when I'm talking to Denise. I can't help it. She affects me in the same way as Josie. I'm hitting back at years of how much better things are over here and you must come over and David's buying a Porsche and our nearest neighbours are the Royals – and all that sort of talk.

'You *must* know more than we do,' I prompted. 'We hardly see her from one year's end to the next. When she arrived this time, she looked as though life was thrown after her and never caught up. And just lately, whenever I go down to the cove it's only Aggie sunbathing, and she says Josie either stays indoors reading paperbacks, or drives off to see friends in that car she's borrowed from somebody and doesn't reappear for a couple of days. What exactly happened to her job?'

'She hasn't been to us since the spring. I don't know what she's told you—'

'Nothing. That's why I wrote.'

'Maybe her affair's going badly.'

'AFFAIR? Not a *wild* affair by any chance?'

A tight silence. 'Perhaps I shouldn't have said anything if she hasn't . . .'

'Oh, go on, Denise. Don't come over all English with the discretion – it's too late now you've dropped the hint. Who with?'

'A college tutor in Oxford.'

'And?'

'He's older than her, married with two children – but *don't* tell Mother.'

'Glory be to God tonight! As Nana Foley says.'

'Oh, how is Nana?'

We wandered off onto a side road, and round all the family *bohereens* I hadn't explored in my letter before I got back to Josie.

'She doesn't eat much, she sleeps a lot during the day and goes out most of the night. She's got this car I told you about. She says someone lent it to her. Could it be the man? How old is he?'

'I don't know. About forty I think.'

'FORTY! But he's nearly old enough to be her grandfather!'

'Do stop shouting, Terry. Of course we all know there are lots of fourteen-year-old fathers about. Anyway, it's not such an age gap. I thought a bit of stability might do her good. She seemed to be crazy about him.'

Stability? With a man already married, two children and an English mortgage hanging round his neck like an albatross? He'd be well into middle-age madness.

'D'you know how much it costs to get divorced?' I demanded. Working in a lawyers' office, you hear that sort of thing in the course of gossip. We might have agitated ourselves into divorce laws for this country but I don't think any of us can fool ourselves it'll make for a more stable society. Denise has been living in England too long.

And there was another thing. In the old days, Denise would have talked glibly about people having affairs in the abstract, and then condemned Josie out of hand. She's something of a moral chameleon, taking on the colours of the landscape she's inhabiting. In Ireland, it was Nana and Mam who dictated the palette for her, and with adultery for the Full Bright Red Hell-fire Treatment in the Afterlife, borrowing someone's husband was something you didn't do. Now, blending into the cosy English background of general hedonism, she looked as though her assumed Catholic views had disappeared altogether. She was arguing vaguely in Josie's defence, and she didn't seem to see much wrong with her course of action from any angle.

I have to confess that before that summer, I couldn't see anything wrong with trying out sex before marriage myself – you might even like the man enough to end up spanseled with the gold ring. But you had to draw the line at men with wives, or the whole affair ended in chaos. Well, in Ballycanty it would anyway. That was what I *thought* I thought. So I got as far as condemning Denise for not condemning Josie; I'm still not sure whether that was because I was feeling irritated with Josie and wanted an excuse to criticize, or because I was irritated with Denise and her Englishness. But my attitude certainly wasn't the result of any moral principles lingering on to be outraged.

If I saw Denise as a chameleon blending into a new environment, I saw the rest of us as poor feathered creatures caught in an ancient and decaying aviary, though it wasn't the rickety birdhouse that was keeping some of us in – only the fact that our wings were still stuck together with the remains of the old Church birdlime.

'Never mind about whether he's married or not,' Denise said. 'He was a lot better than some of the others she's had around. There was a string of them just before she decided she was going to be a nun.'

That really did shock me. I couldn't think of a word to say.

'You didn't hear about that? Oh, before the school job. You know Josie. Probably had a row with the last-but-one, and flew to the other extreme. So she's given up the job? We really haven't seen her since February . . .'

Just then Brendan came in from a film with a couple of his friends, and Denise and I had to hang up. She'd given me some information, but I didn't know how much help it was going to be.

'Hello, Terry!' said Jack Doyle. 'What d'you think of this Aids scandal now? Who are you putting your money on for the Angel of Death? We're opening a book on it – feel free to nominate somebody. I'm glad that ginger stuff's fading out of your hair. I prefer the bleached mouse myself.'

That's Jack for you. I rose above it. 'Are you going on the Sports Club's England trip?'

'As a matter of fact I am, and why would you be asking, Treesa Carmody? You've told us often enough you've no interest in the sports at all.'

'No more have I, Jack Doyle. It was just a polite enquiry.'

I learned to lie from a Jesuit priest who gave us a retreat at school one Holy Week. He told us about withholding information from someone to whom the knowledge would do no good.

I went upstairs to wash my hair. The chestnut hadn't turned out exactly as expected, but as Jack had pointed out, it was fading back comfortably to the colour I would call blonde.

When Sean Butler's piece appeared in the *Irish Times*, my father saw it. It was no front-page shock-horror revelation, but tucked away in the inside, a respectable-length article in a section on contemporary Ireland. My father also told me Sean Butler was a quite well-known freelance journalist, and he remembered reading articles by him before.

The name *Ballycanty* occurred in the first sentence, which must have riveted the eyeballs of every *Irish Times* reader in town once they had the leisure to reach the inside pages, but you had to read on before you found out why Ballycanty featured at all.

I bought my own copy on the way to work, and brandished it in front of Oonagh, who hadn't seen it, over our lunch-time coffee at Whelan's.

'We were right!' My glee was truly unholy. 'Sean Butler was a reporter!' And I read out to her the relevant section.

The rumour in Ballycanty this summer is that the men's sports club annual outing is not all that it appears to be. Traditionally on an all-male spree, the club spends a couple of days in England to take in a match or two – whatever's going – the club is eclectic in its interests. But this year the rumour is that there's an ulterior motive. They've booked the coach and the

56

ferry both ways, and arranged three nights in a hotel just outside London at a discount, but how many men will actually be using the tickets they've bought for matches? Less than half, it's being whispered in the narrow streets of Ballycanty.

Oonagh and I looked at each other over our smoky glass tabletop. That particular fledgling rumour, when last heard of, had precisely four blue eyes and two tongues – belonging to Miss O. Hennessy and Miss T. Carmody. Had our journalist checked the story with anyone else? And if so, who could have been contributing to our home-brooded scandal? For I confess to you, my brothers and sisters – or words to that effect, as those of us gabble off who still go to church for social reasons when we can't get out of it on Sundays – that Oonagh and I had made it up. It had come to one of us, I forget which, on the spur of the moment that night at Miracle Mick's. I had seen the gleam in Oonagh's eye, and she had seen the gleam in mine, and a new little gossip bird was hatched in a matter of minutes. We didn't think any harm could come of it, it was so ridiculous. Now we discovered that the creature had grown a bit without our knowing – or was it just that familiar old bird set to put on a lot more weight?

If they're not going for the sport, what are they going for? Butler demanded with investigative triumph. *For secret testing at an Aids clinic, if rumours are to be believed. Along with the Disco, the Celtic Theme Park out at Castleraine – once the splendid home of the Smith-Bracken family – and the three-screen cinema, the twentieth century has come to quiet little Ballycanty at last. No-one yet knows how many victims Aids has claimed for certain, nor how exactly the disease has been contracted, but estimates of the numbers of men already HIV positive range from one to as many as ten . . .*

The article finished on points general concerning the incidence of Aids in Ireland as a whole, the fading role of the Church, and drugs problems in Dublin, Cork, Limerick. The tone, while tinged with some amusement from the supposed predicament of Ballycanty, was serious. Aids might prove a bigger problem for safe dreamy moral little Ireland than safe moral little Ireland would like to dream. It had been coasting along, relying on standards of behaviour that could no longer be taken for granted. It could yet wake to a nightmare reality.

'Supposing there is a bit of truth in it – that there's more than one or two of them involved?' Oonagh asked. 'I know we made it up, and we didn't even know for certain Sean was a reporter, but he *must* have checked it?'

'I thought he'd have made more of a splash,' I said to Oonagh, losing confidence. 'D'you think anyone'll even see it?'

Overall, we agreed, the article was not the sort of thing to set the country alight, despite its final note of warning. We were half proud of our rumour, half disappointed.

We didn't think.

Up to the time the story was published, most Ballycanteens whispering in secret were concerned to find out who for certain was HIV positive. Names were bandied about, speculation filled up the factual gaps, but no-one really asked how the victim(s) had contracted it.

Drugs were more or less ruled out. Various 'illegal substances' probably drift in and out of town, but you couldn't say that drugs was one of our problems. You couldn't say infected blood from transfusions was a problem either. I don't know a single person who's had a transfusion, except Oonagh's mother after her last baby when she nearly died, and I don't know of any haemophiliacs. That leaves just one thing. Sex.

No-one here admits to being a homosexual. It's been legal in Ireland since 1992, and the age of consent seventeen, which was even lower than England, but in a town like ours you'd live and die a churchgoing bachelor all your days rather than 'come out'. Or you'd get out.

Grandmother Foley takes the credit for this partly, as she told me on one memorable occasion.

'It's the power of the mothers and the grandmothers. No mother wants to admit her son's that way, and no son wants to admit it to his mother. Now the mothers and the grandmothers, we're everywhere in this town! You can fall off your stool with laughing if you like, Treesa Carmody, but I'm telling you we see a lot we don't talk about –' May she be forgiven for that terrible falsehood. '– And I'm not saying it doesn't go on, mind. I'm not saying there aren't some who are that way, God help them. But at least it's not walking down every street bold as brass like it is in England, corrupting the very children. They try to pretend everyone has a chice, you're this way or you're that way. Well, all I'm saying is, God never meant it like that. He made man, and He made woman, and the two of them fit together. Annything else is sheer perversity. Men with men, and women with women – there's no logic in it. You think about *that* now, Treesa Mary Carmody.'

I did. It was the first time I'd ever heard Nana Foley talk about sexual intercourse, and I was shocked to my marrow. It was a true sign of the times. I didn't need Mary Alice O'Shea to tell me – doom was coming upon Ireland all right! No doubt of it.

It only takes one person to read a report like Sean Butler's, then the thing's all over town.

At first there was outrage.

The Aids story was generally assumed to be *our* secret, to be discussed among the inhabitants of Ballycanty for the education and edification of same, not spread throughout Ireland as proof of our public shame. Now this Sean Butler had accepted our hospitality – everyone could testify to having seen him, though descriptions of him differed – but, like the treacherous guest in an old tale, he had stabbed his hosts on departing. If he showed himself again, they'd be making sausages of him.

It never seemed to occur to anyone (well, I have to leave out Oonagh and myself – we felt appropriately guilty after we'd had a good laugh) that Ballycanty must have been feeding him the rumours, retailing and corroborating bits of hot gossip it would have been wiser to suppress, and had only itself to blame. Any journalist worth his label must have checked the story with somebody other than ourselves. Those somebodies had a lot to answer for!

Had Sean Butler's article been the beginning, and end, of it, most of the scandal would have died down and the rumour would have starved away for lack of any proper facts to feed it. But unfortunately it was only the beginning.

Once the feeling of betrayal and the solid damning of two-faced Butler of no known paternity had faded away into the hot night airs, the trouble really started. There was an investigation into the sports club excursion. Then – outrage. Wives were outraged on behalf of their husbands, husbands outraged on behalf of each other (solidarity to the last), mothers outraged on behalf of innocent sons. The innocent sons for their part kept quiet. There is such a thing as tempting Providence.

SEVEN

'I don't think you should go on the trip to England,' Mother said.

Brendan looked all blue-eyed innocence. 'Why not, Mam?'

'You don't know what people will say.'

Mother doesn't openly pay that much attention to talk, because with a family with only one saint in it she's had to get used to a certain amount of negative advertising about *those Carmodys*. So when she warns against gossip, it's worth thinking about, even if you go and do afterwards whatever it was she was advising against.

That's a feature of small towns that never changes: you thrive on the talk until it's about yourself, and then you have to brave it out or it withers you like a poisonous spray over a weed. Generations of gossiping mothers have warned their own offspring not to be the ones to start up anything, and not to be involved in whatever it is, because years later the story will still be hanging in the air and there's no shaking it off. It'll cling to you until you're in your grave. Then the headstone will say something like:

Paddy Ryan

b 18-- d 19--

R I P

T O W T W L

So that's Paddy, with his Latin label (The One with the Wooden Leg). But then, carved in invisible lettering so only the Ballycanteens can read it:

61

He was much too fond of the Bushmills
And fought with the Guards on a Good Friday.

I looked at my 1990s mother with her gin and tonic, and her slim-fit leggings, and her cigarette in her hand. Behind her lurked the shade of her grandmother darning a sock, and her grandmother's grandmother boiling a pot over a turf fire, and all of them with one preoccupation exactly the same, come down through the years unchanged: how to probe the darling life of a secret son. And how to keep him from the razor tongues when she's found out whatever it was he's hiding.

Brendan wasn't deceived.

'What you really want to know is whether I've been sleeping with anyone.'

'I do not,' said Mam. 'I naturally assume you haven't.'

At that very moment, the scene was being played all over Ballycanty by mothers with the identical question: was *their* son one of the ones going to England for a test?

But it wasn't just the sons. Oonagh, Rose and I swapped notes on the number of husbands we knew put through the third degree by their wives. Suddenly the rock-solid fidelity they had all assumed began to crumble. Only a matter of days, and the prophecy of Mr Journalist Butler was being fulfilled – Ireland had been trading too long in outworn currency, minted in a time when nobody who hadn't been consorting with whores caught anything. Of course, officially nobody *had* done any consorting, because everyone would know, and they'd have the priest knocking on their door to do battle for their souls, which could be inconvenient if there was company. Now in the climate of 'galloping decadence' (quotation courtesy of Mary Alice O'Shea), the priest might be wearing out the doorbells and everyone deaf to him. That is always assuming the priest wasn't at a committee meeting, or relaxing behind some notion that things have changed a bit and we're all better educated and therefore more spiritually responsible than we used to be.

After all the talk, there had to be more men with Aids than Tommy Power (still nobody knew about him for certain), so who were they? From being a quiet little place with a normal amount of premarital sex, and the very occasional suppressed scandal concerning somebody's life partner, the whole town was being opened up to public aversion as a sink of immorality.

Now other reporters, alerted by the Butler article, started to trickle in – just the odd one or two at first, asking questions, hanging out at the bars in the hopes of a story. Those recognized as local men were hailed as long-lost friends, clapped on the back, given a couple of pints of Guinness, told tales as long as wet weekends about pigs and markets and old deals over land. Then they got the message and went back home without a word of what they'd come for.

A few newsmen from further afield slunk about planning to blend in with the grey walls outside, and the dark wood inside, and were pointed out straight away.

A short article appeared in a paper in the next county: *Is there Aids in Ballycanty?* and then another in a Dublin paper: *Aids comes to Ireland.* Inevitably the story crossed the water, but hit one of the notorious British tabloids on a day when another government scandal broke, and was relegated to the inside pages.

After that there was a brief lull.

'Do you think Brendan's all right?' Mother asked me, more than once, as Ballycanty grew hotter by the day. It was the usual oblique approach.

'I'm sure he hasn't got Aids,' I said. 'We're not all obsessed with sex in this town. Brendan really does want to go to England for an innocent sports trip. Besides, he hasn't even got a girlfriend.'

'That mightn't stop him going somewhere else,'

Mam said darkly. 'You don't know what seventeen-year-olds get up to these days, or *what* sort of people are coming into the town.'

This was said with all the distaste of Nana Foley; there is a strain of xenophobia in my mother and my grandmother, and it only takes a hint of a threat to the family for a sudden lapse in the acquired liberalism and Mother speaking out with Nana's voice.

I wonder if my great-grandmother's voice speaks out of Nana – I never knew her, or perhaps I might sometimes hear it.

Oonagh and I amused ourselves eavesdropping in the street. Every hushed discussion we happened upon – the sort that stopped mysteriously as we passed and started up again when we were supposedly out of earshot – went something like: 'Sw sw sh sw sw sw *she* mumble mumble so *I* said sw sw . . . she . . . she said . . . sw sw . . . '

Where two or more were gathered together, you could guess the topic.

'D'you think I should let Paddy go?'

'Sure you can't stop him, but they should call the whole thing off now – it's got such a bad name.'

'Have you heard Seamus O'Rourke was one of the first to sign down for it? Him and that John Crowley. I wouldn't be surprised if the two of them weren't at the centre of it. I wouldn't put anything past the O'Rourke boy. He's in with a bad crowd . . . '

So now the names of Crowley and O'Rourke were being linked with Power, and there were three confirmed HIV positive without a scrap of evidence, and the whole sports club trip in jeopardy.

'They'll have to call it off altogether!' Brendan told me, his eyes sparking furiously. 'No-one dares sound keen about going now because whether he has Aids or not, he'll be branded as going over to England for a test. I'd like to wring the neck of whoever started the rumour!'

'I'm here next to you, Brendan, and my hearing-aid's switched up just fine . . . They'll be joining in from Cork in a minute.'

'Sorry,' he said. 'But it makes me mad.'

'There's no truth in it then?' I managed to keep my face blank.

'Of course there isn't! Not that I know of, any road. It was all just a bit of good fun as usual. Now I don't know how much we're going to lose on it. The travel insurance probably won't compensate for cancellation in our circumstances. "Well Mr Carmody, and what would you say were your reasons for cancelling your ticket?" "Intimidation, Mrs Mahoney. Me life's under threat. A lot of ould women spreading the scandal about, just like yourself, Mrs Mahoney."'

For the first time, I felt real guilt. Brendan had worked stacking shelves in the Hyper for weeks to save up for the trip. He and Jack and their friend Mikey were going. Now they'd all be out of pocket. I didn't know how I was going to make it up to him without his either showering me with coals of fire in the form of undeserved gratitude, or suspecting I had something to do with it.

There's no getting a story back. You have to live with the consequences.

It never rains but it pours, as Nana is fond of saying. That's too often the literal truth in Ireland, but it was August, and we hadn't seen a drop of rain for weeks. All the grass was dried up, and anyone who didn't water their flowers found them dead after a day. I'd never seen so many tanned arms and legs in Ballycanty, and the streets had a Mediterranean feel, despite the Irish names over the grey shop-fronts and all that brown paint on the windows and doors. But the kind of rain I was thinking about was Nana's metaphorical sort, and that just tipped out of the sky most of the summer.

It was the third week of August, only days after they

65

officially cancelled the sports club trip, when I opened the front door to a stranger. I wasn't expecting anyone, unless it was Declan.

The man was tall, and well-dressed in casual clothes. He had short curling hair and looked in his early forties. I'd never seen him before.

'Does Josephine Carmody live here?' His accent was English.

I examined him with renewed interest. If it hadn't been for Josie's name coming into it, I'd have taken him for a reporter. My mind leapt for the most interesting conclusion: this was the adulterous tutor from Oxford with the wife and two children? I stored up the details for Denise: quite attractive, pale blue eyes, thin sort of face, broad shoulders and slim body; tallish, curly hair.

'Well, not exactly. This is where her family lives.'

'Do you know where I might find her?' He was studying me with the same attention I was giving him. 'I'm a friend of hers from England. My name is Robert Eaves.'

Denise hadn't given me a name. Josie could have lots of friends in England.

'She's staying in a friend's cottage at the moment.'

'Is it far from here?'

'Nooo . . . not far.'

'Could you tell me how to find it?'

I thought at once of the old Irish joke: *if I were you I wouldn't start from here.* It happened to be true. There wasn't a straightforward route. I could have kept him on the doorstep for ten minutes, and then watched him forget the instructions as he walked away. In the end I asked him in, and gave him a cup of instant coffee while I drew a map. It was easy when you knew where you were going.

I could feel him watching me, but whenever I looked up his eyes were somewhere else.

'How do you know my sister?'

The answer sounded a little reluctant. 'She used to work at the school where my son is a pupil.'

'That would be in Oxford, would it?'

'It would.'

Married with at least one child – it didn't rule him out as the Lover. Josie seducing one of the parents? Or did he seduce her? I couldn't imagine it that way round. His manner was too formal. Perhaps he had a faded wife, and he had been dazzled by Josie.

Perhaps if I'd never been told anything by Denise, I'd have been more free with the questions, but, the way it was, my knowledge inhibited me. I wondered if Josie would be pleased to see him, or furious her hide-out had been given away. I toyed with the idea of misleading him, and then reflected that in the end he'd only ask someone else who would tell him. If he was determined to see Josie, he would.

I handed him the map. 'Would Josie be expecting you?'

'It's possible,' he said. 'Your sister has stolen my car.'

I showed him the way. I felt I owed it to Josie to be around when he saw her, in case he was contemplating beating her up.

He drove a hired car, presumably because Josie had taken his, and negotiated the winding lanes that led west from Ballycanty with an alien's caution. We drove over hills where the summer grass was already brown and dry, and down towards the sea through the woods. The trees were dusty, a worn-out green that was gasping: Give us water – help – water – or we'll fall into autumn and die . . .

I wound down the window on my side, and he wound down the window on his and a warm artificial breeze flowed through whenever we got up a bit of speed.

'How d'you know Josie took your car?' I asked, when he seemed to be getting the hang of the thing.

'*Stole* was the word I used. She left a note in my garage, to the effect that I need not call the police. She

67

omitted to tell me where she was going. I've had quite a job tracking her down.'

'How did you get here – fly?'

'Into Dublin. I should have come into Cork – I had no idea what your roads were like. I hired this car from Dublin airport. I've never come across such an erratic system of measuring distances.'

'That's maybe because we have Irish miles, and English miles, and kilometres.'

He made a sound like *hmph*. 'I intend to go back on the ferry.'

'With your own car?'

'I hope so. I've arranged to leave this one in Wexford, and have it picked up by the hire company.'

'That doesn't seem very convenient.' I tried to sound commiserating.

'None of it has been convenient.' He had a clipped, impatient way of talking. 'I didn't discover the car was missing until after I'd come back from several months' holiday in Greece with my family. We have a house there.'

I couldn't resist the temptation. 'Whatever made my sister think she could borrow your car in the first place?'

The answer sounded perfectly straight. 'She was an au pair for us briefly. I lent her a car once or twice.'

'What does your wife think of my sister taking your car?'

A hesitation, then, 'She doesn't know yet. She's still in Greece.'

This time the tone said: that's enough questions.

I didn't mind. I had plenty to think about.

Denise had said the lover was an Oxford tutor, but if Robert Eaves was the man, what had he been doing taking time off in the beginning of June? Josie had arrived in the first week – surely he would have been teaching then? He couldn't be the tutor. This must be another one! I couldn't imagine Robert Eaves involved in a passionate affair with my sister anyway, and it would have had to be passionate, because with her nothing else would have been interesting despite her pose of bored sophistication about 'wild' affairs. I thought him too staid, too formal to attract the likes of Josie.

There were glimpses of the sea, solid blocks of paint-box blue, before we reached the gateposts marking the cove track, then we rattled down over the potholes and loose stones while Robert Eaves grimaced, presumably at the thought of his Citroën at the mercy of Josie. I pointed out where the path branched to go down to the cove past Josie's cottage.

'You'd better keep on this track down to the cove. That's where she parks your car.'

He grunted, with what I assumed was disapproval.

When we reached the shore, the sea lay dead and calm as it had done for weeks at the feet of the rocks, and the sweep of the sand and little jetty were unembarrassed by anything resembling a Citroën. He looked at me, with suspicion.

'She doesn't usually go out during the day,' I said. 'I expect she's just run into town to shop or something. We could go up to the cottage and see if Aggie's about?'

He frowned. 'Who's Aggie?'

I tried to explain the arrangement. I could see him becoming more and more irritated. 'Want to come and have a look?' I finished weakly.

I didn't have a key, but luckily the door was unlocked. We peered in at the windows first, and then went inside. There were no clues as to whether either of the inmates had just left, or would be back shortly. Cursing Josie, I felt obliged to apologize.

'I'm sorry. This seems to have been a wasted journey.'

'Not at all.'

For the first time since we'd set out he looked at me as though I was a person independent from my thieving sister. Previously I had had the feeling he viewed me merely as an extension of her. 'It was kind of you to show the way. I'll run you back home now and come out here again later.'

I was wondering if I should insist on staying, or offer to accompany him a second time in case his intentions towards Josie were the worst, when the sounds of a car engine and the rattle of tyres over the track brought us both to the door. The Citroën was disappearing down towards the cove.

'At least it's still in one piece!' I said, hoping to assuage any wrath he might be nursing.

We waited in silence until Josie herself appeared below us, her arms round a cardboard box with a milk carton sticking out of the top. She was toiling up the path, which was steep, watching her step on the rocky outcrops, and it struck me how very thin she was. Her elbows stuck out and her face had that shrunk-to-the-bone look people get when they lose too much weight. She glanced up towards us. She seemed to see me first, and then the man next to me. Her face registered shock, followed by confusion. She stopped.

'Robert!'

'Josie.'

That didn't sound loverlike. I saved it up for Denise.

'What are you doing here?'

'I'd have thought that was obvious.'

'You've . . . come for the car then?'

'Very astute of you.'

She bent over to put down the cardboard box and then straightened up. I could sense her thinking furiously.

'Terry, would you mind very much going for a walk for five minutes? Robert and I have a few things to talk about.'

'I don't think we have,' he said shortly. 'Just give me the keys of my car.'

She folded her arms, her head on one side so that her dark hair fell seductively over one shoulder. 'Well, maybe I've got a few things to say to you. You can have the car keys after that.'

'I'm driving your sister back home now.'

She stooped to pick up the box again. 'Oh, she won't mind a couple of minutes, will you, Terry?'

I dithered. I didn't know what answer to give except, 'No. I'll go down to the cove for ten minutes.'

'It won't be necessary—' Robert began, but Josie was suddenly past us and halfway through the cottage door, and he was obliged to follow.

If I'd been Josie, I don't know how I'd have coped in that situation – it's bad enough just meeting old boy-friends in the street. Not that I knew for certain what the situation was of course, but with Denise's information I had some idea. There was always the possibility that Josie had taken the car deliberately to bring him over to Ireland. She might have known he'd come back from Greece before his wife – especially if they'd been lovers. And when did all that happen, for heaven's sake? We'd thought she was working at a school! But why go to the bother of Aggie's cottage and everything – why not just stay in England and wait for him?

I was left marvelling at her. She has a very strong will, my sister.

I didn't go down to the cove, but took the cliff path towards the next bay. I turned to look back twice, wondering if I'd see Josie waving wildly at me for rescue – or Robert running out with Josie after him, a frying-pan she'd never lifted to put on the stove aimed at his head. But there were just the slopes of wiry grass, studded with gorse and small tough plants with dried-up flowers. The cottage was tucking itself down into the hilly folds, keeping a low profile, giving no hint of what was going on under its blue slate roof. I was tempted to creep back, and hang around, a fly with its ear pressed to whitewashed walls.

A lone walker was coming towards me on the cliffs, still far away, and I thought I'd stroll on for a while to see if it was anyone I knew. As we approached each other, the figure looked familiar – a dark-haired young man – then I saw it was Tom Power. Tom Power, subject of all the gossip. We were still some distance away, but he must have recognized me at about the same time, and he raised an arm in greeting.

I always liked Tom's face: not handsome exactly, but attractive, kind, with a way of looking at you with his dark eyes that was half laughing with you, half serious. And he had a quiet voice too, not the average bellow like my brother, effective from one end of a sports field to the other. He was wearing jeans and a shirt with the sleeves rolled up. His arms were tanned, but he looked leaner, and his face thinner than I remembered. There was little trace of the schoolboy about him.

Of course, the first thing that came into my mind was all that gossip. We'd been talking about him, but none of us had seen him for months. I hoped I could behave as though I'd never heard a word of it.

We waited until we were only a couple of yards apart.

'Well Terry, how's yourself? I haven't seen you in a long while!'

'I might say the same for you, Tom. What've you been doing with yourself?'

It was a greeting I could have given anyone, but it sounded to me as though I was referring to the gossip, and I hope I didn't blush. Did he know that the whole town had him down – along with Messrs Crowley and O'Rourke – as HIV positive? And with that thought, it was as though a gag had been tied over my mouth.

'You knew I was studying in England?' he said. 'Of course you did. I've been over there a while. Only another year to go—'

'What was it you were doing now?'

'Engineering. And yourself?'

'At this moment? I'm waiting for my sister to finish arguing with somebody so I can go back home.' I was tempted to tell him she was probably arguing with her ex-lover, but such an admission didn't say much for family loyalty, and the topic of lovers suddenly bristled all over with spikes like one of those mines in an old-fashioned film.

'Which sister would this be now?'

'Josie,' I said. 'She's staying in the cottage down at the cove with Aggie Riordan.'

'Oh, Josie.' Then, 'What's she doing with herself since she was in England?'

'She's only over here for the summer. I expect she'll go back.'

'I always thought she was a great traveller. What's she doing choosing dull old Ireland instead of Greece or the Bahamas?'

'Enjoying the cheap suntan, I suppose!'

'Aren't we all? Isn't it a bit *too* much though?'

The weather. What the English talk about for lack of conversation. I asked him about every member of his family, though they were all still in Ballycanty and I could see them any day of the week. He must have thought it a bit unusual.

In desperation I looked at my watch. It was fifteen minutes since Josie had asked me to go, and I could return.

'I'd better go back,' I said. 'I was supposed to be away for ten minutes.'

'Oh, it's the tactful manoeuvre, is it? I'll walk with you some of the way. Remember when we used to come over here with a picnic to bird-watch? Sometimes I'd like those days back again. It's odd how you can't wait to grow up, but it's not quite what you think when you get there.'

'It's twenty-one you are, Thomas Power, not fifty-one! Well, I can tell you I don't want to go back to school – not for anything. Always more work you hadn't done, always trouble!' I talked quickly, to cover my thoughts. Perhaps he was going to tell me he really *did* have Aids . . . and I didn't want to hear it. It would change everything.

'I thought you were clever enough at the schoolwork, Terry. You come from a clever family.'

'That's Brendan,' I said, as I usually did.

'You didn't want to go on with your studies? You used to want to write books about unsolved historical puzzles. What happened to all that?'

'Oh, that was years ago!' It was; when I was fourteen. 'You don't have to have a degree to write books. Anyway, I was bored with school and all that, and I didn't do so well in my Leaving Cert. And I wanted a bit of fun without all the studying.'

We must have been the only two adult beings in the whole of Ballycanty that summer who didn't speak of the Aids story. I knew why *I* didn't mention it, but it only occurred to me afterwards to ask myself – why didn't *he*?

I watched him out of sight, tramping a track for himself through the rough turf towards the cliff road, and then I went down to the cottage. As a tactful warning, I called out for Josie before I got there.

They both came out, and stood by the doorstep.

Josie looked a bit wild, as though she'd been running her fingers back through her hair, but then she cultivates that look so there was nothing to be deduced from it. Robert was exactly the same as when I'd left: striped shirt, tie neatly done up (in that heat!) and curly hair as before.

'Can you drive, Terry?' Robert asked.

'I can. Why?'

'I'd like you to drive my car if you will.'

'I'll drive it!' Josie shouted suddenly, swinging round to confront Robert. 'I told you – I'll drive it! What do you think I'm going to do with it, for heaven's sake? Head for Dublin or Cork or somewhere?'

Robert didn't even glance at her. 'Terry? If you could drive it to your home, that'd be a great help. I can't get both cars back to Ballycanty otherwise.'

Josie turned on me and yelled, 'Don't you dare touch

it! This is nothing to do with you – I'll drive it!' She was like a fury, stamping her bare foot and shooting sparks out of her eyes.

Robert just looked at me, pleading.

In the end, because it was his car, and I couldn't trust Josie any more than he could, I drove the Citroën, and Robert followed behind in the hired car. We left my sister by the cottage, shrieking after Robert like a banshee, 'You should let *me* drive it! You should let *me*!'

I'd been used to Josie's tantrums in the family, but it was a shock to see her screaming like a spoilt child in front of Robert. Had their relationship – whatever it was – deteriorated so far that she no longer cared how he saw her? Or was this the last-ditch desperation of the cast-off mistress?

Driving Robert's car was an experience. I'd often borrowed the family Ford, but this was in a different league. The track up to the cliff road seemed even worse on the return journey, and I felt as though I were guiding an unpredictable and powerful horse over the potholes, and that it would bolt from my control at any moment. The weight of the responsibility grounded my confidence. I supposed I must be insured on Robert's policy, but I didn't like to stop to get out and ask, in case the answer was no and I lost my nerve completely. We made funereal progress back to town once we reached the public road.

Robert was grateful. He asked if we'd mind if he left his car in our drive for the night – he would be dropping off the hired one the next day, and would make a return journey to pick up the Citroën. I didn't feel brave enough to offer to drive it all the way to Wexford for him. I told myself that if he was fool enough to be involved with somebody like Josie, he could look after his own transport problems – it might teach him to be more cautious in future! Then I caught myself up for sounding like Mam again.

I could scarcely believe he was an Oxford tutor. I had

thought people like that were too mega-intelligent to become entangled with someone like my sister in the first place.

'And what a feeble thing you are, Terry Carmody!' I said to myself that night, in my relatively tidy, Josie-free bedroom. 'You should have stood up to both of them, letting them make use of you like that!'

What did I want to get involved in their stupid quarrels for? I could have walked the four or so miles home with Tom Power, who still, thank God, seemed to have a good bit of life left in him.

EIGHT

The picture of Josie waving her arms about and shrieking stayed in my mind. It disturbed me so much, I
borrowed Father's car to return to the cove to see her
later that evening. Perhaps she'd adored the semi-
detached Robert and that was their final row and she
was suicidal. After all, she was my sister.

You face west driving towards Josie's cove from
Ballycanty, and the evening sky spreads out before
you, pink and gold. Even in August you notice the sun
setting earlier behind the rough blanket of cliff and the
straggling thorn hedges that mark the crazy patchwork
of old fields. Fields are tiny in Ireland – everyone
remarks it. It's partly to do with inheritance, no one
brother wanting to be left out of the family acres, and
Uncle Seamus claiming a share too, and partly to do
with convenience, chance – or the fairies. Uncle Danny
says that out in the Wild West even to this day there are
those who won't change a boundary or move a path
that belongs to the fairy people, and warn you to
beware of their raths and thorn trees. All this makes
nonsense of grubbing up hedges and farming on an
economic scale, but perhaps out there the fairies
continue to jog along doggedly cheek by skin of the
teeth with the EC grants, and computer technology.
Though it may yet come about that what God and
the Church couldn't conquer over centuries, Econ-
omics will obliterate in a few short years, and Old
Ireland will be gone for ever. No wonder Mary Alice is
prophesying doom.

A car came towards me as I approached the track,
and I thought I saw it slow and indicate a right turn

down to the cove. It would have had to wait for me to turn first. The sun was in my eyes, and I could have been mistaken about the indicator; it passed me as I turned into the track.

There was no need to go all the way down to the cove to park. Josie must have heard the car rattling over the potholes, and I saw her dart out of the cottage and then stand by the door.

'I came back to see if you were all right—' I began.

'All right as anybody could be stuck out here in the wilds on their own. I wish I'd gone away properly this summer, not let myself get marooned out here!' She was leaning against the door-frame in a thoroughly bad humour. The door was open behind her, but she didn't ask me in.

'Where's Aggie?'

She shrugged. 'Visiting some friends. She won't be back for a couple of days.'

I was still marvelling at the way she had helped herself to the Citroën. 'You must have known Robert would try to get his car back! He told me you'd stolen it!'

She tossed her hair. 'That's ridiculous. Thieves don't leave notes and sign them.'

'You're lucky he didn't go to the English police.'

'He wouldn't have done that. He's too afraid his wife might have found out. I'm sorry she didn't – I thought she'd be coming back from holiday with him.'

I know I said I didn't want to find out any more about Josie's tortuous private life, but now there were just too many questions clamouring to be asked. 'I can't follow any of this. Why would you *want* his wife to find out?'

Josie frowned even more crossly than before, and folded her arms, shrugging with irritation. 'He ditched me. We were having an affair. It all got too much for him, and he chucked me out, so I thought he deserved it – the car, I mean. It isn't as though he hasn't got another one.'

'So he was your lover?' It was critical to get at least one of the details straight.

She was fiddling with her watch-strap. 'I said so, didn't I? But there was not much love in it. It was an arrangement that suited us both. Robert's one of those weak womanizers – Oxford's full of them. Middle-aged academics bored with their wives, and wanting an external examiner to tell them they're still madly attractive and wonderful in bed.'

'He's a tutor then?' She didn't deny it, so I went on, 'How did he manage to take the whole summer off? He told me he'd just spent several months in Greece.'

'He had a year's sabbatical – he was working on a book. He went to Greece to finish it.'

So far the details fitted with Denise's version of 'the lover', but Josie's jaded afterview didn't tell me much about the actual relationship. I still couldn't imagine what she had seen in Robert, unless it was mere novelty.

'If there wasn't much love in it, why did you go along with it?'

'He had a cottage. He let me live there for nothing.'

The questions were still jostling up, fighting to get to the head of the queue. 'But what about your job? I thought you had to live at the school?'

'Oh, I'd given that up by then.'

'So you'd given up your job before the summer term even started?'

She didn't answer, and I knew I was pushing my luck.

'And Robert—'

She glanced at her watch. 'Robert this and Robert that!' she mimicked. 'What do you know about him?'

'I only—'

'Look, Terry. I don't feel like talking about all this just now. Right? I think it'd be better if you went home.'

So final, it was pointless to argue.

'I will,' I said. 'I only came to see if you were still

alive, and ask you out for a drink. Thanks very much for the welcome and all the gratitude. Next time you have a row with an ex-lover I won't bother.'

Again she didn't answer.

When I reached the car, I heard her shout behind me, 'Thanks, Terry!' It sounded grudging, so this time I didn't reply. The cottage door slammed.

It occurred to me as I rattled back to the cliff road that she'd seemed very on edge, but not quite the way I'd expected her to be. I was putting it down to the fact that she was unnerved by Robert's sudden appearance and the loss of the car, when I reached the turn onto the road. The lane emerges between two straggling hedges and two old gateposts, and there's a bend in the road almost immediately. A car came round just as I was about to pull out. It slowed, and then accelerated past me. It looked like the car I had met on the road only a few minutes earlier.

Two images remained in my mind afterwards. The first was that of the car passing me on the cliff road. There are lots of white cars about, and I'm not observant with the number-plates, but it came to me that it *was* the car I had seen earlier, about to turn down Josie's track.

The second image glittered and teased: the very expensive Cartier watch Josie had been fiddling with. I hadn't seen it before. I wondered if Robert had bought her future good behaviour with it.

It's never my intention to call on Mary Alice O'Shea, conversations with whom can take a turn towards an interview with the Grand Inquisitor, but I was fetching Nana after work in Da's car. She was coming round for tea with us.

Nana and Mary Alice have school, childbearing and widowhood in common, as well as the fact that they've neither of them lived outside Ballycanty in the whole of their lives. They visit each other too frequently, and then bicker with the familiarity of an old married couple though they present a united front in a crisis, especially if it has anything to do with the dire spiritual condition of post-Christian Ireland. Then the only contentiousness will be in outdoing each other with statistics and shocking examples of the fading light of faith in the nation.

No. 36 Dunmore Road has a dark green door, and heavy lace curtains in the windows. There's a fashion for lace at the moment, but Mary Alice's is first-time-round; she pays no attention to trends. When you go in through the front door, the Sacred Heart perpetual light nearly knocks you in the face.

I parked in the street outside, and watched the lace go into its usual spasms.

'It's you, Teresa,' Mary Alice said, when I knocked at the door.

It was nice to be reassured.

'It's Treesa!' she called to my grandmother, leaning her head backwards at a peculiar angle so that the sound would carry through the wall. 'Will you come in for a minute Teresa?' An instruction, not an invitation.

Nana was in the front room, as usual, and sitting in another of the O'Shea dark-red-rep-wing-armchairs with the original antimacassars was Mary Alice's granddaughter, Rita. Rita O'Malley is in training to be the next keeper of the holy well at No. 36. At school we used to call her Saint Rita, and the nuns loved her. She was the year below Rose and me, but everyone knew who she was with her pale hair, pale face and pale ideas glinting through her spectacles.

She's worn contact lenses since she left school and started to work in one of the two Ballycanty travel agents.

'Will you have a small glass of sherry Teresa?'

When Mary Alice offers you a drink, it's a bad idea to refuse − firstly because it's a sign of temporary approval, and secondly because it's an excuse for her to have another glass, and thus an opportunity to score another good mark with her if you need one. Nana doesn't drink, having taken The Pledge, and I don't like sherry – especially sweet sherry.

'That's very kind of you, Mrs O'Shea. I will.'

'Hello, Teresa,' Rita said.

'Hello, Rita.'

Now it's not that I don't like Rita O'Malley – it's hard to know enough about her to like or dislike – but she has the conversational cut and thrust of a Trappist. To tell you the truth, we're all surprised she hasn't become a nun. I suppose it must be difficult to be chatty if you're a saint, with so many interesting topics of conversation lost to you. And of course saints aren't keen on town gossip either: they don't listen to it and they don't pass it on, and if they're as good as Rita, there's not even anything to say *about* them. For the sake of Nana's friendship with Mary Alice, and because Rita doesn't seem to have many friends herself, I try to be nice to her, but it's hard going.

'How's work?' I asked. Her travel agent's is in the shopping mall – a hub of information, you might say, but I wasn't expecting any.

Rita doesn't light up with sparks like Oonagh or Rose when she smiles. Her mouth curves in a quiet way, and she looks at you as though she wants to see right into you. It's disconcerting to the lightweights like me.

'Oh, it's fine. Thanks.'

I waited for her to add something, but she didn't.

'Had your holiday yet?'

'Well no. Not yet.'

Silence.

Her presence has the most curious effect. Gradually all the energy drains out of you, and you sit there, in a strange blank calm, the ideas trickling out of your brain until there's only the clock ticking, and Rita looking you into eternity. I wandered round my head discarding questions like *I suppose you must have sold a lot of holidays this summer?* and *What would you say is the most popular destination this year?* searching unsuccessfully for something that would demand more than a one-word reply.

'Are you planning to go somewhere nice?'

'Oh yes. But not for a while.'

To my relief, Mary Alice intervened with the glass of sherry, and chipped in, 'She's going to Spain for two whole weeks. Isn't she the lucky one?'

Spain . . . with its bullfights, flamenco dancers and beaches – sun, sea, sand, lager louts and the obvious. Rita, in *Spain*?

'You are lucky!' I couldn't afford to go anywhere. 'Will you be spending all the time at the beach, or are you planning to travel round?'

A deep wine colour unexpectedly flushed Rita's fine skin. 'I . . . I'll not be on any beach.'

I wondered for a moment if she was actually going on holiday with a boyfriend none of us had heard about.

Then she said, 'I'm going to Guadalupe.'

All I know about Guadalupe is that it's a village in the mountains somewhere, with a holy shrine dedicated to the Virgin Mary. There was just a hint of defiance about the way she said the name, as though she guessed I would think it a ridiculous destination for a summer holiday.

Mary Alice, picking up her cue, leapt to her defence. 'She's saved up for it all year. She's going on an organized pilgrimage – there's a retreat at the end of it. Isn't she a good girl? Not like the rest of us.'

Mary Alice has a tendency to speak of her granddaughters as though they had never progressed mentally or physically beyond the age of twelve. I caught the look on Rita's face, and felt sorry for her.

It was obvious that by 'the rest of us' and by the glint of her spectacles Mary Alice meant *me*, and Rose, Oonagh and the rest of our crowd – not herself. I wondered if I'd already forfeited her favour for blinking involuntarily in a derisory fashion or looking at Rita as though I might say something critical, and she would snatch the sherry back.

Nana, obliquely, came in on my side, tart with injured family pride. 'Well, it's not everyone as has the opportunity to jine a pilgrimage like that! You are a lucky girl, Rita, but there's no need to go so far to find spiritual benefits. There's plenty on offer down at your nearest church.'

'She knows that!' Mary Alice said at once. 'There's not that many of the young people these days go to church every Sunday like Rita!' She was bristling now like a terrier, guarding the honour of the O'Shea /O'Malley alliance.

Another grandmothers' rubber had started. Mary Alice held the best card in Rita, but Nana wasn't giving up on the poor hand she'd been dealt (me), and she played her one trump.

'Ah, no, Mary Alice. There's more than you would think! My granddaughter Grace has never missed a Sunday Mass since she had her First Communion, and now she takes her children. It's a wonderful thing to see your great-grandchildren lining up in the benches in front of you.'

She took that trick – Mary Alice has no descendants beyond Rita's generation.

Rita and I sat there, two dummies in the one game. I took a sip of my sherry, and Rita took a sip of hers. There was no starting up any rival exchanges, so we both smiled weakly and looked at the wallpaper, which is coffee-coloured, with stripes and patterns on it. It's been the same ever since I've known the house. There's a cabinet in one corner, the glass-fronted shelves piled with O'Shea wedding china, saved unused for posterity. The occasional tables are crowded with framed photographs of children and grandchildren, those who've made it to be priests and nuns in the most prominent position. Mary Alice's wedding blessing, signed by Pope Pius XI, is framed against the wallpaper. Nana's front room has kept up with the times a little better – no yellowing net curtains or antimacassars – but she too has the photographs (Uncle Danny in pride of place), the same pope's signed blessing, and a larger newer picture of John Paul II than the O'Sheas'.

It struck me that Rita lived in a different world. It wasn't that she was excluded from the gossips in Whelan's or the long noisy nights at Reds – she would actually dislike them. All she had in common with the rest of us was that she went to work every weekday and lived at home. I wondered if saints were inevitably lonely people, or just out of step with their times. Perhaps she had been born two or three generations too late. The Ireland she belongs to is that of her grandmother's childhood.

I drove Nana back to our house soon after that.

She said in the car, 'I've never met anyone the like of Mary Alice for lording it over you with all the members of her holy family.' And then, 'That Rita O'Malley's a good girl all right, but she'll never be making the headlines.'

NINE

I had saved my holiday that year, so that I could take two weeks together. The only drawback was that Oonagh couldn't take the same weeks. I didn't have much choice about the dates, and it happened that my Great-Uncle Danny, Nana Foley's brother who is a retired priest, was having a holiday at the same time. It wasn't planned like that, but he had been ill, and Nana was anxious to have him to fuss over for a while.

Now it also happened that Nana had arranged to have her spare room redecorated. The painter wouldn't be finished before Danny's visit, so Mam was to have Great-Uncle Danny – unless the work could be completed in double quick time and the fumes of the paint could expire before he was due to leave. Since Dad sold the old terrace house to buy Mother's dream on the private estate, we haven't had quite enough bedrooms, as I think I mentioned before. When there's a guest, we all have a change around, or one of us is farmed out. It's my room that has the two beds in it.

I could have gone to spend my first week with the Hennessys or the Walshes, but the thought of Josie nagged at me. With no car and no telephone, and even Aggie away for a week with cousins in Kerry, she would be like someone with their limbs cut off. And with Aggie gone, there would be a spare bedroom. I couldn't afford to go away anywhere; the cove – subject to the quality of Josie's agreement – was a solution to the holiday problem. I couldn't see that she'd object if Declan spent his time down there with me. There was no guarantee she and I wouldn't quarrel, but I then could go to Oonagh's.

Josie had looked fiery and defiant the last time I'd seen her, but when I borrowed the car again to drive down and ask her if I could come and stay, she seemed pale and lethargic, with shadows under her eyes. I wondered whether she was moping more about the loss of her adulterous tutor, or the loss of his car.

'It's deadly dull down here,' she said, with no expression. 'There's nothing to do. How will you get into town?'

'I don't need to go into town – I'm not working. I'll bring lots of extra food with me, so you needn't worry about that. And Declan can give me a lift if I want one. He doesn't have to be at the bar until the evenings. What do *you* do with yourself all day?' I saw the pile of battered paperbacks on the floor had grown, along with the piles of ash on the saucers. 'And I could tidy up for you?'

I was sure Aggie had her work cut out keeping the place respectable, and it would be a shame for her to come back to a tip.

'I don't want you messing around. It makes me nervous.' And then, 'Oh well, you might as well come. You can have the loft so you won't be disturbing Aggie's things.'

Then, as an afterthought, 'I don't want you telling tales to Mam.'

'What sort of tales?'

Her gesture embraced the room, the house generally. 'Oh, the mess. The way I live. Whatever.'

The loft is reached by a ladder staircase from the living-room. There's no door to it. If you want to shut yourself in you have to lower a trapdoor from above. It's only possible to stand upright in the middle of the room, and there are two skylights; one facing south to the sea, and the other back up over the gorse and brambles of the sloping cliff. I kept both skylights permanently open, and pulled the bed directly under one of them to catch any passing breath of air. The

87

temperature up there was over the hundred during the day, and only cooled off just before dawn. Even the stars seemed to burn with a white heat that struck the slates.

At first Josie was impossible. Pleased to have me there only for the first five minutes, she subsequently showed an inclination to argue everything. A dark cloud descended on her, wrapping her like an old apple-woman's shawl, black as age and dirt could make it, and she sat about the cottage all day, avoiding the baking sun. The cloud would become impenetrable, and there would be grumblings, and searing flashes it was well to avoid.

I attributed the moodiness partly to Robert's visit. That she was bored was obvious: no car, no telephone, no television – and, it emerged, very little money.

'I thought I'd hitch into town,' she said to me on the second day I was there. 'I know I can get a lift back anyway. Have you got any cash with you, Terry? I'll pay it back when I can get to the bank.'

I had ten pounds, and resigned myself to the gift. I had also brought a huge bag of coins at her request to feed the electricity meter.

'Thanks. You don't want to come, I suppose?'

'It's my holiday. It's like an oven outside. Why would I be wanting to traipse into town when I'm there every day of the week?'

She was putting on mascara in front of a small mirror on the living-room table, eyelash by eyelash. The pale-lipped black-eyed Sixties haunted that summer. With every flick of the brush she was making herself more corpse-like.

'You should eat more,' I said, sounding like Mam and risking an outburst. 'Being so thin doesn't suit you.'

'If you want to stay here Teresa, you'll have to give up nagging at me.'

It wasn't worth arguing, but whereas my mother would have condemned Josie's appearance out of hand, I was prepared to admit that a skeletal frame was ideal for the clothes fanatic.

I spent the day on the beach, and didn't see her return. Later, she emerged from her bedroom in one of those thin floating shifts that look hideous on normal people. 'I thought you'd had enough for the day,' I said. 'You didn't say you were going out again.'

'No. Do I have to?'

She flung that sort of challenge like a knife-thrower, and I became adept at not blinking. 'Is somebody picking you up?'

'As a matter of fact, they are. Now will you stop interrogating me?'

She sat and smoked while she waited, swinging one leg impatiently. It wasn't worth saying any more.

A man called Gus, tanned and flashing with bits of gold, called for her in a big white Mercedes.

I didn't even let myself *think* a reaction until he'd gone: I'd seen the car twice before, both times when it passed me on the road just by Josie's track.

Declan drove down to the cove every morning in his mother's car, and we spent whole days on the beach. We rigged up a bit of shade like a Bedouin tent with some old pieces of wood he brought from the shed at home, and rugs from the cottage, and camped just beyond the reach of the tide. It wasn't cool, but at least the sun didn't fry you up.

'Why don't you join us?' I asked Josie every day.

She stretched her arms out languidly. 'Ugh. I can't bear the heat. It makes me ill.'

'You'd feel better if you came out during the day and went to bed earlier at night.' I sounded just like Mam *again*, which was worrying. Did it mean that that was the way I was going to be as a mother? Mam, despite her latter-day training, was beginning to revert to the Nana pattern. I found myself examining my trains of thought, standing outside my brain to watch it ticking round its hereditary cycle. For example: I never knew what time Josie was going to come in . . . and that was one of Mam's little obsessions with Brendan.

Gus had called for Josie three nights running, and the second one she didn't get back until eleven o'clock the next day. Then she slept until he called for her again that night.

When Declan officially met Josie, I could feel them eyeing each other up. I relied on the evidence of Robert (fortysomething) and Gus (probably the same) for my theory that Josie preferred older men. And Declan? Next to Josie I knew the only desirable body was bone thin, and ivory white, and the only way to wear your hair was very dark and waist long. I was neither fat, nor plain, nor lumpish, but I felt all three.

'What does your sister do all day?' Declan asked me. 'Surely she can't want more than eight hours' sleep? She must be ill.'

When I'd nipped up to the cottage to get us a drink, or use the bathroom, I had found her trying on clothes, or whiling away the hours putting on make-up before she went out. If I stayed to talk to her, it'd be, 'D'you think this colour suits me?' or 'Should I take this up a bit? You don't think it's too long?'

I described the beauty sessions to Declan. 'Perhaps she's in training to be a model. She's got the looks, after all.' I was trying to draw him out with that; he hadn't passed any comments on her appearance.

'Too late,' he pointed out mercilessly. 'If you haven't made it by seventeen you're probably over the hill.'

Now that remark of Declan's brought me up short. I'd been thinking about Josie, wondering how far I could trust a predatory sister with no scruples, but suddenly I found myself thinking about him. As a sex object, Declan was of course wholly desirable, but I wasn't sure what I thought about his attitudes, or even how important they were to me. I was interested in him for one reason: fun. And sex came into that category.

I found myself examining him critically: his smooth confident body, the bones of his face, the thick dark hair I was always wanting to touch, the mind behind the eyes that I wanted to wrench my way and focus exclusively on *me*. He was the best-looking man I had ever been out with, but I had to admit that the effect he had on me was no different in kind from that of my previous boyfriends – until the glamour had worn off them – only different in the degree of its intensity. I now discovered that there were aspects of him that I resented. For example: Josie, beautiful and photogenic, was over the hill at twenty-six; Declan, twenty-one, equally beautiful and photogenic, could let himself run to a seedy middle age, and even as a member of the Balding and Saggy Club and the wrong side of fifty, he would still find women to want him.

I am ashamed of women sometimes, the ones who think any man is better than no man. I suspect that good-looking men like Declan know it, and rely on it, and I resent their arrogance.

He usually went home to change, and drove down to the cottage again to pick me up before going to work at the bar. I either spent the evening with him, or at Miracle Mick's with Oonagh and Rose, until he was ready to take me back again. Sometimes it was nearly two in the morning, but I was always in before Josie.

On the Thursday evening of that week, a man named Oliver called for her. Again, he was much older than her and I didn't like him. He was the Gus type, but dark and Italian-looking, and he had a thin clever mouth and hard eyes. (*Now* I sound like Nana Foley! 'I didn't like him Terry. I can't tell you why. I didn't like his nose/mouth/ears/eyelashes . . .') Josie left with him before Declan arrived to take me to the disco on his night off from the bar.

The earth was like a storage heater. Baked all day by the sun, it threw up heat at night, so that you were still wrapped in the same stifling cocoon of air. At Reds the dancers spilled outside, every door open. Declan and I danced, scarcely moving, our bodies radiating heat.

'Let's go back to the cottage,' Declan said in my ear.

We'd been at Reds a couple of hours by then. I knew exactly what he had in mind. The sex question was growing urgent. Every time he took me back to the cottage, there was a discussion – if you could call it that. More of a 'Yes – No – Yes – *No!*' thing carried on in various ways under the heat that pulsed from Mrs Riordan's slates.

With all the time we spent together, there wasn't much we hadn't done with each other. We'd fooled around naked even on the beach; no-one walks down there and you can sunbathe stitchless if you want to. Car tyres crunch down over the shingle loud as an alarm. I suppose, about the sex, it was finding the ideal time and place that held me back.

'Josie might come in,' I said in his ear, as I always did.

'She won't – she's never back before morning.'

We writhed against each other very slowly while I thought about it. 'You never know,' I said. 'You never know what she's going to do. I don't want her to find out.'

The bass pounded through us, and a voice screamed from the amplifiers. Whatever the words were, there was only one message: SEX SEX SEX. Despite the heat, Declan pulled me even closer and I was excited because I knew it was inevitable we would have sex and that it would be soon.

'Does it matter? I'd have thought your sister would be the last one to worry about it.'

'Why? Has she been giving you the eye?'

'She's *got* the eye – it's purely involuntary. You shouldn't trust her near anything in trousers.'

'What are you telling me, Declan O'Connor? That she's had a go at seducing you?'

'Josie's not my type.'

I would have liked to ask why not, but the music, and the insistent beat, and the entwining that was going on between us made it a bad time for a serious conversation.

'What is your type, then?'

'Come back to the cottage, and I'll show you . . .'

Even the *déjà vu* experience of exchanging amorous clichés didn't put me off and I seriously considered it, sorely tempted. 'But I still don't trust her,' I said into his neck. 'If she came back and found us, I'd never know what she might do with the information.'

I asked Josie about Oliver in what seemed to be a favourable moment.

'Oh, he's a friend of Gus's.'

'But who's Gus? How did you meet him? I've never seen him round here.'

'He's got a house near Carlow. I met him at a party.'

It was hard to know how far to probe before she would flare up in a fury, and threaten to pack me back to share a room with Great-Uncle Danny. That was nonsense, but it meant I wouldn't get any more out of her.

'They seem quite old to me – Gus and Oliver.' I tried hard not to sound like Mam and Nana Foley in chorus, but like *me*: I thought they were old. I calculated Josie wouldn't want to be made to feel aged in comparison with a sister of twenty-one. 'I'd have thought you'd prefer younger men.' It was really astonishing that Josie of all people should be a victim of the Balding and Saggy Club.

I got it wrong. Of course it made her laugh with superior indulgence, and she could patronize me in the older-sister-with-experience role.

'They're the ones with the money! What good are the boys? They haven't got a bean. How much does Declan spend on you?'

'Well, nothing really, I suppose. Why should he? We buy each other drinks, or our own drinks. I earn my own money.'

'There you are then!' She was triumphant, as though

93

she'd proved her point at the end of a long and hard-fought argument. 'You'll be the one doing *all* the paying in the end! Men exploit women every way they can. I like to make sure it's reciprocal.'

Reciprocal – like Declan and me buying each other drinks. But I didn't want to get stuck on an altercation about that. I tried a new tack. 'I didn't think you'd kept in touch with many of your old friends once you went to England, but you have a better social life than I do!' I aimed to make it flattering.

'Oh, I've kept a few links, but you only have to go to one good party and you make a whole lot of new ones.'

'So this Gus – and Oliver – they're new ones?'

'And why not?'

'Nothing. What happened to Robert, by the way? Taking his car back seems a bit final.'

'I suppose it is.' She tossed her hair back. 'Oh he can go to hell.'

A relationship with married Robert might have spelled sorrows vast as those of Deirdre, but Denise had had a point when she had first told me about Robert: at least he was more respectable than some of the other men Josie was going around with.

It wasn't just that Gus and Oliver were complete outsiders. We none of us want to go out only with men we know in town, but family ties extend like a net all over the county. You can bet your last Irish penny that *somebody* in Ballycanty knows every intimate detail of the background of the boy from fifty miles away you thought had escaped the grandmothers' dossiers. I had always regarded it as an irritation, but for the first time the network appeared as an advantage. It is no more than a vetting process, and you know who are the bad lots to avoid. If you choose to seek them out, you can't say you weren't warned.

I didn't have much of an opinion of Gus, and I certainly didn't like Oliver, but I didn't know anything to the discredit of either of them that might make Josie stop and think.

TEN

Rose, Oonagh and I met in Whelan's on Saturday. The three of us hadn't had a good gossip for over a week. It's always more crowded in Whelan's on Saturdays, and we had to postpone the serious talk until we had a table to ourselves. There were people in and out of the place the whole time, and what with the tortured violins of the chair-legs screeching across the tiles and the intermittent percussion of the coffee machine, the noise was terrible. We had to exchange our confidences in a nervous shout, ready to cut down the volume every time the machine was switched off.

Rose was due to start her holiday from Monday, and we thought we might arrange to do a few things together during the week.

'That's if I can prise you away from Declan,' she said. 'I saw you wrapped round each other at Reds on Thursday night. It looks serious.'

'It is,' I said, and our three heads bobbed in towards the centre of the table like hens pecking for the same corn. 'It's got to the crunch. Do I or don't I?'

'What's stopping you girl, for heaven's sake?'

'Well, I'm not sure.' It wasn't that I hadn't given it some thought; I'd given it plenty. 'There's the Cork affair – is it on or is it off? And then there's the problem that as soon as you have sex with someone, there's a kind of obligation there. And if you stop going with them, or you change your mind about the sex, it's very hard to tell them you don't want it.' I had to raise my voice suddenly in the middle of that. We instinctively looked round to see if anyone had overheard. Then we laughed.

Then Oonagh said, 'It was like that with me and Dan at the end. I don't think either of us wanted it, but each of us just went on, so as not to hurt the other. That made it worse.'

The voice of experience hardened my resolve, for the moment. I wouldn't give in to Declan. Just yet, anyway.

We swapped a few speculations about Rose and Mikey Duffy – was it on or was it off? – while Rose laughed, and then she lowered her voice in that wait-till-I-tell-you way and our heads ducked in again.

'Mikey told me Orla his sister-in-law won't let his brother have sex with her until he has an Aids test! What do you think of that now?!'

Oonagh leaned back to light a cigarette. 'She's not the only one. Half the sports club wives are now in favour of the trip that was cancelled, the rumour has them so worried! They'd rather the tests were done in England – it's more anonymous.'

'Anonymous! What's anonymous about it, for the love of Patrick?' Rose demanded, too loudly in a sudden lull, and was Hshd! to a hoarse whisper. 'After the fuss there's been, the whole country would know that was what they were going for! If they'd just gone ahead in the first place, no-one would have been certain of it. They can't reinstate that trip now because it's too late for it. They'd have to get up another one.'

'Well, there'll be no more Aids in this town!' Oonagh announced. 'And there'll be no more sex either so you'd better make your mind up double quick about Declan, Terry. They're all going out to buy padlocks for their trousers. They say there's been a run on them at Mooney's. My Grandpa Joe couldn't even get a lock for his garden shed.'

'I've heard some stories about your Grandpa Joe,' I said.

'Aw, he's too old for Aids, girl.' Oonagh waved her hand dismissively, and we laughed. It was still the stuff of jokes.

Rose sipped her coffee, her eyes on me. 'Talking of men, I heard your sister Josie has quite a string of them after her. Someone saw her at a party in Cork the other night. They said she was off with THREE at the one party.'

'CORK? That's miles! No wonder she gets in so late!'

'Has she still her job in England?'

For the honour of the Carmodys, I said she had, and then distracted them.

'Talking of Aids,' I lowered my voice to the hoarse whisper, 'I forgot to tell you. I met Tom Power walking on the cliffs. He looked the picture of health! I don't think I believe that story about him any more.'

'You can't tell when they first get it. It takes its toll over a few years.'

'Since when did you become such an authority, Rose Walsh? Any road, I'm telling you now, he looked perfectly fit and he sounded cheerful. We didn't talk about Aids at all.'

'Not at *all*?' Rose's blue eyes were goggling. 'With all the scandal careering round the town? That's significant.'

'I heard that it's true.' Oonagh took a long breath through her filter and let it out slowly sideways in a smoky plume. 'They say his parents are destroyed. He's had the tests in Dublin.'

'What did I tell you?' said Rose.

I was seeing Tom walking towards me on the cliffs, tanned, grinning in recognition as he drew nearer, his teeth white. It was then that I realized the voice that was speaking to us over our own, and over the noise of Whelan's, was familiar.

'Hello, ladies!' it was saying. 'Oonagh, isn't it? And Terry? Do you mind if I join you?'

I looked round, straight into the wicked blue eyes of Sean Butler.

My first thought was: how much has he heard? And my second was about Tom Power. Not for anything would I give him information. The further he was led away from Tom, the better, in case Oonagh's news was true.

Oonagh said with a certain delighted edge to her voice, 'Well, if it isn't the journalist! Playing us along for a lot of bog ignoramuses. Working in the paper industry indeed! I'm surprised you've the nerve to show your face around here, after wrecking our lives on us.'

Mr Sean Butler gave us a look, first one and then the other, shrewd, and full of amusement, and he didn't stop to negotiate further his right to join us but took a spare chair from the next table and sat down.

'And what wrecking would that be?' His eyes quizzed us again, and I thought not for the first time what a very attractive man he was.

'My brother wouldn't speak to me if he knew I'd told you the rumour about the sports club,' I said. 'He lost his deposit on the holiday when it was cancelled.'

'Cancelled, was it?' says he, all innocence. 'Well, that's news to me.'

'Tch tch tch, and you an ace reporter! We weren't born yesterday,' I said. 'Only the day before. You must be following the story. What else would be bringing you down here? And by the way, this is Rose Walsh.'

Rose shook hands, very demure. We'd told her about Sean Butler and our night at Miracle Mick Dooley's.

It was so warm when we came out of the disco that same Saturday night. Rose was still in there, but Oonagh had had enough and gone on to Mick's with a crowd of others.

I knew I'd had too much to drink. I couldn't focus properly, or stop myself from laughing at things that weren't really funny. Declan couldn't have had as much as I had. He seemed perfectly normal.

We sat on the concrete wall for a while that is the car-park boundary in front of the great barn of the disco. There were other couples on the wall too, a few yards between each pair as though, by tacit agreement, illusory hospital screens separated us all, no couple paying any attention to any other. The barn acted like a great sounding-board for the bass from the speakers inside, and the deep tribal beat came out even more strongly, while the lights flashed red, blue, yellow in the summer dark.

'Unattractive sort of place, isn't it?' Declan said. 'The whole outside needs whitewashing. Can't you imagine a visiting Martian taking a look at it and thinking we were all mad – deafening ourselves with the amplification and jigging round in the heat in the middle of the fields?'

I laughed; what he said seemed wittily original. 'Perhaps they'd think it was a ritual – for the crops or something.'

'The only crops you'd get in these fields are weeds.'

It was a stupid conversation. What we were really saying was something quite different. He put his arm round my waist and we started to walk slowly along the road, away from the other couples, towards the open country.

The grass was dry, and the ground hard. I didn't mind. I could have been lying on rocks just as comfortably. My bones, floating in alcohol, had become soft and accommodating, as though ready to mould themselves round the shapes of the stones and clods underneath.

'Mm,' I said. 'It's so warm. I could go to sleep here. G'night.'

Declan laughed, and put his arm over me. 'Don't go to sleep yet . . . '

I even thought at the time: there's something so phoney about men and their heavily loaded sentences before they make love. Do they overdo the meaningful bit or what? It'd be better if they just shut up. We kissed. Despite the drink, and the drowsiness, I could feel my body wake up. I remembered what I'd said hours before to Oonagh and Rose, but because of the drink and the way I was feeling, and also because I knew it was pretty safe, I didn't put up any resistance.

I'd done it before. It's never like the films, all that panting, and moaning, and ecstatic sighs and groans at the end – unless of course you're putting it on because you think it's expected. Declan felt very heavy, and because of all the alcohol I suppose it wasn't that brilliant from my point of view, but I didn't really care. After the putting it off for so long, and the build-up, it didn't even seem a very significant act in the end, though I said in my head, 'This is it! This is Declan. We're making love . . .'

Even that didn't make it real. And while it was going on I was asking myself, 'Is this love? Is it *really* love?'

My heart beat faster, and I thought I must move or he would think I was no good at it, and ditch me for someone else.

Perhaps before midnight in an August heatwave, lying on a strip of field beside a hedge, constitute neither the right time nor place.

Ever since the spring, when we'd kissed on our first meeting in the disco, dancing in the noise and smoke and dim light that I suppose are the modern catalysts for romance, there had been this possibility of more than kisses. The expectation of it had built up almost to fever pitch. It was first a curiosity, and then a physical compulsion that fed on a preoccupation with sex, but I couldn't fool myself now that it had had much to do with real love.

Then, because it was Ballycanty and because it was that summer, I suddenly remembered Tom Power, and after that I couldn't keep the thought of Aids out of my head.

How did I know Declan was safe?

We none of us knew anything for certain any more. There was the girl in Cork. I'd vowed that he wouldn't have me while she was still on the scene – the straightforward her-or-me as in the soaps – but it wasn't as simple as that. Aids is like a good old-fashioned Irish family curse that targets its generations and wipes out the whole future. You can cut off emotional ties from someone, and they become like a part of a plant that's lopped off and dies, but something that's passed in the blood is a physical legacy, and it lives in you, and can be passed on to others, until *you* die. Who had been before the girl in Cork? And who had that girl been with?

I was convinced that I was filled with death. Disease was already creeping through my veins. Soon it would eat into my flesh, my bones. With the corruption that had invaded my body, I could feel myself already turning, not to dust – nice dry clean dust like the ashes the priests used to mark your forehead before Lent – but to a horrible ooze, a dark stinking clinging decay. I looked at my arms, examining them for tell-tale marks. They were pale, silvered by a sinister moonlight.

It was the first time I understood that there might be other ways of looking at sex, and I hated myself for throwing away what might have been an exclusive gift. And Declan for accepting so casually what could be, literally, my life.

My father has a critical attitude to 'modern love'.

'They've destroyed romance, Terry,' he says. 'Youth today, you want everything *now*. But real romance is about longing, about sublimation, even about denial. It's about waiting for the place and the time to be right. Sometimes they never will be, and that is what makes the real thing so powerful.'

'Where did you get all that?' I asked him once.

'You think the twentieth century has a monopoly on romance? You want to read some of the old Celtic stories. There's sex and violence for you, but people had to suffer for what they wanted. They knew how to commit themselves to an ideal, or to someone else. To commit everything that's in you with no guarantees beforehand – that's a responsibility you take on yourself, and a risk. That's what raises it above the sordid and above the mere animal.'

Now I wanted to say to him: 'Do you really think I don't know what risks are about, Da? I've just taken a risk – I've just played Russian roulette with Aids. And speaking for the rest of my despised generation, I can't be the only one on a hot August night . . .'

But then I thought: perhaps we want it all now because we are afraid to wait. Underneath we fear more than any other generation that there is little worth striving for, and that our tomorrow is more under threat than ever before from forces over which we have no control. And of course we don't believe in the old-fashioned sort of immortality any longer. Fame is our immortality NOW, so we're all busy living lives packed with the right sort of action for our best-seller biographies.

As for protected sex, there's no such thing! There's blood, and adrenalin, and whatever chemical it is that drives you towards the act, and in the heat of the moment you take the risk – no advert ever invented is going to stop you then. And we all know Death can shoot through latex, so what's the point in pretending that it can't?

A cynical, bitter sort of humour came on me as my perspectives shifted.

'Declan,' I said. My voice sounded too loud in the night even though I was talking quietly. 'Did you wonder if I might have Aids?'

If he hadn't, I despised him for being stupid. If he had, I despised the cynicism that made him calculate the odds in advance. Then I despised myself for just letting it happen.

'Come on Terry! What sort of a person do you think I am?'

He sounded shocked, but I wondered if that had less to do with the subject of Aids than with the question itself. It was too crude, too real. Even if a lovey-dovey bit after sex was meaningless, he expected to go through the form.

He still hadn't answered my question. I wanted to know. I resented the calculation, if there had been calculation, and the cold way he would have looked at me, sizing it all up. It pigeon-holed me with girls who go along with just any man out for a good time. It meant he didn't think of himself and of me in a context in which there might be a possibility of marriage. Not that the idea of marriage to anyone had seriously crossed my mind. It was somewhere in the future, and I wanted a lot more fun first, but the vague *possibility* of marriage somehow put a better gloss on what we'd just done – made it less animal – though I didn't stop to apply my father's reasoning just then.

'I want to know,' he said. And then, 'I didn't think you were that sort of girl.'

THAT SORT OF GIRL!

And we all thought that phrase had died somewhere in the last generation! The magazines, the newspapers, educating us all with the received wisdom of the sociologists, tell us attitudes have changed. *It's all new, it's all different in our late-twentieth-century world*. I looked at Declan in the dark field and I thought *No it isn't*. Nothing has really changed, the New Man has just gone to a different designer for the externals, that's all.

I wouldn't talk to him after that, even though he tried to coax me out of a bad humour. It wasn't until days afterwards I realized that of course *I'd* been weighing up the risks, wondering how many girls he'd slept with in the town, deciding it was unlikely he could have connected with the deadly bloodline that had infected Tom, and maybe Seamus O'Rourke and John Crowley too. I had come to the conclusion that the danger was the usual one – getting pregnant – and it was up to me to calculate the likelihood of that.

He drove me back to the cottage in silence. There was no point going back to the disco. I was filled with resentment, and anger I wouldn't, and couldn't, try to explain. I felt cheated of something, though it was hard to know what exactly. He was puzzled and became resentful in his turn.

The cottage was in darkness. Declan stopped the car by the path, and walked down to the door with me, which he always did. There was a glimmer of moon on the sea and the rhythmic shushing of the waves in the invisible cove below the black line of the cliff.

'Will I come in?' There was no telling from his tone whether he wanted to or not. It was what he always asked.

I gave him the usual excuse. 'No. Josie might come back.'

He didn't argue. 'Will I see you tomorrow?'

'I don't think so. I've to go home to lunch to see my uncle. It'll probably mean the whole afternoon.' I knew he was working in the bar in the evening.

'All right.' Silence, then one last try. 'Why are you angry with me, Terry?'

'I'm not.'

'There were two of us wanting that, you know. It wasn't just me!'

'I never said it was!' But even as the words came out I asked myself, Is that what I actually thought, though – that he wanted it and I gave in? 'Oh . . . just go home!'

He shrugged. 'Suit yourself.'

The path was a pale thread winding up through the folds of the cliff. I could see his dark figure clearly, moving with long strides away from me. I didn't wait to see him disappear.

I had rung Oonagh from home at lunch-time, and arranged that she would drive us somewhere for a drink in the evening. Afterwards she would give me a lift back to Josie's cove. In Oonagh's car we took the coast road and headed west.

'This sex thing,' I said. 'Is it all a big con, do you think?'

'What do you mean?'

'Grace says women always come off worse in every

situation. D'you think sex is the big late-twentieth-century lie?'

She was onto it at once. 'This means you and Declan have done it, or you're still thinking about it?'

I wanted to sort my feelings out a bit before I told her. 'I'm thinking,' I said, with my Jesuitical evasion in mind. 'You see, what gets me is this . . . Women weren't supposed to talk about it before, and they weren't supposed to want it. Now they talk about it all the time – all the magazines are full of it – your freedom, are you enjoying it, are you getting enough of it and all that. But the one thing you're *not* allowed to do is *not to want it*. It has to mean there's something wrong with you.'

'You don't mean to tell me, Terry Carmody, after all these years that you're not interested in sex!'

'No, but I'm serious,' I said. 'In the old days if you went out with someone, according to Mam anyway, they were lucky if you let them kiss you! They still wanted the whole thing I suppose, but they didn't expect to get it, and it was a big deal if you let them have it because you were allowed not to like it. So in a way, you had *more* power, not less.' I wasn't sure I was explaining myself clearly, and I was warming to resentment on behalf of myself and all the other women I was beginning to see as exploited. 'Now sex is expected because of course we're told all women like it, and so it's no big deal any more. It's like paying the tip in with the restaurant bill – the waiters expect the ten per cent, and you pay it automatically whether the service has been any good or not. Sex is just part of the package of going out with someone – the automatic ten per cent at the end of the bill. But just supposing, despite the magazines, you don't think it's that fantastic after all?'

'Ha!' said Oonagh triumphantly. 'You *have* had it with Declan, and it wasn't that great!'

There wasn't much point denying it. 'OK then, I have,' I admitted grudgingly. 'We had sex in a field and

105

it's death to romance. But don't spread it around!'

'Cross my heart and all that. Honestly, Terry, what's the matter with you? Of course I won't!'

'All right then, but that's not what I was talking about.' I felt irritated that she could treat the subject as merely a piece of new gossip, when I had been struggling to explain something that seemed suddenly important. How could I tell her that underneath the search for meaning, most of the time I felt like crying, and that life was one big disappointment? I abandoned the attempt.

'Anyway,' I said, 'the thing is that I don't think I really want to see him again.'

Oonagh shook her head, her eyes still watching the road. 'I don't follow this. I thought you two were supposed to be crazy about each other?'

'Crazy *for* each other maybe. I don't know. I don't know what our feelings really are – if we've got any at all!'

'I'm not sure that's the way Declan sees it.'

'Oh, he probably wanted a bit of the lovey-dovey stuff afterwards – but what's the point if it doesn't mean anything? I asked him about Aids, and had he thought one of us might have it, and he was shocked.'

'Men are very squeamish – and conventional. They like to have this detached attitude – sampling lots of women before they get tied to one, but they're outraged if they find the same detached attitude in a woman.'

Was I really detached? Was Declan outraged?

I tried out Oonagh's view of it – I hadn't looked at it from her angle before – but it seemed to me that there was still something missing from the picture.

We drove out to a little fishing town beyond the cove. There was one bar in it, and we took our drinks out to the sea wall. A screaming crowd of gulls cruised and ducked after a shoal that was invisible beneath the opaque surface of the sea. We sat on the wall to watch the evening light.

*   *   *

106

Josie had a casual attitude to locking the front door. Sometimes she did, sometimes she didn't. But because Aggie was more conscientious about it, the cottage being her aunt's, I thought we should get into good habits. I'd left the key under the mat for Josie when Dad had come over to fetch me for lunch with Uncle Danny, just in case she returned before me. Oonagh dropped me at the cottage, but she didn't stay. Josie wasn't back, of course.

The living-room light-bulb died only seconds after I had switched it on. I was in blackness for a few moments and then began to see the shapes of things again. There were spare bulbs, thanks to Aggie, in the dresser. I turned on a bedroom light to see better, and opened one of the top drawers. I could feel two boxes at the back, pushed under some papers. I had to take the whole lot out before I could get at the bulbs, and then had difficulty twisting the old spent one out of the socket.

With the light on, I began to put back into the drawer all the things I'd had to take out: envelopes, bits of string, clothes-pegs for the line in the side yard. There were two paperbacks I hadn't read, so I left them out, an old newspaper, a couple more envelopes. The bigger of the two envelopes was slightly torn, and the contents began to spill out. I put the edge of my hand across the top to stop them falling – glossy photographs – and one slid over my fingers. I had looked at it – large, black and white like a publicity photo – before I was even aware of it. It was a nude pose. A girl on a bed. She had a kind of halter round her neck, and a whip in one hand. She wore a pair of long leather boots.

It was a few seconds before I realized what I was looking at. Then I saw that the girl was Josie.

There were six photographs in all, and the rest were in colour. They weren't exactly 'posed', and looked as though they might have been taken on a different occasion from the first. I wondered afterwards if they'd been done with a time-switch on the camera, for the private entertainment of the couple featured in them. It was too horrible to think that there might have been a third person involved. My hands were shaking when I put them down. I'd have given anything not to have seen them, but I found myself having to look again. I couldn't believe it. Josie, photographed having sex with a man. There was no doubt that she and the man both knew the camera was there.

I pushed them back, flung the paperbacks in on top of them, and slammed the drawer shut. I felt as though I was going to be sick; my heart was pounding and I could scarcely breathe.

I must have sat there for hours. I turned off the light, which brought in too many moths through the open windows. They banged against the lampshade, and fluttered against the scorching bulb, seeking the brightness and their deaths. I thought about what had finally happened with Declan, how it had not been about love, or romance, but something merely animal that did not satisfy, and I thought about Josie, until the two separate experiences started to overlap at the edges and to merge, and Josie's further tainted mine.

The dark began to change outside the window, though the heat still lay over the cottage like a thick pall.

Why had she done it? For kicks? For money? Was that how she'd been making her living, not at the school at all?

I wondered if I should tell someone. Not Mam. Not Father. They'd be more horrified and upset than I was. Not Brendan. Not Grace. Should I ring Denise? I thought of Oonagh – just the act of telling her would be a relief. But after the orgy of gossip we'd indulged in, I couldn't trust her not to pass it on.

ELEVEN

Josie came back at about half ten on Monday morning.

I was sitting at the table with a mug of coffee in my hands, and propped up against a biscuit tin was a newspaper Dad had brought over the day before, when he'd fetched me for Sunday lunch with Uncle Danny. Shining straight through the cottage windows the sun was relentless as ever, and the sound of the sea came up from the cove.

I hadn't slept at all, and I still felt sick when I thought about Josie. There was no need to look at the photographs again. They were etched on my memory with corrosive acid. I didn't know how I was going to talk to her.

She breezed in with a blast of expensive perfume and stale cigarettes. Her face was carefully made up.

'I thought you'd be on the beach by now. Oh, good. A paper.' Then she saw my expression. 'What's the matter with you?'

I didn't look directly into her eyes. 'I've seen the photographs.' It came straight out. It wasn't even what I'd been thinking I might say, and it didn't occur to me to lie.

'Which—' She looked genuinely puzzled for a moment, then her hand flew to her mouth. 'Oh my God. What were you doing prying in there?'

Her flare of defensive anger made me furious, and fatigue pushed me towards hysteria. I jumped up and the coffee went all over the table and seeped across the newsprint in a brown stain.

'I wasn't prying!' I shouted, banging my fists down. 'I wish to God I'd never seen them – they fell out of an

109

envelope when I was looking for a light-bulb. How could you, Josie! How *could* you!'

She was flouncing about now, moving objects from the table to the dresser unnecessarily, bashing Mrs Riordan's cushions, all injured something you could hardly call innocence, the way she does when she's caught on the wrong foot.

'I don't know why you should be playing the moral judge, Teresa. You're not so pure and white yourself. It was only a bit of fun.'

'Have you shown these to Aggie?'

'Of course not. She doesn't go round snooping like you —'

'I told you I wasn't snooping! And how can you call this sort of thing *fun*? It's pornography and you know it!'

'Don't be stupid,' Josie said between her teeth. 'They're not for publication.'

'What are they for then – the family photograph album? Was someone paying you, is that why you did it? Is that where your money came from, and not from the school at all because you were lying about your job?'

'Of course my money came from the school! You can ring them up and ask them if I worked there!'

'You're not working there now, though. How long is it since you gave up your job? And that old goat in the photographs – was he before or after your married Robert, or just a bit on the side when you got bored with waiting for your tutor to slip away from his wife to the cottage he was lending you?'

I thought she would throw something at me. She looked wild, a bright spot burning in each pale cheek.

'You've got it all worked out, haven't you? How dare you judge me!' She was almost screaming at me. 'You're just a child! You live in this backward, priest-ridden pox of an island and you don't understand a thing!'

I was too angry myself to point out her inconsistencies. 'And aren't you the English sophisticate! You know it all, don't you? Despising your poor ignorant Irish sisters who haven't caught up with the ways of the world yet! Well, if that's the life you live in your precious England it's the life of a whore! It *stinks* and I'm glad I don't have anything to do with it!'

I could feel the whole exchange tipping towards a childish slanging match; we'd be at the hair-pulling next, and it was too important for that, so before she could reply I ran up the ladder to the loft. 'I wouldn't be staying here a minute longer,' I shouted as a parting shot, 'if I could get home!'

And with that I slammed the trapdoor and piled cushions and books on top of it. I felt dizzy with rage and had to sit down.

It was an uncomfortable afterthought that she might there and then set fire to the cottage beneath me. There'd be nothing for it but to get out of the skylight and jump into the turf from the roof, but better a broken leg than a skin like a roasted hen. I started packing my things.

She was banging about downstairs and cursing, and then the front door slammed and all was quiet.

In spite of Uncle Danny's occupation of my room and the prospect of nowhere to sleep that night, I walked all the way home once Josie had gone, told Mam she was impossible and I didn't want to stay at the cottage another minute, and moved my stuff with Brendan's help and Father's car once he had come back from work. Mam said I'd have to sleep on the sofa-bed in the sitting-room while Uncle Danny was there – Nana's spare room still wasn't finished. I said that was fine by me.

As for Josie, she could go to hell as far as I was concerned. I kept that sentiment to myself, though nobody was surprised that I'd had enough of her.

111

I rang up Rose once I'd got back home from collecting my belongings. We agreed to take our bicycles and pedal out towards the coast – in the opposite direction to Josie's cottage. I told her I didn't want to meet Josie, but I said nothing about Declan.

I was still off Declan; I didn't even want to think about him. In justice I had to admit to myself that it wasn't entirely his fault – the responsibility for the event had been six of one and a half-dozen of the other, as Mam would say – but our relationship had become inextricably confused now with Tom Power and Aids and Josie. I found myself wishing Declan and I had never even met. Life was too complicated.

On Tuesday I went out with Rose again. We found a very private little beach, and had it and a couple of bottles of wine to ourselves all day. Rose prattled about Mikey Duffy, and I thought on and off about Declan, and wondered if he had come to look for me, or made any effort to contact me, and then pushed the whole business to the back of my mind. That night I'd promised to stay home for supper, so there was no danger of meeting him unless he turned up on the doorstep demanding to see me.

'So how's life with you, Terry?' Uncle Danny asked when I got back from the beach.

Uncle Danny is the old-fashioned type of priest, like Father Jim Lafferty. Even though Danny is retired he wears his collar on holiday ('Once a priest always a priest and you never know when someone'll be dying on you').

'Fine,' I said, dazed with the sun and drink. I don't know what it was unless the stupor combined strangely with the sight of the collar, but I had to fight off the temptation to go into instant confession mode. I'd have to be at my last gasp before I'd confess to my uncle, but my mind was chattering to itself, and I had to be careful not to say the words out loud: *Someone I know has Aids, my sister is posing for pornographic*

112

photographs, stole a car, and has affairs with married men, I've just had disastrous sex with my boyfriend and although I don't think I could be pregnant I might be and then I'd want an abortion which I can't have in this country and I just might have Aids too and I don't know what to do about anything. 'Yes, fine,' I said.

The pregnancy fear took me by surprise, but I suppose it's always nagging around at the bottom of your subconscious even when you know it's so unlikely as to be impossible. Guilt, of course. At the back of your not-quite-ex-Catholic mind, you're just waiting for God to punish you. He gave up thunderbolts and fireworks after the Old Testament, so now he just sees to it you get pregnant, or catch Aids, and despite changes in modern attitudes to single mothers ('Did you know that single girls account for *forty-five per cent* of first pregnancies in this country?' – the outraged voice of Nana again making herself heard above all the conflicting babble in my brain) and all the new drugs, your whole life is ruined. In my more rational moments I think this is nonsense, but it's hard to be rational when you haven't slept enough, and you've drunk too much, and the world in your immediate vicinity reveals itself to be much nastier than you thought.

'That's grand. It's grand to be your age, Terry. Life's only just beginning and everything opening out before you.' He was looking me dead in the eye. 'Don't spoil it.'

From anyone else I'd have dismissed such a speech as the usual set of matching platitudes, but from Great-Uncle Danny – well, I seriously wondered if he couldn't hear all that hopeless wailing going on in my head. He used to be my favourite uncle, when I was still young enough to make such distinctions.

By Wednesday morning there'd been no call from Declan. I was relieved, and insulted. I'd have liked him to have tried once, so that I could let him know for definite I didn't want to see him. It would have given the whole thing some point – even if it *was* only a full stop.

I wondered about Oonagh's view of his involvement, that he mightn't see it in quite such a harsh light as I did, but his silence seemed to prove her wrong. He must have discovered in the field that he wasn't really in love with me, either. Good. That would mean we were both happy.

Rose and I were scanning the papers for another piece by Sean Butler. We hadn't fed him anything particularly erroneous, but the fact that he'd turned up must have meant he was onto something. I wondered what more he might have heard to bring him back down to Ballycanty.

It was Great-Uncle Danny who told me about the dangers of dancing, and it was I who told him that priests were always fat. I was sixteen at the time, as I've said before, so have no excuse for the lapse in manners. He countered with the lesson that things are not always as they seem, and instanced the saintly Franciscan priest Padre Pio, who might be supposed to be a healthy eater from his photographs, but who in reality lived on little more than a few slices of bread a day.

Great-Uncle Danny has always been spherical. He wears small gold-rimmed rectangular glasses to offset the roundness of his face and his bald head with its circling fringe of white hair, and his round stomach. He has lost some weight recently on account of his illness, but he is still a plump little man, and over the years I have discovered that his shape, like Padre Pio's, bears no direct relation to his eating habits. Perhaps gluttony amongst the clergy is not as common as it might appear. Dancing, as I now know, is not always about dancing.

Uncle Danny, for all his age and roundness, is a great walker. I could feel an unspoken pressure from Mam that I should spend some time with him before I returned to work, and he went back to his priests' retirement home and saying Mass for his local nuns. But living between Josie's sordid secrets that haunted my dreams, and my own hedonistic daytime world of sun, wine and Rose, I wasn't sure I wanted to expose any of my thoughts to the perceptive gaze of my priestly uncle.

Tramore is a seaside resort not so far from us, and used to be one of our favourite holiday places when we were children. There's a wonderful long stretch of sand there, and its name translates from the Irish as 'The Big Strand'. It's a good mile to the end of it.

When Uncle Danny asked me to drive over there with him, I couldn't refuse. Nana was there as well as Mam, and her look said: *Go with him. I'm telling you now, Terry. It would please him.* I couldn't see Rose that afternoon, and Declan was out of it, so I thought I might as well.

We sang old Irish songs on the way, and Uncle Danny told me a few holy jokes, and I told him a few unholy but respectable ones. Approaching the town from the west, there is a view I particularly like, a long perspective east across the two arms of the bay. The Metal Man is on his pillar on the cliffs just ahead, and far across the blue floor of the sea is Brownstown headland. The bay itself is a golden C shape in the sun, flooded with turquoise when the tide is in. Little purple orchids grow in the turf at the Metal Man's feet in the spring, but when Danny and I got out to admire the view only the dried-up heads of sea pinks stood above the wiry grass.

There is a place to park along the sea front, back from the wall that keeps all but the worst storms from washing over the little golf course behind. The tide was far out when we arrived, and there were acres of shining buff-coloured sand, quilted with pebbles like the buttons in a satin cushion. We walked an erratic path in the direction of the sandhills at the far end of the bay, picking at the stones that caught our eyes. For once there was a sigh of a breeze to stir the hot air.

'This is a fine place,' Uncle Danny said, stopping to take in a deep appreciative breath. 'Are you enjoying your summer?'

'So so,' I said. 'It's not as quiet as usual. You know what's going on here?' I meant the Aids stories. No-one had mentioned them at the family meals I'd attended.

'I do.'

We walked on again, stopping and stooping to the pebbles like the oyster-catchers and dunlin that run back and forth with the autumn tides. Tom Power and I used to chase flocks of them, delighted by the way they moved with such speed on little clockwork legs thin as wires. Uncle Danny in his black priest's suit collected a whole fistful of stones, gleeful as a child with the brightest ones.

I was eaten up with the desire to talk to him about Josie's secret. I had come to the conclusion that he was the only person I could tell, the only one I could trust. He wouldn't be personally upset by it in the way Mam or Father would be. He was a priest, and he might have heard the same or worse in the confessional. I told myself I needed to discuss it, not because I couldn't keep a secret, but because I didn't know what to make of such knowledge – hug it to myself and let Josie go her own way to a nasty end, or try to make her see sense? Danny was a spiritual adviser; that was his job. He could tell me what to do.

'Uncle Danny,' I said. 'I want to tell you about something. But it's a dead secret. I don't want anyone else to know.'

'Look at that now!' He was examining a shining stone. 'Did you ever see such a colour? So what's this, your confession?'

'No,' I said.

'No,' he said. 'I suppose you've given that up a long while ago?'

'Well, I have. I can't see any point in it. Lots of the things I used to say, I don't feel sorry for now. Any

116

road, it's a bit like going to a psychiatrist or someone, isn't it? You feel a bit better about yourself when you've offloaded a few worries.' I knew he wouldn't agree with me, but I didn't want to waste time on that subject. 'It's not me I want to talk about – it's Josie.'

His white eyebrows shot up. 'You want to tell me *her* confession?'

I hadn't thought of it like that. 'Maybe, in a way, I do. I know some things about her. They're not good things, and I'm afraid for her. It's all since she went to England.'

'Ah England!' he said, and it sounded like the opening of some dreadful old poem. 'England the Oppressor, the Ravisher of Ireland, Enemy of the True Religion – England the Provider of jobs on building sites, and Seducer of our souls! The Gall – the Saxon, mortal enemy of the Gael.'

'What?' I said. 'You're not going to recite are you, Uncle Danny? Because if you are, I'll just walk on a bit until you've finished.'

I hoped he wasn't going to go historical on me. It was a hobby of his that used to fascinate me, but it was hard enough to find words about Josie without having to cut through an Irishman's lament.

'Wait now,' he said. 'England. We all wanted to go to England when we were young. That's where the money was, that's where we thought we'd see a better life, but we weren't prepared at all for what we found when we got there. That's the way it used to be, anyhow. But with the world shrinking the way it is, and Ireland's own little economic miracle, it's my belief that if we want to go to the bad, England these days will be providing no more than the signposts.'

'Well, yes . . .' I said. Was he saying that Josie had an innately wicked streak in her? It was interesting that he'd caught onto the theme that had always irritated me about Josie's so-called 'sophistication'. But how to tell him about it since I didn't know how Josie's downhill slide had come about, and I didn't want to be unfair to her? In the end, it seemed easiest to launch in with the worst bit.

'She . . . well, she has some pornographic photos — of herself. That's the most worrying thing.'

I don't know why I should have thought that any worse than her affair with the married Robert, which is good old hell-fire adultery on a priest's scale of things. But the adultery seemed to me more 'contained'. It was a straightforward breaking of the rules, while the pornography was a more complex matter.

I knew that once you'd done that sort of thing, of course, it made it easier to repeat the experience. It's like the very first time you have sex; you lose your virginity, so it's a big deal. You might feel terrible afterwards. You might even confess it. But after that, the next time, it's not such a big decision any more, and you think, 'Oh well, why not? I've done it before.' And you also think, 'It might be better this time,' and so you go on. Perhaps adultery is like that too — perhaps all sin is like that, even murder. I once heard a radio programme about a Mafia killer. He said the first time he killed, it was terrible. He felt he'd stepped over a line that had suddenly put him in a different, dreadful world. But the next time he killed, it was just part of his job.

Well, Josie and her pornographic photos. I suppose, now I look back on it, I could understand the adultery, but not the pictures because they seemed to be something subtle and perilous, as though Josie were fooling about on the edge of a dark pit full of terrible dangers and she didn't even see that it was there.

Uncle Danny didn't comment one way or the other, his bright eyes still scanning the sand. 'Did she show them to you?'

'No. I found them by accident.'

'She knows you've seen them?'

'She said it was just a bit of fun.'

'And what did you say?'

'That it was almost like being a whore — letting men

look at you like that, make use of you.' Those hadn't been my exact words, but I gave him the gist of them.

'A bit of fun,' he repeated, pocketing a sea-smoothed white marble. And then, '*Almost* like. You're making a fine distinction there, are you?'

'So are you telling me you're not?'

'I'm asking you – is there a distinction?'

I thought for a moment. It was harder than I'd imagined. I had been expecting him to give me a straight answer, lay down the law, and say: *That's it. Take it or leave it.* 'I suppose so. She's had an affair with a married man, and had sex in front of a camera, but it doesn't have to mean she's done the same as a whore.'

'Was she paid for the photographs?'

I was shocked that such a nice old man as Uncle Danny should ask such a mercenary, down-to-earth question. I'd asked Josie the very same thing, but in my case it's what you'd expect. 'I don't know. I don't think so. And she doesn't see it as particularly wrong.'

I felt I had to try to stick up for her, to be fair to her.

'Doesn't she? She hid the photos, didn't she? Would she want your mother to see them?' Put like that, the answer was obvious. He gave it for me. 'Of course she knows it's wrong.'

'But you could say she's just got a different set of values.'

'You could and you'd be right. Why not say each set of values is as good as the next? Why condemn the paedophile, or the murderer? Now look at it from God's point of view – how do you think He sees her set of values?'

God is always a problem for me. How can you have any real belief in an omniscient, omnipresent, omnipotent character who looks like Santa Claus minus the red hat? And how can you believe in his ultimate love and kindness when he lugs round a great sack full of sharp stones which he dishes out randomly instead of presents?

'I don't think I believe in God any more.'

119

If I'd said that to Nana Foley or Mary Alice O'Shea, I'd have had a lecture as long as a wet week about losing my faith, and they'd be down at St Anne's praying the Novenas for my enlightenment. Uncle Danny didn't bat an eyelid. That's what gives me a bit of confidence in him.

'Look at it this way, then. Who would you say had the better set of values: a woman who steals other people's husbands and displays her body in ways that even you don't approve of – and remember it's *you* who are disapproving of her or why are we having this conversation? – or a woman who doesn't, for the very good reason that she might ruin herself and others?'

It was a catechism class answer, and I wasn't a very good advocate for Josie. I knew I wouldn't get the better of him in an argument; he was far too practised at it for me.

Fine, I said to myself. So what Josie's doing isn't something you can admire, and I was right about that. But the problem remains.

'What am I going to do about her?'

'Are you really asking me to speak to her about it?' he asked.

I kicked at a pebble, shining russet like a cornelian. It flipped over on the wet sand, leaving a scuffy little mark that began to sink back into itself. We were close to the water now, and a spent wave left a line of vanishing bubbles only inches from my toe.

'No,' I said. 'I don't think I am. She wouldn't listen anyway.'

'No more she would,' he agreed. 'And she has a good idea what you think of all this?'

'She certainly has – that's why I left the cottage!'

'Then there's not much more you can do for the present. You'll have to wait until she's in a more receptive frame of mind. So what about yourself, Terry?'

I hadn't planned to talk about myself. Apart from the Declan business, there didn't seem to be anything much to talk about, and I wasn't going to discuss that.

'What do you mean exactly? I'm not sure.'

'Then, where, say, would you like to see yourself in ten years' time?'

'I don't know.'

We stopped walking. Uncle Danny turned and looked out to the bright blue line of the horizon, dividing the scarcely moving sea from the still sky.

'If I were you,' he said, 'I'd go back to school.'

TWELVE

The second piece by Sean Butler appeared in the *Irish Times* on Thursday – a whole page this time, with a picture. In the absence of an Aids victim ravaged by the disease, or the Angel of Death herself looking either vengeful or pathetic depending on the mood of the story, they settled for a view of St Anne's from the main street – fine double doors, tower and all – with a tree, lamppost and a bit of the shopping mall off to one corner. The sacred and the profane, as my father pointed out over breakfast.

Uncle Danny remarked that it was inevitable that the Church should be involved, whether it knew anything about the Aids scare or not.

'The Church is news these days,' he said, 'and not just in Ireland. Worldwide interest, but – wouldn't you know it? – all scandal. And in the absence of a case of child abuse by the clergy or a married priest still functioning in the parish, there are any number of official spokesmen ready to leap into the void, opening their mouths before they've received convincing signals their brains are alive.'

'Those poor devils of newsmen have to eat, after all,' Da said. 'And the retractions, apologies and further comments can be spun out for weeks after that if there's nothing else stirring in the world.'

Nana Foley rang us at lunch-time with the news that Father Jim had been telephoned less than an hour after Sean's article appeared. Someone wanted to know the truth of it, and whether Father Jim could shed any more light. Father Jim is a wise man. He couldn't. The caller had been ringing from the offices of a Dutch newspaper.

I'd never fallen out with Rose before, but that afternoon I came near to it.

We started off amicably enough, dissecting Sean's article on our beach over another bottle of wine, taking it in turns to rub each other with the tanning oil. Rose is very fair-skinned and has to be careful; I have to be careful myself, but I'd a whole week's start on her, with Declan under our Bedouin tent. We all know about skin cancer, but who wants to go round washed-out in a blazing summer? – apart from Josie, and she looks positively ill without all the fashionable face-paint.

Rose was indignant. 'He must have been there before he spoke to us – sitting with his back to us! That's where the joke about the padlocks came from – he overheard Oonagh.'

'Yes, but what about the rest of it? Who did he get the numbers from?'

According to Sean, there were now rumoured to be as many as *thirty* diagnosed Aids sufferers in Ballycanty alone, and fears were growing that the scourge was spreading round the county. Gossip and innuendo were undermining the fabric of all our lives in the town, dividing husband from wife, mother from son, boyfriend from girlfriend. (Had he heard something about Declan and me?) Suspicion was poisoning the very air of Ballycanty. The 'Angel of Death' theory brooded over the town, and the Angel herself was, or had been, extraordinarily busy enticing the young men into her lethal embrace. The big news was: our own Sean Butler claimed not only to have information as to her identity, but to have been negotiating an exclusive interview at some unspecified date in the future!

I was annoyed. Sean Butler was *my* protégé. He had no business to be wandering off investigating on his own.

'How is it that *we've* heard nothing about this person – if she exists at all? Don't we live here with all the gossip thirty-six hours of every day? He's just a mischief-maker, if you ask me,' I said, unasked. 'He's got to write something to justify his existence. If he doesn't find anything, he makes it up. It's sad what journalism has come to.' That had been more or less the tenor of my father's speeches at breakfast.

'Sure it was always like that. Sean's been very careful – he hasn't named anybody.'

'There isn't anybody to name, that's why, and he can't list the victims. There's no reference to Tom anywhere, nor Seamus O'Rourke nor John Crowley. I think he's just lighting a few fires to see which one's going to cook his supper.'

'Or burn it. Talking of burning, it's your turn to do my back. And pass the bottle.'

She lay with her head on her arms while I rubbed the oil over her.

'Ah, it's a wicked world!' she said happily. 'What would we have to do with ourselves all day if there was nothing to talk about? How many sins do you think we're committing by just being here? For example – take gossip now. About Sean Butler – what you said about him could amount to detraction. I'd even go as far as to say calumny. You've called him a malicious liar.'

'But *I* wasn't telling lies – only speculating!'

'The likes of him could be claiming just the same as you. Well, I'll settle for detraction then. Immodesty – there's another one for you. Neither of us is wearing a top . . .'

She was off, running through the sinner's gamut – lust, impure thoughts, sloth, drunkenness, giving bad example. Only someone with a collapsed-Catholic mind could have thought up such a list to rejoice in. At least you're never bored in the Roman landscape, I'll say that for it; the spiritual pitfalls pepper the ground like shot from an enemy gun.

That last idea occurred to me at the time, but I didn't mention it to Rose. I was laughing with her at first, but, underneath the humour, her refusal to take anything seriously was beginning to irritate. Was Josie's life with all its risks something to laugh at – or even the way my affair with Declan was turning out?

I put the top back on the sun oil, and pushed it under the towel to stop it from frying us. I found myself following a train of thought that traced its provenance back to Uncle Danny. 'What would you say filled your brain all day, Rose?'

'You mean apart from men? Clothes, soaps and local scandals.' She turned her face sideways on her arm, and looked at me. 'Of course, when I'm at work, most of the time it's bank stuff – figures, pieces of paper, people's accounts, that sort of thing. You can't afford not to, or you'd be out on your ear. There's the coffee-break, and lunch-break and tea-break – then it's back to the usual things. What else is there? Why are you asking?'

After my conversations with Uncle Danny, the poverty of such an answer struck me for the first time.

'My uncle says I'm wasting my brain. He says when the novelty of earning my own money and spending it like water wears off, I'll be bored to destruction, because there's nothing worthwhile in my mind. And as I'll never earn much more than I do now, there won't be the yachts and the international playgrounds to distract me in the future.'

Rose smiled and shut her eyes. 'There's always the video games, or you could marry a millionaire. Who's the richest man we know in Ballycanty?'

No answer required: it was the standard joke. Eddie Mooney is fifty. He has a cattle farm and owns the hardware shop in the main street. He dresses like one of his own farm-hands, and has the reputation for being the meanest man in the whole county. He's worth hundreds of thousands, and they say he won't have a wife because he doesn't want to throw away a few pounds a week on the cost of her keep.

For once I didn't laugh. Rose's contribution had scattered all the serious threads I had been trying to draw together.

'Uncle Danny says we're *all* wasting ourselves!' I insisted. 'We live in only one dimension, as though this world is all there is.'

'Well he would say that, wouldn't he? He's a priest.'

At the back of my mind was the shadow of Tom, and what it would be like to be facing certain death so much sooner than you expected. I was determined she should at least consider this. 'When did you last go to confession, Rose?'

'Ah, it's lost in the mists of time, girl.'

'*When* was it?'

She took another swig from her glass, propping herself up on her elbows. 'I don't know. I didn't go last Easter, or the Easter before that – two years ago? Three – four?'

'Does your mother say anything?'

'What business is it of hers? But if she asks I say I'm going somewhere else, to keep her happy – outside Ballycanty so I don't know the priests. What about you – when did you last go?'

'After the first time I had sex with somebody.'

She turned her head sideways again, laying her cheek on the back of her hand. Her blue eyes were filled with lazy amusement. I thought what a wonderful model she'd make for a pagan Goddess of Abandon, with her curvy body and her hair falling over her bare shoulders.

'Now who's this mysterious *somebody*, Treesa Carmody? Is it that you've been having more of these secret affairs than you're after telling?'

'It's not mysterious at all!' I said crossly. 'I told you years ago!' She was about to stray again, so I tried to head her back onto my track. 'Do you really think there's nothing wrong with sex before marriage?'

She gave me a sudden suspicious glance. 'What's the

matter with you? I'm beginning to believe that conversation with your Uncle Danny should carry a mental health warning. I can't see that there's anything wrong with it – apart from the obvious things like Aids and diseases and getting pregnant. Everybody does it. It stops you marrying for the wrong reason – you know, in the old days they wanted the sex and that was the only respectable way to get it.'

'Maybe.'

'So what do *you* think?' she demanded.

I didn't know, that was the problem. First there was my father's definition of romance to fit into the equation, and then I thought of Josie. I didn't answer directly. 'What about kinky sex and that? Or taking part in pornographic films – do you think there's anything wrong with that?'

She gave it all of five seconds' consideration. 'Children now, you shouldn't involve them, but otherwise where's the harm in it? It's just a bit of fun between adults. Why this interest suddenly?'

'Oh, I just don't know any more. I used to think the no-sex thing was all the priests and that, and I couldn't wait to find out what it was like, but perhaps it isn't such a good idea. The consequences aren't always fun.'

'*Consequences!*' She was contemptuous. 'And all this stuff about confession is the way to make it all right? Rush off every time and tell the priest – is that what you're saying? Well, these days you might find that the priest has something even more interesting to tell *you*.' She sounded very scathing now – and her mockery wasn't entirely reserved for the priests. She had set herself apart, scrutinizing me as well as our notorious clergy, and from her different piece of ground she didn't think much of my patch at all. 'Why should I listen to some old hypocrite sitting in the box telling me what to do, giving me his forgiveness when he's done worse than me? What do I care about his forgiveness? It's *my* forgiveness he should be asking, for behaving so badly when he's set himself up above me and everybody else!'

'You know it isn't like that, Rose! It isn't *his* forgiveness he's giving you—'

My voice had taken on more of an edge than I'd meant, and again there was that accusing look from her. Up to that point I had been imperfectly parroting Uncle Danny, but I'd just run out of lines. For lack of his knowledge I was a hopeless advocate. To tell the truth, we'd had the same sort of discussion over a family tea, only I'd been the one to argue Rose's case then. Now I felt I had to be fair to what Danny had said, since he'd beaten me fairly and squarely on theological ground, and I'd been left with the unexpected and humiliating revelation of my ignorance of the religion I'd all but given up.

Rose's tone was full of mockery. 'You've changed your tune about all this! What's happened – fallen out with Declan?'

Yes, of course I had! You might say that my general dissatisfaction boiled down to that fact and not much else. But I hadn't told her about the field episode, and now I didn't want to.

I thought about my lack of answers for a few moments before I opened my mouth and then, because I couldn't adequately explain whatever the problem was, and because I didn't want to fall out with Rose too, I backed down.

'I suppose there's no point confessing what you're only going to do again,' I said, with a mental apology to Uncle Danny.

She gave me another wary glance. Then, 'That's just how I feel!'

The warmth returned to her voice, and she rolled over slowly onto her back, holding her glass to the sun in a mock toast. She was almost naked, and again I thought of the pagan goddess. '"The firm purpose of amendment" . . .' she said. 'Well, I haven't got it. Here's to the next time!'

'Venus Walsh,' I said. 'The New Irishwoman.'

I'm still not sure of the quality of insult I intended.

The next morning, Mam asked me to go down to the presbytery for Brendan.

'He's gone off with Jack and he won't be back until tonight, and this has got to be sent today!' She thrust a folded paper in front of me. 'It's some course he wants to go on – it only needs Father Jim's signature. You wouldn't ever take it down there for me, Terry? I'd see to it myself only I promised to go over to Nana's, and I don't want to disappoint her.'

'If he needs a priest to sign it, why not ask Uncle Danny?'

'Oh these applications, you know what they're like. Bank manager, parish priest, but no relations! What would you do if you lived out on some farm in the wilds, I'd like to know? You will take it?'

'All right,' I said. 'I'll take it in before lunch, then I might meet Oonagh at Whelan's.'

The presbytery door has a brass knocker on it, hand-polished every day by Brigid Flynn. I knocked.

Nothing happened.

I knocked again. After a silence, there were sounds of someone inside. Through the frosted glass panels I saw the shape of the black suit and pale head of Father Jim. He put the side of his head to the door, as if listening. It seemed foolish to knock again, since I could see him there.

'Father Lafferty? It's Teresa Carmody.' I thought the name Carmody might mean something to him.

'Who is it there?'

'Teresa Carmody, Father. I've come to ask if you'll sign a form for Brendan.'

'Who's that?'

'TERESA CARMODY, Father.'

'I'm not seeing anybody today, Teresa. Is it urgent?'

'Well, no, it's just a—'

'Post it through the letter-box, and I'll give it my attention later.'

I could see him through the panels talking to the wall. Each time I spoke, he leaned his head against the door, confessional style.

'Is it Father Jim you're wanting?'

Brigid Flynn was suddenly at my heels, a little guard dog in her fifties.

'Father Jim!' She gave a bark and a sharp rat tat, though we could both see him through the frosted panels. 'It's me, Brigid! I've got Treesa Carmody here. Let us in!'

She turned to me. 'It's no good me using my key. He's got the whole place chained and barricaded.'

'Ah Brigid – it's you is it?'

There was the rattle of a bolt being drawn back, and then the figure behind the glass ducked out of sight and there was another rattle. A key jiggled in the lock.

The door opened a crack, stretching two safety chains across the breach in the defences. Father Jim's long nose appeared, and disappeared, and then one pale blue eye shining through the lens of his glasses.

'And it's Patrick Carmody's Teresa, is it?'

'Yes Father. I've got a—'

'You'd better come in quick. I didn't recognize your voice. There's no-one hanging around out there, is there? You know, journalists and that?'

'No, Father.'

'Come in, Teresa. Come in Brigid.' The safety chains were off, and Father Jim was pulling me in through the door.

'They're demons,' he said. 'Demons. I wouldn't want you to be thinking I'm comparing myself to St John Vianney now, but I'm beginning to appreciate what he must have had to put up with for all those years, with the Devil banging around night and day and no proper rest. They'd be up the drainpipes and in through the windows if I didn't have every one of them locked.'

I could hear Brigid rattling the bolts and chains, and locking up behind me.

'What's happened, Father?'

He shook his head. 'It's the reporters. Ever since that piece appeared in the paper yesterday, they've given us no peace, have they now, Brigid? I don't know what they think I could have to say about the matter.'

'Is that why you're keeping the curtains drawn, Father?'

It was hard to find your way in the house.

'Those long lenses of theirs – you never know what they'll be taking their pictures of next. I'm glad Brigid was with you – there's no knowing what sort of non-sense they'd be writing about young girls coming to the presbytery! It's a strange age we live in, and no mistake. Now, what can I do for you?'

'It was like getting into Fort Knox!' I told Brendan afterwards. 'The alarm bells start ringing when you put your foot on the doormat, and a steel gate drops down from the ceiling. If you're quick enough, you'll get over the death traps in the floor, and then this giant boulder comes rolling—'

Brendan gave an ostentatious yawn. 'You should be telling that to the journalists,' he said, in tones he had cultivated as peel-the-skin-off-you. 'They'd pay you for it.'

It crossed my mind then that Brendan might have discovered the source of the sports club Aids rumour, but my brother is very straightforward. If he *had* heard, I'd know about it.

I did wonder if they'd pay me for a description of Father Jim's kitchen. It's a health hazard. He won't let Brigid cook for him, and she doesn't live in. I don't know whether he has a particular devotion to St John Vianney (hence the reference?) but perhaps he's trying to emulate the saint's holy diet of a pot of potatoes boiled up at the beginning of the week to last all the way through until the next; he ate them with vinegar.

131

Father Jim buys food in bulk down at the Hyper – four dozen cans of sweet corn, six dozen cans of luncheon meat, ten boxes of instant-soup packets. No wonder Father Aidan is keen on accepting invitations if there's a meal at the end of them.

Mam would have died of disgust over the tea towels. I suppose he has a washing-machine?

THIRTEEN

Now I wouldn't want you to be thinking we had anything to do with the other Aids scandal that broke in our part of the world at the end of that summer. It's true that Ballycanty isn't a million miles away from the other place, and there were some who made malicious remarks about 'copycat scandals' and 'publicity seeking', and some who thought there must be links between the Aids victims, but I'm telling you that our story broke first, and followed its own peculiar path, independent of the other.

I think it was the weather, myself. Baking heat over Northern Europe, and great holes ripped in the ozone layer. We're not used to it.

There were terrible droughts in England. Denise told us about them on the phone. Only months earlier we'd been watching the pictures of the floods and people wading round their living-rooms, while in Holland they'd been praying the dykes wouldn't give way and the water destroy the country entirely.

Mary O'Shea had an explanation for the whole thing, and only nodded when yet another scorching day dawned, just as she'd done when it had been tipping down rain all winter, and pursed up her lips in the What-did-I-tell-you manner: it was the beginning of God's judgement on us. But I read somewhere the Dutch crisis had been the fault of the Government not spending enough money to maintain the dykes and build new ones, and Denise said the English summer water problems were due to privatization, and not enough money being spent on mending the leaks in the pipes while the directors were all awarding themselves huge salaries. When I pointed this out, Mary Alice said that was just what it was about: God's judgement was to let us make a mess of it ourselves, without Him sticking His oar in and saving us from our difficulties. He was fed up with us not believing in Him any more. That's my understanding of her prophetic utterances, anyway.

So out of the blazing blue had come Sean Butler's second story, with promises of future revelations, and within hours newsmen from all over Europe were flying in to Dublin, Cork, Waterford, fanning themselves with their newspapers, and fighting each other for the hire cars. Now Waterford International is in the middle of a field and the jets fly in over the five-barred gates. I'd say it wasn't what they were expecting.

The very afternoon of the day I visited Father Jim, the doctors' practice was besieged with foreign callers, and next morning you couldn't walk down the street without having a microphone shoved in your face, and the shiny black nose of a video camera sniff you out. They were avid for *the name*, competing for the story almost before Sean Butler himself had seen his piece in print. The way they looked at it, Ballycanty was so small, everyone must know the identity of the Angel of Death. It was only a question of getting someone to talk.

The sports club story was raked up again, of course. The fact that the trip had been cancelled and nobody had gone to England didn't convince the 'investigative' journalists of anybody's innocence. You'd have thought the whole town had spent the previous winter in immorality, playing a game of pass-the-parcel with the Aids virus.

Father Jim, fortified by his barricades of supermarket tins, lay up in the presbytery, and refused to make a statement to anyone, referring all enquirers to the Bishop through Brigid Flynn, who was well trained to see them off.

*   *   *

We never fathomed the Rita O'Malley story. It was hotly debated long afterwards who had started it. I had my own suspicions, but there was no proving them. Perhaps this was the point at which the gossip bird was posing as a phoenix – become an independent creature that relied on no one individual to feed it, it constantly renewed itself. We scarcely recognized it any longer.

It was Saturday, another grill-you-on-the-pavement blue day, the day after I'd been down to Father Jim with Brendan's application form, and the TV men were persecuting the passers-by in town. Rose rang me in the afternoon.

'There's something going on at O'Malleys' out on the coast road!' She sounded excited. 'There's about a dozen reporters camped in the garden – no-one can get in or out! Mam had a call from Mrs O'Malley could she fetch the groceries for her from the Hyper – they're starving in there. Down to their last rat!'

'It can't be to do with the Aids story – it must be something else.'

'Mrs O'Malley said it was terrible. Newsmen trying to get in by the back door, and everybody filmed and photographed who goes in or out. There's a great hairy German on the front doorstep, and he keeps pointing a camera through the letter-box. They haven't had any post now for two days – Jacky Dooley took one look at them and pedalled off down the cliff road like a man late for the races.'

It sounded like a story all right. We took the groceries with us on our bikes, and a pair of binoculars, and toiled along to look.

The O'Malleys' house is a grand new one with a blue slate roof with dormer windows to it, and three bathrooms; Mam and I inspected it when they were building it. There are five others in the row, each slightly different, with half an acre of garden apiece. A low wall, Spanish colonial style, runs along the front, with two gates and a horseshoe sweep of a drive. The rest is lawns, all brown and dried-up that summer, a bit spare for my taste at any time of year, with not a tree in sight, and the cliff road all but blown away by the gales in winter. Mr O'Malley's not had a lot of luck with his viburnums, despite treasuring them like children.

We stayed back at first, getting the lie of the land among the gorse bushes on the hill opposite, with the box of groceries. We could see well enough. There were hired cars parked right along the lane. Two reporters were sitting in one sharing a packet of sandwiches; the others were on the walls by the gates, or on the lawn. I looked out for the hairy German, but there was no-one on the doorstep. All the curtains were drawn.

We watched for a while, the binoculars passing between us, but nothing happened until a curtain moved upstairs and Rita's expressionless face looked out for an instant. It was as though an electric current passed through the army outside. Car doors slammed, figures raced for the drive, and all those on the lawn clapped camera lenses to their eyes. Small white explosions everywhere. It was like a mad fireworks party in the scorching sunlight. Rita's face disappeared again.

'I think it *is* something to do with the Aids story!' Rose said with a flash of inspiration - if it *was* inspiration. There's no getting the truth out of Rose. 'Let's go down and we'll find out what's going on.'

We left the bikes, and came down off the hill slowly, threading our way through the gorse and tussocky grass, taking it in turns with the grocery box. Mrs Walsh had stacked it for a siege.

'Turn your ankle now, Rose, and you'll be front-page news,' I said.

'I could get us in the paper if you like,' she offered, innocently.

'Thanks. I'd never live down your sort of publicity.'

But despite my shrunken-violet act, I had my first experience of what it's like to be a naked celebrity.

When we reached the road, everybody, I mean everybody, turned to look at us.

'Are you coming to see the O'Malleys?' one of the reporters asked.

Before I could gather two wits together to give an answer, Rose was in the middle of it. And I'd thought it was Oonagh who was the actress.

'I might be, so I might,' said she, in her best simpering Irish voice, with one of those charm-the-money-out-of-your-trousers tinker's smiles.

'Do you know them?' He was an Englishman.

'What's that worth to you?' Simper again.

He laughed. 'A drink at the pub tonight?'

'Aaah, surr, and you flying off this very evening in one of those helico-peters with all your wicked stories!'

A group was gathering. Some of them laughed, and the Englishman grinned.

'You don't want your picture in the paper, then?'

'And me last year's Beauty Queen in Ballycanty? There's no novelty in it.'

'Do either of you know Rita O'Malley?'

Rose jumped in again before I could open my mouth. 'Rita! And isn't she my sister-in-law!'

'You're married to her brother then?'

'No. She's married to mine.'

'She's *married*?' He sounded surprised. The others pricked up their ears, and a notebook came out. The three closest to us had tape recorders.

'Twice – the first time in England so it didn't count.'

You could see the words flashing up on their mental autocues: Married – bigamist? – divorcee? – England . . . They were all gathering round.

'So your name must be O'Malley too, from a different family?'

'No. The same. There's a terrible lot of inbreeding round here. There's not an O'Malley with their two eyes set straight in their head. We're plagued with the squints.'

There was scribbling going on in some quarters. 'And what's your name?'

'Rose O'Malley.'

'Get us out of here!' I said in her ear. 'Or I'll drop the box on your foot.'

They were onto me. 'And are you Rose's sister?'

'No. Just a friend.'

'A friend of Rita's?'

'I've never met her in my life.'

'You live in Ballycanty? Your name is?'

I said the first one that came into my head. 'Oonagh Hennessy.'

'She'll kill you for that if it gets into print, Treesa Carmody,' Rose said afterwards. 'You came across as a terrible eejit out there.'

Rose got us out of it, but she was thoroughly enjoying herself. She swept them all with a smile she'd borrowed from Joan Collins in our childhood days of watching *Dynasty*. I recognized the set of the teeth, but it was there the similarities ended.

'I'm sorry gentlemen, but I can't answer any more questions now. I'll talk to you later.'

'Are you going inside?'

'No more questions.'

She barged on straight through them towards the front door, pulling me by the hem of my teeshirt, while I struggled after her with the box.

'MRS O'MALLEY!!'

A face appeared at an upstairs window, just above the porch, and disappeared. There was the trundling of a heavy object being moved, and the rattling of chains, bolts and keys and the door opening a crack while one of Mrs O'Malley's eyes appeared in it, and then I thought of what Rose had said about the squint and could hardly keep from laughing.

'Is that you, Rose Walsh? And who's that—?' The crack widened half an inch.

'Teresa Carmody is it? Come in both of you quick. They're a lot of wild animals out there.'

Mrs O'Malley looked harassed. The heavy object had been a large bookcase. We helped her push it back against the door.

'It's to keep that German away. It gives you a terrible fright coming downstairs first thing in the morning to see bits of him staring at you through the letter-box.'

The house was half dark, and like an oven. 'We daren't open any of the windows.'

'Where's the German now, Mrs O'Malley?' Rose asked.

'Oh, I expect he's drying himself out. Rory tipped a bucket of water over him from the landing window.'

'What's going on, Mrs O'Malley?' I asked. It surely couldn't be the Aids scandal in that household. But it was.

'It's Rita,' Mrs O'Malley said. 'They think she's the Angel of Death.'

Getting in was child's play to getting out again. Two hours passed. The vultures, as Rory called them, remained on the lawn, and the cut and thrust of a return match with them paled next to the challenge of escaping right under their noses. Rose and I, sweating in the gloomy heat of the house, fantasized with hilarity about tunnelling our way down to the sea and then swimming round the cliffs, or waiting until dark.

'Some of them were there last night,' Rita said miserably. 'The cars were parked there since half nine. They must've slept in them.'

In the end I rang home.

'Come and get us. It's a siege. Don't answer any questions.'

It was Brendan who took the call. 'Wait by the front door,' he said. 'Be ready to come out the minute I get there!'

Ten minutes later Father's car screeched into the drive, with Brendan at the wheel. Strictly speaking he hadn't got his licence then, but it was an emergency. Jack Doyle was sitting in the front beside him. They pulled up at the front door, tyres smoking, and Jack fell out of the front passenger seat to wrench the back door open. You couldn't work it from inside – there was something wrong with it. Rose and I, with Mrs O'Malley's pink cellular blankets over our heads, ran out and dived into the back, the whirr and click of camera shutters deafening us. I flung myself onto the floor, and Rose on the seat, and we lay there laughing helplessly under the covers. Jack just made it into the front before Brendan took off again through a swarm of reporters who scattered, squawking. One of them jumped sideways into Mr O'Malley's viburnums, crushing them as he subsided.

A car gave chase, but Brendan lost it after a couple of turnings. It takes a native to get the lie of the *bohereens* round Ballycanty. And it's no use trusting the signposts, such as they are.

The pressmen laid siege for two whole days, during which the final wave of summer tourists was held back, due to the shortage of hire cars. Parties of Ballycanteens took trips along the coast road to see the newshounds, and stood afar off, marvelling. There was some coming and going amongst them; a few gave up, while one or two new ones arrived.

'D'you know what Joe Finnigan's charging for one mouldy sandwich?' Rose asked me, eyes agleam. 'That's one bit of bread halved, mind.'

'Depends what's in it.'

'A dead lettuce leaf and a bit of cheese even a mouse couldn't but cough back at you. And the-day-before-the-day-before-yesterday's bread.'

'Eighty pence?' I guessed weakly. It had to be an extortionate sum judging by Rose's glee.

'*Three* pounds thirty! And they've been paying it! He's making enough to retire.'

Joe Finnigan kept the only shop on the cliff road – milk, bread, tins, that sort of thing.

'Mind you, some of them are getting wise to it.'

There was no doubting the enjoyment she was deriving from it. 'They're making deals with each other and sending one fellow out, while the other one grows roots in O'Malley's lawn with his camera glued to his eye! Did you ever hear anything so ridiculous now?'

FOURTEEN

'Poor Father Jim!' Mary Alice O'Shea announced, when she dropped in to see Nana Foley. 'He's been hiding in that presbytery for days. Brigid guards him for the week-day Masses, and he sends Father Aidan out on his errands because Father Aidan's got no authority to make any kind of a statement, though we all know what's happened about *that*, but Father Jim will have to come out tomorrow for Sunday Mass unless he's going to let that Father Aidan shoot his mouth off again, *and they'll all be waiting for him.*'

She pronounced the final words with the grim relish of an old *tricoteuse* by the guillotine, discussing the next day's tumbril-load.

She turned to me. 'So you're here, Treesa, and how's your mother?'

'She's fine, Mrs O'Shea,' I said. 'I've just been bringing over some cakes Mam made for Nana. They're to console her now Uncle Danny's going back to the nuns.'

She nodded. That was just what she wanted to know. 'And how's that sister of yours, Josephine now?'

The choice of 'sister' straight after 'mother' was significant; so was 'that' sister of yours. Decoded, her social enquiry meant a lot of things: it meant Mary Alice had been hearing gossip, and she disapproved of what she heard; it meant that Josephine had somehow been distressing her mother; it meant that by distancing herself (*that* sister of *yours*) Mary Alice dissociated herself from anything Josie might be doing, and out of respect for Nana, who was after all kith and kin, she wasn't going to say any more, but I was to pass on Mary

Alice's disapproval to Josie and stop her doing whatever it was that had got her talked about.

We didn't say any more about *that* sister, but cut back to Father Aidan.

Now Father Jim's usual assistant had been away for a while; the Bishop was letting him do some study course in Dublin on Catholic marriages in a feeble attempt to thin out the queue of divorces-in-waiting, so Father Aidan Burke was being lent to say the extra Masses along with the occasional Sunday one, and do the visiting while he was away. Father Aidan is the new breed – white open-necked shirt and a cross on a piece of string. First time I'd seen a priest like that, I'd mistaken him for a New Age monk and treated him with unnatural respect. Some of the New Agers take themselves very seriously, whereas you can laugh and joke with the young priests.

Anyway, all week Father Jim had been conducting the usual morning Masses for the good old souls who go to them, and whose dull and holy presence was sufficiently un-newsworthy to keep the hounds off his back. But on Friday, as soon as the Mass was over, he'd had to sprint for the presbytery straight through the sacristy and across the garden, to slam the door before the pack was onto him and his narrow face grimacing out of the next morning's papers.

So, for want of anything else, they'd come up with the headline: *Local Parish Priest Strangely Silent on Aids Scandal*, beneath which they'd assembled a few speculations about festering sepulchres whitewashed with Church connivance, and expanded on the likelihood of any one, or all, of them containing the true substance of the Ballycanty affair. It's the season for *outing* Church scandals. We've had plenty, nationwide, so it takes a lot of innuendo to sell the extra newspaper these days. We're almost blasé about it. Still, we like to read whatever it is, and Father Aidan, asked to comment on the situation, had obligingly done so and supplied a bit more copy.

Poor old Father Jim. Having escaped the photographers, he hadn't been best pleased to see Father Aidan's face grinning out of the *Irish Times* over his cornflakes that very morning. In the piece that accompanied it, Father Jim had been made to appear a villain for holding the Church paintbrush, while handsome Father Aidan had delighted the press by his cooperation in criticizing the alleged whitewash – and shown his lack of wisdom to the rest of Ballycanty in that he had had anything to say at all.

Mary Alice had been to early Mass and had the whole story from Brigid Flynn. She relayed it in the half-hushed tones of one with a scandal to tell.

'You know, poor Father Jim had told him again and again to have no truck with the newspapers, and to keep away from the photographers. The devil's agents, the lot of them. Any road, as Brigid said, Father Aidan's a good-looking man, and it must be a terrible temptation to him, the way it isn't for Father Jim now – and wouldn't you know it? Father Aidan's already been photographed by one of the English papers too! Father Jim must've missed that one. Well now, the gist of what they've made of it is this: Father Jim if you please has been keeping the truth from everyone – he knows what's going on and he won't say for the sake of the Church's good name! Anything about the Church and they're onto it, whether it's true or not, like a lot of flies after the rotten meat. And Father Aidan has a way with the women.'

Nana Foley shook her head, more in sorrow than charity. 'I'm thinking he won't be keeping his vocation long.'

St Anne's was built at the beginning of this century. My father says it would have been better if they'd let it alone after that; it was never meant for all the changes of Vatican II, and has been destroyed by the modern iconoclasts. It's a bit on the deprived side, but I don't mind it – I'm not in it often enough. And what are churches supposed to look like, anyway? Father says they took a lot of the paintings away, and several of the statues, and brightened the whole place up with the pink and yellow paint. The new altar is so far forward it's where the communion rails used to be, and Father Aidan stands in front of it like a chat-show host when he's giving his sermon, crooning into the microphone. Father Jim doesn't like the microphones; he stands well back in the pulpit and shouts.

Oonagh, Rose and I all went to Mass on Sunday with despicable motives. We knew the church was going to be packed, and we knew why – the word had got round like lightning.

Against all the odds, the O'Malleys were going to try to break through the siege at their doors and were coming to Mass, braving the microphones, cameras and continuous fire of incisive questions. I rang Rose and Oonagh to tell them, because Mrs O'Malley phoned Mam and mentioned it.

We got there early, and sat waiting, wondering if they'd make it. Not a head turned in Rita's direction as she slid into one of the side pews just before the Mass began, but nudges worked their way along the rows, and everybody knew where she was. The entire family had come – Mr O'Malley, Mrs O'Malley, Rita, Rory and Roisín.

'Did they bring the dog?' Oonagh whispered across at me.

The reporters, on the trail of Rita, came to Mass. You could tell some of them had never been inside a Catholic church before – sauntering in, touching things, examining the candles and the statue of St Anthony as though they were in a museum. I suppose most of them thought they were.

The majority sat at the back, to make a quick getaway as soon as Rita left. A man came and sat down next to me. He leaned towards me.

'What are you three witches doing here? Hello Terry Carmody.'

I turned to have a look at him, and for once there was no pleasure in my surprise at seeing him. 'Well if it isn't Sean Butler! And what would the likes of you be showing your face in Ballycanty for, after all the trouble you're causing us? More mischief I suppose?'

I must have been hissing quite loudly. A pair of old ladies (Briege Kavenagh and Carmel Smith – Carmel was married to an Englishman and had left him) two rows in front turned round.

'What trouble would that be now?' he hissed back.

'Writing all the things Oonagh and I were telling you – in confidence mind – about the terrible afflictions of the town.'

'In confidence was it? And there was I thinking you were wanting a wider audience for your talents. And how is Oonagh – and Rose?' He leaned forward, craning along our row.

Briege, her head turned right round like an owl, gave another baleful stare.

'Just fine!' hissed Oonagh. 'I suppose you're in here after the O'Malley story like the rest of them?'

'And what would make you suppose that?'

It was then it struck me that among all the reporters on the O'Malleys' lawn, there'd been no Sean Butler.

'You're here,' I said. 'What else?'

He gave me an amused look. 'Keep your voice down. What are your bets for the subject of the sermon?'

'When it's Father Jim it's usually the collection plate, or falling Mass attendance and the new catechesis programme. He shouldn't be saying this Mass – it's Father Aidan's turn – but we all think Father Jim isn't trusting him any longer to be discreet. He thinks having his face all over the paper will turn his head.'

Denise told me that in England on the few occasions when she's remembered her religious roots and been to Mass, everybody sings. In Ireland, a strange dumbness descends for such a musical nation. We stand there and stare at the books. I've heard this attributed to our competition with the Protestants in the bad old days. The Church of Ireland was always singing hymns, but we had the Mass, in which you didn't have to sing, and our silence made the point that we weren't having any truck with the heretics. But that sort of division doesn't matter much any more: there's so few of them, and we're all half lapsed anyway. We still sit in silence with the organist playing away to himself during the hymn spots – old habits die hard, especially laziness. And of course you can say the prayers at high speed, but you can't gabble a hymn or everyone falls about laughing.

The readings offered a choice of Moses, St Paul and repentant sinners, and the story of the Prodigal Son for the sermon theme. Father Jim prefers male lay readers, but the feminists have overpowered him, and it was two women that day. Father Jim of course read the gospel, so I was sure he'd go for the Prodigal Son, if it wasn't the collection plate. Instead, he went for the press.

Now as I said, Father Aidan likes to stand in front of the altar when he gives the homily, and sometimes he sits in his chair trying to pretend it's a chat over a cup of tea with friends – which we all know it isn't; nobody would be allowed to go on the way he does in a free conversation. Brendan says he's only waiting for him to get out the Val Doonican guitar, and the pity of it is the Church is so behind the times – when it's finally got round to updating, what was once a new trend is already dead and buried. It's pathetic really. But Father Jim Lafferty, against the wishes of the Bishop, preaches an old-style sermon from the pulpit.

If it's true that everybody has one good book in them, then it could be true that every priest has one really good sermon in him. That day Father Jim gave his.

There was a blinding blue-white flash of bulbs as he got up there, gathering himself for the fray, and the entire congregation was distracted by the photographers clustered in the aisles.

Father Jim cleared his throat and began.

'I'd like to welcome you all here this morning. It's good to see so many familiar faces again, and I hope you'll be here again next week. Now I'd like to say a word or two to the gentlemen of the press, as I can see you're all here: *I know what you're here for*. You've been persecuting me for the best part of a week, and the poor parishioners that've been coming to my door.'

Nobody knew whether that was meant with good humour or bad. I slid my eyes sideways towards Oonagh next to me, and then the other way towards Sean, but he was leaning back, one arm along the pew as though he were sitting on a park bench, with a slight smile arranged on his face.

Father Jim gave another little throat clearance. 'You want an interview you say. Well, I'm giving you an interview – now. I'm giving you my prepared statement, in public, so that there'll be no mistakes. But you won't like it, and I'd even put money on it that you won't be printing a word of it, because it isn't quite what you want to hear.

'Now the first reading today was about idols – the Israelites worshipping a false God they had made for themselves. Well, I can see I'm losing your attention already. Who cares any longer about a lot of old nomads in homespun clothes wandering round somewhere south of Sinai? – wherever that was exactly. I've heard the Bible scholars are still quarrelling about it.

'So who cares, some of you are thinking, about worshipping gods anyway? They're none of them real. One false god is as good as another . . .'

Oonagh gave me a nudge.

'"Ah!" I can see you thinking, "he's going to talk about modern idols – money, political power, fame." Some people are famous for being famous these days, and others for just looking like someone who's famous, so perhaps you think I'm going to go for the more obvious – pop singers, sports people, Hollywood actors? Well, I'm not. I'm going to talk about the Angel of Death – or to be precise, the *Angels* of Death. There's more than one of them.'

There was a hiss as from a snakepit while a few hundred people drew breath suddenly.

I leaned forward and Rose leaned forward and we found ourselves looking at each other, then we looked at Oonagh between us, then all three of us turned to look at Sean, and he raised his eyes to the yellow ceiling.

'You gentlemen of the press, you're looking for *an* Angel of Death. Powerful phrase, isn't it? Good headline stuff, but you toss it about a bit lightly, don't you? Do any of you know what an angel is?'

Another nudge from Oonagh.

'You'll all tell me very learnedly the word comes from the Greek for messenger. So if you believed in God you might say that it was a person God used to give a message. A person, very ordinary. So why not have a headline: Messageperson of Death? We mustn't use exclusive language in this enlightened age, so by the same token this "angel" you're all looking for could as well be a man.'

A *man*? – Father Lafferty loudly introducing the homosexual theme no-one had dared so much as hum under their breath? I gave Sean a dig in the ribs here. Wasn't he claiming to know the identity and promising an exclusive interview?

'Now the doctor can be a messageperson of death,' Father Jim was saying, oblivious of the undercurrent he had caused. 'And that makes it very ordinary, takes too much of the drama out of it, doesn't it? Messageperson . . . all the supernatural mystery's gone.

'But *Angel* of death – you're borrowing power from an idea that's rooted in more than just the earthly.'

Father Jim raised his eyes to the yellow ceiling Sean had just been inspecting, while his voice took on a heavy sarcasm. 'It's amazing what people will believe in – magic stones, flying saucers, even spontaneous combustion taking place in a human body with several pints of its own fire extinguisher built in.'

Then he took his eyes off the ceiling, leaned forward, and said with slow emphasis, 'There are probably those among you who would be prepared to entertain quite seriously the idea of *aliens landing from outer space*. But I bet none of you could bring yourselves to believe in the theological definition of an angel if I gave it to you. Nevertheless you use the word, because it gives a certain false glamour to the message-person.

'Death, now. There's the other powerful word. The end of human life.' He snapped his fingers. 'Out like a light. Nothing . . . Well, that's what some of you think, though you might call yourselves Catholics. Others believe in reincarnation – coming back as an ant, that sort of thing. But we won't go into a subject as contentious as what happens to you after death, because whatever your standpoint, we can all agree at least with my first very limited definition.

'So, gentlemen of the press, you're looking for the messageperson of the end of human life. Or "angel" as you prefer to call them, because "angel" pitches us all against some mysterious power. Thus the angel you want is a sort of supernatural destroyer.

'Let me help you a bit there. The angel you're looking for is a fallen one – a devil – so your headlines should read: "Devil of Death", since that's what you mean. Nice alliteration, isn't it? But of course you believe in devils even less than you believe in angels, and the word "devil" has been much overused, so it doesn't have quite the same *punch*. Now you're stuck with angel again . . .

'"If it bleeds, it leads", isn't that what your editors say? And "the public has a right to know", isn't that what *you* say? You all pretend to morality – you all pretend with your investigative journalism that you're rooting out evil, exposing hypocrisy, showing us the truth, cleansing the world of wrong.

'Now there's one question I'd like to ask *you* before I finish my sermon, which has gone on long enough: are you really setting out to be such knights in shining armour? Or are you all thinking of your pay packets, your reputations, and your own path to fame on the back of someone else's misery?

'Now as this is a sermon, you can treat that question as conveniently rhetorical. But let me tell you, when we're talking of *real* devils and angels, no human being can ever be either a devil or an angel – human beings are a different order of creation. You still want to use the labels? All right then. Angels of death – messagepersons with a certain false glamour who seek to put an end to human life as they know it – bringers of destruction. Who are they?

'It's true that a certain amount of destruction has gone on. Reputations are being destroyed, idly, wantonly. The good name of the town is being destroyed in the same way. And because individuals' lives are suffering, because the town itself is suffering, soon people's homes will be affected, and people's jobs. Already members of families are suspicious of one another.' He leaned forward again, fixing the little knot at the back of the centre aisle with his glasses. 'And what about the job security of anyone who is suspected, however wrongly, of having the Aids virus? Who'll want to work with them, or eat food processed by them, or be served by them in a shop, or treated by them in a hospital? And after that, who'll want to come as an ordinary tourist to a town stricken by a twentieth-century plague?

'In your pursuit of the "truth", you want to destroy some poor sick woman – or women – even though none of us knows for certain whether she or they exist, and you'll destroy a few more in the search. What is it that you have been doing since you arrived?

Persecuting me in the presbytery by preventing me from going about my work. Persecuting my parishioners with your impertinent questioning. And persecuting a young girl and her family by laying siege to her in her house for two days with no evidence to go on whatsoever!

'Now, gentlemen of the press, I'll tell you who are the angels of death. *You* are.'

And that was the end of Father James Lafferty's sermon.

I didn't dare look at Oonagh, or Rose, though Rose had the nerve to stare very fixedly at Sean Butler. She told me afterwards he'd caught her eye and winked.

I didn't like to add up all that we three witches, as Sean had called us, had contributed to the destruction process that was going on. We couldn't have denied it. Although Father Jim had taken his aim at the press, some of the shot had scattered our way. There were not many of us there, keeping our heads down, who could call ourselves angels of the blameless kind even by the loosest definition of the word.

Rose and I retrieved our bicycles from the gorse bushes above the O'Malleys that Sunday evening, while most of the press, undeterred by Father Jim, were still hanging round in the hopes of a story. Finally somebody influential in the town took pity on the O'Malleys. I think it was one of the Gardaí myself. So with a roar of Rent-a-car engines the press pack was off, back up the coast road towards Ballycanty and then north to lose itself for a while in the *bohereens*. They'd been tipped another name. Oonagh thought it was Kitty O'Reilly's – a poor old soul of seventy scratching a living with her hens.

I hoped that no-one would so much as breathe the words *Tom Power*, because I heard back at work on Monday that he'd been taken into hospital, and nobody knew exactly what was wrong with him.

But I was forgetting the point of the Rita O'Malley story.

Rita was the one I told you about before: the only bona fide virgin over the age of eighteen in the whole of Ballycanty.

FIFTEEN

Like swallows sensing the chill of autumn the pressmen took off, and with their departure a kind of
flatness descended on the town. It was still hot; oc-
casionally clouds traced a wispy veil across the sky,
but there was no sign of any rain. My holiday was over.
It had been an eventful two weeks – Josie's secret vices,
the final crunch with Declan, Sean Butler's article, the
O'Malley siege, Father Jim's attack on the press. I told
myself I was getting used to living purely for sensation.

There was no Oonagh at work on the Monday morning to exchange news with in Our Ladies' Boxroom,
and she was off sick for two days. I hadn't been at
Miracle Mick's the night before (that was the Sunday
night of Father Lafferty's sermon) so I hadn't seen her,
and when I rang Mrs Hennessy after work to ask how
she was, she told me Oonagh hadn't been to Mick's at
all. She had gone to visit a cousin on the Sunday afternoon, and hadn't felt well then, so she was staying on
a couple of days until she was better. It was nothing
serious; just a stomach bug.

I met Rose for lunch, and we discussed Oonagh's
absence, speculating on its probable causes – everything from morning sickness (unlikely in the post-Dan
era) to genuine stomach-ache. Underneath the super-
ficial chat, I was thinking about Declan. He had rung
me the night before.

Mam had picked up the phone. 'It's Declan for you,
Terry,' and then into the mouthpiece, 'She's just here
Declan—'

I'd pulled a face at her and shaken my head to show

I didn't want to speak to him, but she pushed the receiver into my hand and went out of the room. She likes Declan; she and Nana have knitted their way through the complex patterns of his genealogy, audited his father's computer business (successful), and Declan is always polite when he calls. His label is 'The Right Type'. I'm sure Mam never exercises her imagination as to what we might get up to when we're alone together, and what she doesn't know doesn't bother her. Nana probably guesses, and says the appropriate number of rosaries. Although I hadn't discussed my break with Declan at all, Mam must have deduced from his glaring absence we'd had some sort of disagreement.

'Terry—?'

I can't say I felt a thrill or a glow at the sound of his voice as they do in romances. I just felt nervous the way you do when any relationship has gone wrong, and you still don't know whether it's worth trying to put it right or not.

'Declan—'

'I haven't seen you for over a week.'

'No.'

'I called round – Monday evening I think it was. You were out.'

It was the night I'd gone cycling with Rose. I didn't explain.

'I wondered if you'd be at Mick's tonight – and if you'd acknowledge my existence if you were? I'd like to talk to you.'

'You're talking to me now.'

The way I said it was childish, and I wouldn't have blamed him for putting down the phone on me.

'Then I'm asking you Terry – will I see you tonight at Mick's?'

Giving a straightforward answer seemed like too much of a commitment. I edged round it. 'I was thinking of going somewhere else? There's too many of our crowd there on a Sunday night.'

155

I instantly regretted that – I hadn't thought it through. With Oonagh or Rose around, there would have been no opportunity for in-depth discussions about *our relationship*.

'I'll see you at John Dooley's then.'

I didn't argue with the statement. I supposed I'd agreed. Reluctantly.

John had some of his Old Faithfuls at the Grotto on Sunday nights; without them the bar would fall down. But it is Mick who draws the younger crowd, so there were none of our own set at John's. We sat in a corner, and tried, after the usual preliminaries, in as outwardly casual a manner as possible, to indulge in the first 'meaningful' conversation we'd ever had.

It was Declan who started, and he went straight for the jugular, as they say in thrillers.

'What are you trying to blame me for? Taking advantage of your intoxication to have my evil way – is that it?'

I couldn't claim that, so I kept quiet and rustled the potato crisp packet to cover our voices.

'If you want a sex life, you've got to take responsibility for it.' He sounded tense.

'When I did, you didn't like it!'

'*Talking* about catching Aids you mean? Where's the responsibility in that when it's after the event?'

'Ssh! You just didn't like it when I showed that I was detached as you are about the whole thing! Men hate to think that women can beat them at their own mean game.'

'You're the one talking about detachment, not me. And who says I'm playing a mean game?'

'I suppose you just want me to be a clinging lovey-dovey little eejit!' I accused him, my voice rising incautiously. 'You'd hate it if I really were! You'd soon be bored with me!' I thought about the detachment. It wasn't what I'd expected to hear. 'Are you telling me you're not detached, then?'

'No, Terry. I'm not detached. I care about you a lot.'

'What about your girl in Cork? That's not "caring" in my terms – wanting me for the summer when you can't have her, and then going back to her when term starts and I'm forgotten about! I don't want that sort of arrangement.'

'It isn't that sort of arrangement. I told you – I've finished with her.'

'You expect me to believe that?'

He looked me directly in the eyes. 'Yes.' And then, 'You've got to trust *somebody.*'

It struck me that everything we had spoken so far could be the lines out of a TV soap. Was this life imitating art? Perhaps there *was* only one way to play a scene like this. What a pity that, to save yourself time and emotional hassle, you couldn't just buy the script and read it out!

It was Oonagh who had hinted that Declan might not be so detached about our relationship as I was. I couldn't yet bring myself to trust him, but I could trust her; she could have no ulterior motive in it.

'Look Terry, can't we just carry on as we were for a while? You've got all these ideas about the way I am, but you haven't bothered to check them out. Don't you think *that's* mean?'

'All men are the same in the end. Men are there to be enjoyed, and when you don't enjoy them any more it's time to move on to someone else. That's what Oonagh says.'

'What's the matter with you? You, Oonagh, Rose – so sharp you'll cut yourselves! You're in training to be the three old maids of Ballycanty – three old birds twittering on like your Nana and mine, and Mary O'Shea! Only you'll none of you be grandmothers except by accident. You're all the same – no commitments. So careful of your real feelings you'll end up without any!'

There was a sting of truth in that. I hit back. 'Declan – I'm only twenty-one and you're only twenty-one!

157

What is it that you want us to commit ourselves to, for heaven's sake?'

The interview ended unsatisfactorily. He was pressing me for a decision I couldn't yet make. I wanted much more time to find out what sort of feelings I had – if, of course, I still had any such things left in the emotional storecupboard which, according to him, I was so jealously guarding. From his point of view there was no problem: the answer was either a yes or a no.

'All right then Terry!' he said. 'You can have time. As much as you want!' And he slammed the money for the drinks on the bar and walked out.

Another soap line. I found myself embarrassed, and disturbed, but not exactly heartbroken.

John Dooley had been watching us discreetly over the bar, and he caught my eye.

'Bit of a tiff there, Terry, was it?'

'Oh no, John. Just a lively exchange of views.' I wasn't going to let him think I was upset.

He gave me a friendly wink. 'Never mind, love. Whatever it is, a pretty girl like you has no need to worry. He'll come round.' John Dooley is good at dishing out the publican's flattery. He's easily old enough to be my father, and those clichés are too familiar.

I thought about what he'd just said as I left. It wasn't so much Declan who had to 'come round' as me. And Declan probably wouldn't be 'coming round' in another sense either – his parting words had sounded final. He'd twice been the first to make a move. I couldn't think that he'd be prepared to risk it again.

I walked home.

I didn't give Rose many of the details. Just that we had agreed to cool off for a while. There was still so much going on in the town, and it wasn't the time to be brooding on a hot summer romance suddenly gone cold.

*   *   *

Hospital beds always look like something out a space-age factory – it's to do with all the metal and the pulleys and the castors underneath. They speak very clearly of impermanence; the bed can be wheeled away at any time and the occupant with it.

I had to nerve myself to visit Tom Power. He'd been in hospital for five days. He'd been taken in with a respiratory complaint, everyone said, and the way they assured you of it and looked at you at the same time, you knew the information was loaded. Just because he couldn't breathe properly didn't mean he hadn't got Aids as well. In fact, it probably meant he did have Aids. Who caught pneumonia-type illnesses in a blazing summer unless there was something more sinister wrong with them?

Tom was in a room by himself. The curtains were hospital chintz and there was a jug of flowers on the bedside cabinet to make it seem more cheerful. But the walls were that pale green somebody once thought was psychologically beneficial, and I thought how if it had been me lying there they'd have reminded me of the next spring I might not see, and I'd have been profoundly depressed. Especially with Van Gogh's sunflowers on the wall, which would remind me of the next summer as well.

A drip was rigged up beside the bed, with a thin plastic tube snaking down towards the patient's arm. I didn't look too closely. Hospitals make me feel sick at the best of times, and if I were the type for panic attacks I'd really indulge myself.

I was ashamed of it even at the time, but I couldn't help feeling that the very air around me was contaminated with Aids; that just by being there, and breathing it in, I'd end up like him. You have to remind yourself firmly how Aids is caught.

I didn't want to be there, in that place or that atmosphere, but after a while I would walk out. I tried to think of how much less Tom wanted to have anything to do with any of it.

He must have read my less acceptable reactions in my face those first few seconds, before I got a grip on myself. He was so changed – pale, and thin, thin. He had sunk in on himself. His eyes were ringed with shadow, and I could see fear in them – of rejection, of my embarrassment, of me – that I wouldn't be able to handle it, and that would make it all the harder for him. He gave me a grin, but only his mouth worked. His eyes were resentful as well as scared. I was well, and alive with a future, while he was sick and there was only the present.

I had to swallow hard before my voice came out. 'Hello Tom!' False cheerfulness bounced off those sick green walls. 'I brought you these—' I didn't mean to chuck the flowers at him like a live grenade, but they fell out of my hand as I thrust them out to him, exploding onto the bed in a tangle of colours and stems. They were florists' dahlias. He looked at them, and indicated the arm connected to the drip with his other hand.

'Sorry. I'm not supposed to move it. If you ring for Anne she'll bring a jar or something.'

'Anne is it? What's happened to "nurse"? I can see you're getting on all right, Thomas Power. Up to the old tricks, is it?'

As soon as the words were out of my mouth, I saw how stupid they were. I was just babbling to keep away silence. Old tricks. Sexual innuendo might be the last thing he wanted, but I wasn't supposed to know that, and I made it worse.

'Sorry, I shouldn't have said that.'

He gave me a look. 'Why not? It's like a morgue in here.'

Morgue. That used to be a joke too.

I tried again. Again the note was false. It came out fussy and brusque like the words of an old-fashioned matron hidden behind her starch. 'You're not supposed to be having parties, in the name of goodness.' I picked up one of the cards by his bed. 'How can you be bored with all these visitors I hear you're getting?'

We went through the litany of names then, finding something gossipy to say about each one, but he wasn't really interested. Both of us were just filling in the blank.

I thought: how can you even pretend to be interested in the minutiae of other people's daily lives when there might be so little left of your own? All jokes had lost their humour. We were making a feeble noise – a whimper against emptiness.

After a while Tom put his hand over his eyes. 'You'd better go, Terry.' His voice was choked, but at last it was all real, and we couldn't keep up the pretence any longer. I sat down on the very edge of the bed, and suddenly it was easier.

'Tom,' I said. 'You don't have to answer this, but you know what people are saying about you—' My heart was beating so fast it was like going into a school examination. 'Have you got Aids?'

'Yes,' he said.

'Who knows about it?'

'The hospital staff, I suppose. But they're not saying anything for the sake of my family. They don't want it talked about. I've only told you now.'

I looked at him very hard. 'Why me?'

'Because you're the only one who's asked. And because you won't tell anyone else.'

I was stabbed with guilt – a guilt far worse than what I'd felt when they cancelled Brendan's trip to England. The Aids rumour had been the breath of life to Oonagh, Rose and myself all summer. We'd made jokes about it, speculated on the victims, laughed about the tangle of relationships that must be involved. We'd hugged it to ourselves gleefully, then dropped hints, then spread it around, and then made up stories. And now Tom trusted me.

'Tom,' I said, and I looked him in the eyes though I felt that my face was on fire. 'I swear to you I won't tell a soul. I *swear* to you.'

161

He seemed surprised by my vehemence. 'I know you won't, Terry.'

I saw that he was dejected again. 'You don't look so bad, you know. You'll pull round again.'

'You say that because it's not you,' he said. 'You don't know how it is until it's you. This isn't the first time I've been in hospital.'

'But people don't really know very much about Aids even now!' I protested. 'I've read of babies born HIV positive and then mysteriously the thing reverses itself and they're fine a few years later—'

It was a pathetic straw, and he wisely let it whirl past.

'Don't, Terry. It's no use. You know, Father Aidan was round here yesterday. He was trying out the jokes, but I saw that he was scared. He didn't know what to say.'

'Oh, come on Tom—' I was going to say *He's always visiting the bedsides of the dying*, but I changed it in the nick of time.

'—he's a professional. It's his job to talk to people in hospital.'

'Not people my age, with Aids.'

I was sure he was right, but I brushed it off. 'Perhaps it's *his* age that's the problem. He hasn't had time to clock up the experience. You mean he didn't have you reaching for the rosary on the spot?'

I felt I'd struck a wrong note again. Old-fashioned repentance. Was that really appropriate to Tom? It was a question I couldn't ask.

SIXTEEN

Mother was worried about Josie.

'How is it that Aggie's as brown as a kipper and Josie still looks as though she's been playing the ghost of Hamlet's father?'

I thought of Oliver, and Gus, and the never-home-before-dawn lifestyle, and hoped I knew the answer.

'I wouldn't lose sleep over it, Mam,' I said, with the callousness of one who guessed too many of her sister's sins. 'She's trawling the discos for talent every night until the early hours. Aggie looks a wreck too, but she sleeps it off on the beach while Josie stays in bed.'

I was beginning to feel bad about Josie. I hadn't spoken to her since the row over the photographs. I didn't want to see her – she was already wandering in a world I had only read about, and she was losing herself. I still felt contaminated by what she'd done, as though touching the photographs and being her blood relation had covered me too with an indelible stain.

Then when I thought about my walk on the beach with Uncle Danny, I realized I had been trying to ease the responsibility for the knowledge onto him. Adroitly, he'd turned the conversation round to me, and then left me with it. I came to the conclusion I might be casting Josie off when she most needed help.

The whitewashed walls of the cottage threw the sun back into your eyes like daggers, and the grey slates shone as though covered with cooking oil, ready to fry you up. Only the cool green window-frames and the green door were good to look at.

Aggie was on her way down to the cove. I shouted

after her and waved. She waited until I'd got as far as the cottage.

'Just got up?' I asked.

'Something like that! I'm going for a swim. Is it me you've come to see or Josie?'

'My sister.' But even as I said it, I could hear sea fingers touching the shingle, stroking, rolling the pebbles gently. Cool cool inviting water.

'Inside,' Aggie said with a wave in the direction of the cottage. We both glanced at it, and the dazzle struck back at us. The sun burned on our heads and our arms and our feet.

'I'll come for a swim with you first,' I said. 'I don't suppose Josie'll be going anywhere this time of day?'

'No more she will. Will we go down?'

I like Aggie. She has the red hair that old people used to call unlucky; Nana says there are some who would take another road rather than meet a 'foxy woman' or let her cross their path. Aggie doesn't go brown the way my mother described. The sun covers her with golden freckles, so many they join up over her nose, and on her forearms. The rest of her skin stays milky white, and she curses it. She looks at you straight, and has an easy sense of humour. Without her humour, she and Josie would probably have murdered each other. They all say her pupils like her.

We lay on the beach after our swim, and talked for a bit. Then I went back up the cliff, leaving her to her book.

I called out for Josie, then pushed the front door and stepped inside. It was no cooler, but the blinding glare had gone.

Josie was there. I thought I saw her rubbing her eyes just as I came in. They looked red, as though she'd been crying.

I thought: *I came to ask how you were. We haven't seen much of you lately* – polite conciliatory openers, but they weren't right. Being too kind and polite would make it look as though I were the one in the wrong.

Josie stared at me, neither hostile nor welcoming.

I said, 'Is anything the matter?'

She turned away abruptly. 'No, of course not.'

There was, and she meant me to ask, to go on prob-
ing while she denied it until wearied by the pressure
she gave in, and allowed herself to wallow in the sympathy offered to her. She always used to be like that,
and I was irritated already; would we have to go
through a whole Josie charade before we either estab-
lished that I *wasn't* to know what was the matter with
her, or that I *was*?

She started to comb her hair. I couldn't see her
expression.

'Mam was worried about you.'

She shrugged, in silence. Then, 'I saw you go down
to the cove with Aggie. You were a long time.'

'We swam. The water was grand.'

'What did you talk about?'

I thought I'd take a short cut. 'You, if you want to
know.'

Her spine went stiff. 'What did she tell you?'

I stared at her. Not what did she *say*, but what did
she *tell* you. Then there was information about Josie to
be exchanged. I already knew about the photographs,
so it wasn't that.

'That she thought you were too thin, you smoke too
much, stay out so late even she can't keep up with you.
And breaking up with Robert hadn't done you any
good.'

She moved so that I could see her eyes directly in the
mirror, and she looked at me. Defiance. 'What business
is that of hers – or yours?'

'None. We just thought you were very keen on him.'

'I found we didn't believe in the same things.'

Edgy, humourless Robert, the academic. No. He
wouldn't have a lot in common with Miss Good Time
Girl.

'What sort of things?'

'Oh, life. You know.'

It wasn't worth pursuing. She would only become more irritated.

'Aggie also said you fainted twice. Once when you were driving her car. It was lucky she was with you.'

'Not while I was driving it. I pulled off the road. You're not to tell Mam.'

'What's the matter with you?'

I couldn't see her eyes now.

'It's a hot summer. I can't stand the heat.'

'It never bothered you before.'

'It's never been this hot before. Not here. It's different in Greece and places like that. You're prepared for it. You wouldn't know. You haven't been there. It's different, that's all.'

It sounded plausible, and I wasn't going to argue about the way the sun struck different parts of the planet. I'd been thinking about the fainting business all the way up the path from the cove. Josie had had fainting fits before, when she was at school. Nobody ever found out why, and in the end the doctor came to the conclusion it was the way adolescence affected her. I'd had my own theories that it was to do with lessons she didn't like, but when I accused her of it, I found there was no real pattern to it, and the next time she'd fainted just before one of the lessons she did like. Just to spite me, I suppose. Now I had another theory. I came straight out with it. 'Are you pregnant?'

I'd worked it out. She'd got pregnant, and Robert had chucked her. Either she'd had an abortion in England and come back home for the summer to recuperate, or she was still carrying the baby and starving herself to induce a miscarriage. Or perhaps she thought if she was very thin it wouldn't be so obvious later on, and she could have it in secret? Anything was possible with Josie, but I wasn't wholly convinced by that last theory myself: secrecy wasn't her line. She was much more likely to draw attention to herself by making a stand for single mothers. Had she already told Aggie whatever it was, and Aggie had been trying to throw me clues to cushion the shock? How on earth would Mam take it? I had a pretty accurate idea what Nana Foley would say.

'No. Of course not.'

She sounded indignant.

I suppose if you're as sophisticated as she is, it amounts to a deadly insult for someone to suggest you might have conceived a baby by any other means than a designer test-tube. I braved an explosion.

'Did you have an abortion in England?'

She swung round this time, her eyes blazing some message, but I didn't know what. 'No! Once and for all, I was not and am not pregnant!'

We glared at each other, and I knew she was weighing up the advantages of an outburst, while I was preparing to give as good as I got.

Then I said, 'I'm going back to the cove to join Aggie. So I'll tell Mam you're all right, then, despite looking like a lump of uncooked dough?'

'Who wants to get skin cancer?'

Skin cancer. Her latest fad. I should have guessed.

'I don't care,' I said. 'I might die before then, and you only live once.'

The comforting cliché, opiate of the intellectual coward according to Uncle Danny.

There was silence, though it was not because Josie was fazed by the platitude. I've seen her switch on the tears to order, but I'd have sworn that time they were genuine. She just stood there, and the tears rolled down her face.

'Oh God,' she said. 'Oh God.'

The photographs, the life she led in England, stealing Robert's car . . . ? I couldn't guess what it was. All of them, none of them. I felt her misery wash over me like a wave, and I began to cry with her. We put our arms round each other, and sobbed against the chair she'd been sitting on.

I don't really know why I cried then, but, at that moment, life was suddenly stripped of all its sparkle.

We'd been given a lot, Josie and I: parents who were still together, reasonably affluent, and who did their best for us; adequate doses of intelligence and good looks apiece – and what was it all for? Already Josie seemed to have a string of regrets behind her, and I had my own growing list of them. But why laugh and joke and look for enjoyment the way both of us had, when in the end it only compounded the miseries?

After what seemed a very long time, Josie said, 'You'd better know. I have got something wrong with me.'

'What?' I asked, as we wiped our eyes with the back of our hands, and sniffed.

'The doctors aren't sure. I've had it for some time. They think it's something wrong with my blood. Don't tell Mam.'

An invisible fist punched my heart. I couldn't breathe. The word Aids instantly flashed up in my mind like a neon sign.

'What do they think it is? How serious is it?'

'It's . . . I . . .' She just looked at me.

I couldn't think. Josie. Josie might be dying! My sister dying. First Tom Power with Aids, and now Josie dying of – what? Some blood disease. Leukaemia? Or something she'd caught on her travels abroad? To my knowledge she'd been nowhere particularly dangerous from a health point of view, but her look had told me *serious. Very serious.*

No future perhaps for either her or Tom . . . Take it all now. Fear. There is no certain future.

Again I thought of Oonagh and Rosie, and how we'd joked, and guessed, and started rumours like hares, just to see how they'd run, and all the time we were playing with the idea of death.

'It could be a mistake,' I said. 'If the doctors don't know what it is – it might not be too bad. You could get better any day!'

'Yes.' But the way she said it made me think she'd given up hope.

'Mam'll have to know,' I said, when I could speak again. 'How are you going to hide it from her? What are you going to do?'

'She mustn't know!' she said fiercely. 'She mustn't! I'll tell her I'm having treatment in England. And as you said yourself, I might get better.'

That sounded so forlorn, I started to cry again.

'Does Aggie know?'

'Yes.'

'Anybody else besides me?'

She hesitated. 'Only in England.'

Denise? – no. Robert perhaps? Maybe that was why he hadn't gone to the English police about his car. He'd felt sorry for her.

'Does Robert know?'

'He does now. But he doesn't care.'

I felt a flare of sisterly indignation – callous bastard! Cowardly, weak, unsympathetic – a whole string of maledictions ran through my mind but I didn't voice any of it. There was a finality in Josie's tone that inhibited further questions. She might be wayward, difficult, selfish, but a love for her I never knew I had swept me suddenly. She was Josie my sister *with* all her faults.

This new picture of Josie haunted me. I was distracted in the office, and out of humour with our lunch-time meetings when Oonagh came back to work.

'What's the matter with you?' Oonagh kept asking. 'You're like the death's head at the feast. Life's wonderful!'

Death in Life at the feast of summer – not for me but for Josie.

Oonagh had just been on a clothes-shopping spree in Dublin, and for her life certainly did look wonderful. It was her second weekend in Dublin, and I wondered if the new glamour was to be cast over a new man. We went for a walk together after work, down towards the cliffs. The grass was burnt and the sea still shone a hot

169

blue. I couldn't tell her what I wanted to talk about at Whelan's.

'You've got to swear you won't breathe this to a soul – I mean it, Oonagh.'

She looked startled. 'I won't tell anyone.'

'Swear you won't!'

'I promise, Terry. Isn't that enough?'

'All right. It's not my secret.'

'I won't tell,' she said again.

I told her about my sister.

SEVENTEEN

After Oonagh, Rose knew. I couldn't forget Declan's jibe about the three of us – 'old maids of Ballycanty – so sharp we'd cut ourselves' – and I found myself testing our reactions against his judgement of us. With such a secret between Oonagh and me, it wasn't possible to keep it from Rose. For once, it was not something she could turn to a jest.

We decided to keep the secret between the three of us, and planned to take it in turns to try to cheer Josie up at weekends, or on the odd week-day evening, organizing ourselves into a little band of 'carers'. I was certain Josie would be angry about Oonagh and Rose knowing; we would have to be so discreet about our offers of entertainment as to be almost ineffectual, to prevent her finding out. I suppose it made us feel good about ourselves. Sharing the knowledge with the other two certainly helped me.

I noticed that Josie wasn't particularly grateful for my invitations and attention, but it was hard to think of anything else to offer. She still went out late, and stayed out. I didn't blame her now for the awful Gus, and worse Oliver. They were a way of forgetting.

She had talked of going back to England, but said Aggie had persuaded her to stay on until the end of September, unless there were any medical appointments she had to keep. There weren't. So Aggie thought she would be better with people she knew, rather than trying to bear it alone.

Once Rose was in on the secret, our lunch-time meetings at Whelan's were resumed. At first we were careful not to mention Josie, in case anyone overheard.

But coded enquiries became full-blown discussions with only names omitted.

What had happened to my sister was beginning to seem to me like a judgement on the three of us. I even began to see it as significant that the long hot spell over the country was changing at last. A wind began to blow in from the Atlantic, pushing clouds before it that patched the land with shadows, though still no rain fell.

I need not have felt guilty about telling the others of Josie's illness. The secret to which she had sworn me leaked out in other directions. Josie herself told Grace – sweet, sympathetic Grace – who was more upset than I had been, and cried for two days, until her husband Kieran had to find out what was wrong with her. So he knew.

Grace told Mam, with Josie's reluctant permission, because she thought she ought to know about her own daughter, the matter was so serious. Then Da knew, and with so many shocked and doleful faces, Brendan guessed there had to be something going on and nagged it out of me.

It was Brendan who had the least sympathetic reaction. He has never got on with Josie since he's been old enough to have a mind of his own. He thought he detected a discrepancy.

'What's she so worried about skin cancer for when she's supposed to be dying of something much worse?'

Is any one killer disease worse than another? I was taken aback by Brendan's callous remark, and even more shocked by his follow-up.

'What's she got? She can't tell us. Are the doctors over there stupider than ours? I can't believe it. *Blood disease* – my foot. I don't believe a word of it. I'll bet she's pregnant.'

I defended Josie hotly, inspired by guilt as much as genuine sisterly feeling. Brendan's cynical detachment reminded me of my own where Declan was concerned, and it was an unattractive response. 'She's not! I asked her.'

'She's had an abortion then and it's gone wrong, or she's regretting it.'

That had been one of my very first suspicions of her, and had come to mind once or twice since, but I was certain she would have told me. I knew about the photographs, after all, and I thought: surely you couldn't have anything much worse to admit to than those?

'I'm certain it's not that. You'd have to be very unlucky to have something go wrong with an abortion these days, and if she was regretting it, she'd be defiant and you'd never guess – you know Josie. Of course she's ill! You only have to take a look at her.'

Brendan shrugged. 'So would you look ill if you stayed out of the sun and ate some faddy diet of tobacco and red wine.'

Mam's explanation of Brendan's reaction was that he was too young to take it in, and frightened by the idea of it.

'Don't blame him, Terry. You're older – you can come to terms with something like that better than he can.'

I didn't see that at seventeen I'd have found Josie's illness any harder to bear than I did at twenty-one, but I tried to make allowances. Perhaps boys were different. After all, Da preferred to shut himself off from it, and avoided any discussion of the subject, whereas Mam and I needed to talk about it.

Mam was out the Saturday morning Josie came to raid the fridge.

Josie had 'borrowed' a few things before, but this time an unnatural hunger had come over her. She had hitched a lift into town with Aggie, and I supposed that her finances must be in a very bad state from the acquisitive way she examined the kitchen.

'Aren't there any more yoghourts in here?' she

asked, opening the fridge door wide, and picking through the likely pots.

'Mam's gone out to the Hyper. She'll be getting some more.'

Before I knew about her illness, I might have remonstrated with her. She should have been buying her own food, since she had firmly decided against accepting our hospitality in other ways. Now she was seriously ill, it seemed unchristian to deny her anything: serious illness in someone suspends idle criticism and critical judgement alike – it anaesthetizes them. Well, I'd say that's true for most people, though it clearly didn't apply to our next unexpected visitor that morning.

There was a ring at the door, and when I went to open it I found Mary Alice on the doorstep. She was looking for Nana, who was to join her on one of the Active Retirement outings that afternoon.

'She said she'd be round here this morning. I thought I might catch her before she left.'

'Will you come in, Mrs O'Shea? She hasn't been here yet.' The words were out before I remembered Josie.

Mary Alice saw Josie through the kitchen door; the kitchen opens onto our living-room.

'A little bird told me you're not so well,' Mary Alice began.

My sister gave her one dark searching look, and then said dismissively, 'I'm fine.'

Mary Alice wasn't to be shaken off. 'Well now, I was talking to your grandmother, and she seems to think you're not well at all. Are you seeing a doctor?'

'I'm fine, Mrs O'Shea. There's nothing wrong with me.'

It was Mary Alice's turn to give the piercing glance. 'Your health's not something you should be taking chances with. You should be going to a doctor, while you're over here at any rate. It's a lot of responsibility to be putting onto your Mam, if there is annything seriously wrong with you.' Undeterred by the stony silence she went on, 'Are you planning to stay on in

174

Ireland now, or will you be going back to England? Your grandmother was telling me you have a boyfriend over there.'

'I don't know how she got hold of that!' Josie was sparked into annoyance. 'It's not true.'

'What, a beautiful girl like you and no boyfriend? That's a shame now.'

My sister said nothing and glared, while I racked my brains to work out how Nana might have discovered the story about Robert. About Josie's illness Mam must have told her – but Robert? Nana could have been ringing Denise on the quiet, but Denise wouldn't have given her that sort of information. Mam then – had she been phoning England and passing on the gossip to Nana?

Josie clattered upstairs after that, and I heard her knocking about in the bathroom, and then in my bedroom. I knew she wouldn't come down until Mary Alice had gone.

'There's something very wrong with that one,' Mary Alice told me, shaking her head. 'What's she been up to over in England?'

'Wouldn't we all like to know, Mrs O'Shea!' I said it very lightly, teasing, to suggest that Josie hadn't been up to anything at all. I wondered: did she or did she not *really* know about Josie's illness? Mary Alice is very astute, never mind her sixth sense for things going on and whatever revelations she might be having from On High.

She gave me her brightest gimlet look. 'Now, Teresa. Don't you be following in her footsteps.'

An image of Declan and myself in the field flashed into my mind – and there behind the hedge was a fit old lady with a spray-on perm pedalling past on her bicycle . . . Surely not! I had to tell myself severely that it was nothing but guilt again, distorting the facts. But she was back to Josie.

'She'll come to a bad end, that one, if she's not careful.'

'Is that a prophecy, Mrs O'Shea?' *Or*, I was going to add, *a bit of wishful thinking*? There was no humour in my voice. I wanted her to know that we were all supportive of Josie, and she wasn't to be presuming on her friendship with Nana when it came to making the disparaging remarks.

It was fortunate Mary Alice was herself amused. 'Get along with you. I don't think there's annything wrong with Miss Josephine Carmody that leading a better life wouldn't cure, and that's my honest opinion. She's got you all flapping round her, but what is it you're after?' Then the amusement began to fade. 'Making yourselves feel better, is it? Because I can tell you, you're not doing annything for *her* but make her worse. If she's as ill as it's said, she's no business to be putting all that responsibility on Aggie and the rest of you. She should be seeing a proper doctor, a specialist – unless she's planning to come home to die and your Mam is prepared to look after her. Now I'm telling you this because underneath all that silliness you're a sensible girl. Your Nana and your Mam don't know what to make of it, and one of you has got to be thinking straight.'

If I'd been shocked by Brendan, it was nothing to what I felt after hearing Mary Alice! I know she's been a nurse, and nurses have to brisk themselves up to the harsh realities of death and all that, but did she have to put it so bluntly since she must know – judging by the long conversations with Nana behind her words to me – that Josie's illness was serious? My reaction showed in my face.

'You don't think I should be saying things like that?' she said, fixing me with the eye again, but this time she lowered her voice so that there was no chance that Josie upstairs might hear her. 'Well, I'll tell you something about your sister. She's a good little actress, but she'll find she's overdone it one of these days, and then how's she going to get herself out of it?'

'What do you mean?'

176

She didn't answer directly. 'You get her to go to a doctor. She shouldn't be walking round like that without some medical supervision.'

'I've tried,' I told her. 'She says she's seeing a specialist in England. I suppose she doesn't want to confuse the treatments.'

She gave me one more look, and then began arranging herself to go back to her bicycle. 'Tell your Nana when she comes round I'll be ringing her to fina-*lize* the details of the cinema trip. I'll be on my way home now.'

'I'll tell her, Mrs O'Shea.'

'Mind what I said now, Treesa Carmody.'

'I will, Mrs O'Shea.'

'It's only an easy step to regrets you'll have all your life!'

I could imagine myself telling Rose about her parting shot.

'I'll remember, Mrs O'Shea.'

I thought she'd grow roots in the doorstep.

After she'd gone, Josie gave me hell about passing on gossip. She'd worked out during her session upstairs with my nail varnish that I must have told Nana about Robert, because I was the only one who'd met him or knew anything about him.

It was useless to point out that Josie herself had driven up to our front door in his car, and that the whole street had commented on it. They would naturally assume it belonged to a boyfriend if it wasn't hers. Perhaps some of them had even seen him fetch the Citroën from our drive, after he'd retrieved it from the cove and I'd driven it home.

She refused to listen, so rather than argue with a sick woman, I went out and stayed out until she'd left. Then it struck me she hadn't argued at all about Mary Alice knowing of her illness. Perhaps her deductions on that score had been the same as mine: Nana had found out from Mam, and passed on the news.

I thought a good deal about what Mary Alice had

plainly come to tell me: that she had her suspicions of Josie's illness. But why would Josie lie – what would she gain from it except a bit of extra attention, which she didn't seem to want?

There were no yoghourts in the fridge later. Mam had given her the entire new supply, because she'd asked for them.

We were still prepared to 'look after' her, our little team of carers, doing our best to atone for all the mischief we'd stirred up. We thought we'd better just hold ourselves in readiness for the time when she might seriously need us. For the moment there was little we could do, especially as Oonagh was away for the weekend again.

'I think she's gone to Dublin,' Rose told me. 'D'you suppose she's keeping him quiet?'

'Keeping who quiet? You mean a new man? You know Oonagh – she'd have told us. I think she's on another buying spree.'

We discussed Oonagh's glamorous new office wear.

EIGHTEEN

The papers came too late for Da that morning, after he had gone to work. He usually leaves just before eight, and I don't have to go for another half-hour. He reads his way through a couple of Irish papers and an English one every twenty-four hours. That day they were in a folded pile on the dining-table where Mam had put them, the English paper between the pages of the *Irish Times*, and I saw it first as I opened them up to glance through the news while I had my third cup of coffee.

The photograph leapt out before anything else. It was half a front page, in colour, and hit me in the eye. There she was, Josie, her hair just caught by the breeze. She was posed beautifully, with her soulful eyes and pale skin, a model for some expensive magazine. In the background the sea, flecked yellow-green where the sun caught it, peaked in little snow-capped waves, and above and behind Josie a painter's cloudbank built up in magnificent plumes and puffs of grey on gun-metal and brilliant white. It had to have been taken in the last few days. It was a striking picture, and a haunting one. Very clever. It said TRADITIONAL IRELAND right at you – beauty, wildness, sadness.

I don't know why I didn't read the words above it. I thought, what on earth is Josie doing on the front page of an English paper? My brain stumbled round the question – is this something to do with tourism in Ireland, or has she made it into the world of top modelling unknown to us all – or is it as a porn queen she's finally hit the headlines?

Then I read the words.

I felt like someone who has been searching for a way into a building by pushing foolishly at every obscure little exit, when the word ENTRANCE is written up in bold capitals over the front door. IS THIS THE FACE OF DEATH? the headline screamed at you. Then, in a more subdued shout underneath the picture: *Alleged Angel of Death Josephine Carmody photographed near Ballycanty. 'I'm the one they're all looking for.' Read our exclusive interview inside.*

I sat in front of the paper, staring at it. Josie! Josie? But she had said she had a blood disease that the doctors couldn't identify. A blood disease.

She'd been afraid to tell us the truth. But to announce it in this way – had she shouted it stark naked from the rooftops in Ballycanty she couldn't have set herself up for more of a scandal. Aids must have affected her brain, unless it was just one last pathetic bid for the fame and attention she felt cheated of. And the fortune of course – the 'exclusive interview'. They must have paid her for it. But how had they got the story in the first place?

My eyes went back to the picture. She looked so young, and sad. I don't know why, but the callous thought came into my head that the whole thing had been carefully staged: the backdrop, the lighting effects nature had obligingly provided, and Josie – not scowling and resentful of her fate, but speaking through her soulful dark eyes of a whole lost generation. It was a masterpiece of news management.

I'd thought I was immune to shocks by then, but my knees gave way as I tried to get up from the table.

'Mam,' I said. 'Have you seen this?'

'No. What is it? Did you put the kettle on?' She came to look over my shoulder. Then she said, 'Oh my God.' And sat down very quickly. We read it through together in silence, leaning towards each other. Mam said again, 'Oh God.'

For a while, there was nothing more to say. The front page was so big – so monstrous – abruptly it had become the whole world and we couldn't take it in. We sat there, staring.

Finally Mam asked, 'Is it true, do you think?'

'It must be.' My brain was ticking round like the hands of a very large clock, heavily, laboriously. 'She told us she had a blood disease. And the signs have been there of something serious. You know – all that shutting herself up in the cottage. She's been looking so ill. And then going out after a social wild life. Trying to forget about it, I suppose.'

'I suppose,' said Mam. Silence. Then, 'Wouldn't you think leukaemia, or whatever it was meant to be, was serious enough?'

There was something odd in her tone, and I looked at her in astonishment.

'Then you *don't* believe it?'

She shook her head, helpless. 'We've all cried in secret over Josie's illness, but now she says she's got something worse and announces it to the world – well, I don't know what to believe . . .'

An image from a sheaf of photographs spilling over the top of the dresser in Mrs Riordan's cottage flashed up in my mind, and suddenly *I* could believe it. Although Josie might be capable of anything when it came to grabbing headlines, with the kind of life she was leading Aids was no remote threat but an occupational hazard. But Mam didn't know about those photographs, and it was better that she shouldn't.

She was still coming to terms with Josie on the front page.

'Does she want to ruin us? Have you thought of how this is going to affect us all, Terry?'

'Don't get cross with me, Mam! I've nothing to do with it!'

We both stared at the picture again, at Josie's eyes, at her blowing hair, at the whole cloudscape of heaven behind her. Then Mam leaned towards me, and, slipping an arm round my shoulders, laid her head against mine.

'I'm sorry, love. I'm just so mixed-up about all this – it's such a shock. I can't understand it—' Her voice split suddenly, and she put up her fingers to wipe underneath her eyes. 'Have you a tissue, Terry?'

'No, Mam. I'll get you one.' I wondered why I wasn't crying. Perhaps it was because I had had more shocks about Josie than my mother.

'Never mind. Get me my cigarettes, will you? And ring your father. D'you think he's seen this by now?' She gestured towards the photograph.

'I don't know,' I said. 'The papers came a bit late today. I suppose that Jacky Dooley was reading them instead of delivering them.'

'Or stopping to discuss the news on every doorstep,' Mam said with bitterness. 'Ask your father to come home, will you?'

I watched her. Her hand shook as she held the flame of her lighter to the cigarette in her mouth. Perhaps she still saw Josie as a difficult, dissatisfied little girl, and ached for her.

When I thought of that, all I could see was a difficult dissatisfied grown-up girl with Aids, who for reasons best known to herself was making a public display of herself and bringing shame on us all.

I was so startled by the ring at the door that I jumped, the way actors do in a farce. It was Jack Doyle coming to call for Brendan. His father drove them both to school every day, but he usually sounded the car horn as a signal. If I hadn't known he'd seen the headlines just from the fact that he was ringing the bell, Jack's face – solemn for the first time in Irish history – would have given it away.

'Is Brendan coming today, Terry?'

'Why shouldn't he be coming?'

Jack was fazed for an instant. Then he met my eyes. 'Has he seen the papers?'

'No,' I admitted. 'He hasn't.'

'I think he should – before he gets there, like. Everyone will be talking about it.'

I hadn't seen very many of the implications of Josie's public confession myself at that stage, but I guessed Jack had been struck by nothing beyond the sensation factor.

'You'd better come in. Will your father wait just a minute?'

'Oh, sure.' Jack wiped his clean dry shoes emphatically on the doormat. In the middle of summer. When he'd never been known to do such a thing before.

It was the one bright moment in an otherwise black day.

I suppose Brendan's reaction was predictable, but its vehemence took me by surprise.

'How could she do this to us? How could she?'

I thought of what Mam had said before about his not being able to come to terms with Josie's illness; he had refused to believe in it all along. 'It's a stunt! She just wants to see herself in the headlines!'

'She's ill,' I said. 'Maybe she doesn't care any more what people think. Maybe she just wants to set the record straight.'

My brother's face had grown red, his eyes bright with angry tears. 'Don't be more of a fool than you can help, Terry! It's all a stunt!'

'Ah come on, Brendan.' I tried to pacify him. I could see he was going to upset Mam further. 'What's the point – what has she to gain? She's ruining herself. Of course it must be true. And we all knew she was ill.'

'Then she should be ashamed! If she's really dying of Aids wouldn't you think she'd want to do one last decent thing for her family, and shut up about it? So why's she telling the whole of Ballycanty – the whole of Europe? Anyone capable of reading an English newspaper now knows that my sister's slept with so many men she can't remember the number!' I thought he would cry then, unless his fury was a way of dispelling his tears and his shame in front of Jack.

'She's *ill*, Brendan,' Mam said, almost pleading with

him. 'You have to accept that, unless the doctors can prove otherwise. There's no cure for Aids. Just imagine what it's like to live with that knowledge!'

'They're working on cures, Mrs Carmody. They're finding new drugs all the time. They could find one before Josie—'

Poor Jack. He wasn't used to playing the role of comforter. Everyone left the knife-edged little pause alone.

'She's not ill!' Brendan was beginning to shout. 'She's been behaving like a whore all summer, and now she wants a bit of mileage out of it before she goes off again and leaves us in the mess she's made of our lives!'

Mam's eyes met mine.

'You go to school now, Brendan,' I said. 'It's not much use you wasting your day at home. Show them we don't care about the gossip. The sooner you go the better. There's no point making a nine days' wonder out of it.'

His resentment exploded round us like fireballs. 'Josie's already done that! I could kill her!'

Mam began to cry. 'Brendan, don't go on like that. If it's true, then she's going to die – have you forgotten?'

'Did she have to tell the papers? She's boasting about it! Did she have no thought for the rest of us? That's what I can't forgive her for!'

'Nobody will be blaming you for it,' Jack said awkwardly. 'Will I go and tell my father you're coming, or not?'

'Be grateful she isn't your sister, Jack Doyle.' But he was no longer shouting.

When Brendan and Jack had gone, I rang Father. My hands were shaking just like Mam's, so that I could hardly hold the phone, and I dialled Da's office number wrongly the first time.

'Patrick Carmody.'

I knew from the curtness of his voice that my opening question was unnecessary.

'Have you seen the papers yet, Da?'

'Terry – I just have. I'm on my way. Tell your mother not to answer any calls until I get back, and not to open the door to anyone. D'you hear me now?'

It was a real crisis. My father is usually what you might call humorous and discursive, but when life goes wrong, he switches into another gear: curt and very efficient.

'Stay at home until I'm back.'

I rang McCormick's and spoke to Mary Brennan. My mind was entirely a blank as to how I'd begin.

I asked her if she'd seen the papers.

'I have,' she said. 'It's a terrible thing, Teresa. I'm very sorry for you all. How's your mother?' Mary has a deep voice, and she sounded as though there had already been a child death in the family. That made me angry. She's a professional and should know better than to anticipate disaster in such blatant tones. Perhaps it was the nature of the scandal that brought out the drama in her.

I explained that I would be late as I didn't want to leave my mother, and I was waiting for my father to come home.

'That's all right, Terry. We'll manage all right. You stay with your Mam now.' The voice was full of a most uncharacteristic (where I was concerned anway) sympathy.

Why did I have the feeling Mary had just been in discussion with Norah in the office next to hers, and possibly with Old Joe McCormick himself, and that the scandal was screeching gleefully round the offices already?

'Where *is* Josie?' Father asked, the instant he came through the door.

'At the cottage, we think,' Mam said. 'Shouldn't we go down there at once? To see if she's all right?'

'It's not her health I'm worried about.'

I shot Da a look, wondering if he was going to prove

another sceptic like Brendan, and maybe Mam too. Was I the only one who could believe in Josie's Aids? But it wasn't the moment to ask.

We had all imagined a rerun of the O'Malley scandal, only with Josie as first siege victim, and then ourselves. I had even been toying with the idea of a quick raid on the cottage, scooping up Josie the way Jack and Brendan had snatched Rose and myself from the O'Malley front doorstep, and then a dash for Dublin where we could lose ourselves in the maze of the city. It might be only a matter of hours before the first of the newshounds was on Josie's track. Now my father alerted us to a much more serious threat.

'It'll take the reporters some time to get to her, but it's not the reporters I'm concerned about. What about Josie's "victims"? What about their families? They all of them live just down the road. You don't think they're going to be in a forgiving frame of mind when nobody even knows who's got Aids for certain, and they've just seen her plastering herself all over the front page of a newspaper as the Angel of Death?'

I stared at him, taking it in. 'But who are the victims? We've only heard three names this summer, and only one of those is definite.'

Da gave me a hard look. 'There are three things *I* know for certain. One: this town has been obsessed with Aids all summer and there could be any number of men infected – from none to several dozen. Two: my daughter hasn't been living the life of a Carmelite. Three: she has just confessed to spreading the Aids virus. Whichever way you look at it, the consequences will be no fun for her or anyone else. Do you know if she's seen a doctor while she's been over here?'

That opened up what threatened to be a long discussion. When I'd suggested a medical consultation to Josie, she'd been adamant that she was seeing a specialist in England, and that there was no need for anyone else. Father insisted that if she was to remain under our roof, she was to have a test and register herself again with an Irish doctor.

I remembered what Mary Alice had said.

'Da,' I said, after the matter had been back and forth a few times, 'Brendan thinks it's not true about the Aids. He doesn't believe Josie – and I think Mrs O'Shea didn't believe she had a blood disease. What do you think?'

Again, he looked at me long and hard. 'She should see a doctor. Then we'll know the truth of it.'

He ruffled my hair, and pulled me against him, my face pressing into his shoulder. 'Don't you be doing this to us, Terry, will you?'

His voice was rough suddenly, and I was surprised by the intensity of the pain in him.

One hot night in a field . . . Was I no better than Josie? Setting out on the same road, only for me it was still no more than a little *bohereen* while she had found her way to a lethal public highway?

I heard Mary Alice's voice: *underneath all that silliness you're a sensible girl . . . and one of you has got to be thinking straight . . .*

'What'll I do, Da? Come with you to the cottage and fetch Josie?'

'Go to work,' he said. 'You'll have to face them all some time. Get it over with before they've time to add too many little embellishments of their own to the story.'

It was horrible. I noticed the difference as soon as I went out. People I knew well looked at me, and then their eyes switched away as though they thought they'd ignore me, and then they'd look back at me again as though they thought, 'I must act normal' and then they'd say, 'Hello, Terry!' and hurry past. It was all so quick you could think you were imagining it, but it happened several times. I was a walking plague, trailing a cloud of disease behind me that would envelop them if they weren't quick enough. I imagined them putting their handkerchiefs to their mouths behind my back and trying not to breathe until they were in new air, the way you do when you get caught up in the exhaust from a bus. By contrast, you could easily tell the people who hadn't seen the paper.

When I reached McCormick's the first person I met was Oonagh. She was coming out of the boxroom as I was going in. I thought, 'If she does that to me I'll die,' but of course she didn't. She took three quick steps backwards, pulling me with her and shutting the door. We were squashed against the basin.

'Terry, have you seen the paper?'

'I have,' I said.

'It is true?'

'And we all thought she had a blood dis—' I only just got the words out, because I started to cry. It was the first time I'd cried that day. To begin with, I'd been in shock. Then I'd had to be strong for Mam, and then I'd felt I should try to support Da, and then it was not letting the Carmodys down in front of the whole of Ballycanty. There was no need to act for Oonagh.

She put her arms round me. 'Don't, love. Would you like to go home? Would you like me to speak to Mary for you?'

'No. No . . . ' I sobbed. 'Going home would only make it worse. You don't know what it was like, coming here this morning! The way people looked at me – you'd have thought I'd got Aids as well as Josie!'

'Oh, the old hypocrites in this town!' She sounded really angry. 'In church every Sunday gabbling through the prayers they don't mean and then at the very first test of basic Christian charity they fail—'

'But it's not everybody, Oonagh.'

'No, it isn't. Well, we'll know soon enough who are the sheep and the goats! But why did Josie tell everyone this way? Why let them have the story and make such a public drama out of it when she must know how it would react on her family?'

I'd been thinking about nothing else for hours.

'Perhaps she thought there was so much rumour flying around it was the best way of putting the record straight.' I hadn't really believed that when I'd said it earlier to Brendan. It was too straightforward, too rational for Josie. 'But did she go to the press, or did they find her? Remember Sean hinted that he knew who it was? I didn't look at the journalist's name. Did you?'

She shook her head. 'Have you seen her? I don't suppose you've had time yet.'

'Mam's going down to the cottage now. Father's taking her. Josie'll be on her own, unless she's managed to contact Aggie – Aggie'll be back at school.'

'Don't you worry about it. D'you hear? I'm taking you to lunch in Whelan's and we'll show them that we're not the least bit interested in making scandals.'

I had to smile then. That, coming from Oonagh!

NINETEEN

I went down to the cove that evening after work. Mam
had been out twice to see Josie with Father, but the
cottage had been locked both times and there had been
no answer. We all of us speculated as to whether Josie
was inside or not. It was impossible to tell. She might
have shared our fears of predatory journalists, or an
army of avenging furies from Ballycanty ready to seek
retribution for the lives of their men.

Mam had had nothing to say to the three newspapers
who rang up during the course of the day. No doubt
they would be trying anyone and everyone to fill them
in with a bit of detail on the Carmodys. Some enter-
prising newsman had even traced Nana, and regretted
it. Then Oonagh had called me as soon as she arrived
home from work to say that she was sure she'd seen a
journalist in the town, someone she recognized from
the heady days of the O'Malley siege. It was urgent
now that we should reach Josie before the press did.
Though, as Da had already pointed out, she had more
to fear from Ballycanty itself than from the papers.
Those had already done their damage.

'You go, Terry,' Mam pleaded. 'She might talk to you.
Honest to God, I didn't even know what I'd say to her
if she opened the door to me.'

'I don't know either, Mam.'

'Ah, go on Terry. If she'll talk to anyone it'll be you.'

I wasn't so sure of that – Aggie was her chief confi-
dante. But term had already started and Aggie was
living back at home. Mam had rung her when she got
home from school, and Aggie said she hadn't been able
to make contact.

It was about eight o'clock by the time I finally set off to visit Josie. Brendan had arranged to borrow the car to meet a friend, so we agreed that he would drop me at the cottage, wait five minutes, and if I didn't re-appear in need of an instant lift home, he would assume she was speaking to me and call to pick me up again at about ten. If my interview with Josie went badly before that, and she took it into her head to throw me out, it would still be light enough for me to walk home, and maybe hitch a lift if anyone passed.

Brendan dropped me about halfway down the track, in case Josie should see the car and think the whole family had arrived to harangue her.

'Give her a piece of my mind for me while you're at it?'

'I will not!' I said. 'Anyway, she's made a getaway by now if she's got any sense left. We're wasting our time.'

That was what I hoped. My visiting Josie wouldn't do any good at all if she'd set her mind against coming home. I still didn't know exactly what I thought about her. I wasn't even sure I could be kind to her.

While Brendan was turning the car round, I went down to the cottage and banged on the door.

'Josie! Josie – it's me, Terry! Let me in!'

I tried the handle, but the door was locked. The cottage had a deserted look, but I told myself that was entirely a subjective view. Most of the time it looked deserted, even when Josie was painting her nails inside. I banged again.

'Josie – I only want to talk to you for a minute – open the door!'

A long silence. I could imagine Brendan sitting in the car and looking at his watch. The walk home stretched out in my memory like a piece of elastic. I was just about to give up on my sister and run back up to the car when I heard the key being turned abruptly, and then the door opened.

'What do you want?' she said, very unwelcoming.

My feelings towards her had gone through too many changes in the course of the day for me to be aware of any one emotion at the sight of her. I tried to concentrate on the fact that I believed her to be dying of Aids, and therefore I had to forgive her any rudeness.

'I just came . . .' I began weakly. 'I just came to see if you were all right . . .'

'You mean you've seen the paper?'

'Well, yes I have. Have you?'

'Aggie brought it to me this morning.'

'But I thought she hadn't been able to contact you!'

Josie's eyes narrowed. 'Ah. The network's been checking up, has it?' She peered out round me, up towards the track. 'Did you come on your own?' I nodded.

'How did you get here? Where's the car?'

'Brendan brought me. He's gone off now to see a friend, and he won't be back until ten to pick me up.'

'You'd better come in.' She turned away from the door and I followed her meekly into the living-room. 'What would you have done if I hadn't been here?'

'Run after Brendan, or walked back home. Have you been here all day? Why didn't you answer the door to Mam? She was – good heavens, Josie, you're packing!'

'Full marks. I am.'

Two suitcases were open on the floor, and clothes were draped on the table and every chair.

'Where are you going?'

'Back to England. I'm not just sitting here waiting for the press, and anyway, I've had enough of this place. Now I'll be branded as the Scarlet Woman – murderer of all those fine young men. I'm surprised Father Lafferty hasn't been down here with the book of exorcism rites already. I suppose the gossip's flying.'

Her tone of resentment surprised me out of my emotional neutrality. 'But you must have known it would when you gave that interview! You posed for the photograph – you must have known they were going to publish the whole thing! Did they pay you?'

'It's none of your business, but they did, as a matter of fact.'

'A lot?'

'That *is* none of your business.'

I guessed from the evasion it probably had been a fairly substantial sum, and some of it was now going to pay for her trip back to England.

'How did they find you out?'

She didn't answer, but began folding skirts into one of the suitcases.

'Josie, you told the reporter you'd slept with lots of men – you couldn't remember how many!'

'Did I?' She sounded so vague, it was as though she were talking about something as trivial as the number of cans of lemonade she'd brought for a picnic. 'I don't remember.'

I was looking at her, and the mess around her as I talked, and, exasperated by her general carelessness and complete lack of concern for the family she'd just put through twelve hours of misery, I began to understand the way Brendan had reacted. Then my eye was caught by something familiar on the table. I pounced on it.

'You've got it here!' I said accusingly. 'Look – it's in black and white!' I shook the newspaper in front of her, and then read the lines aloud. '"It was revenge," dark-eyed Aids victim Josephine Carmody admitted yesterday. "It's impossible to imagine how anyone feels when they find out they've got Aids – until it happens to you. You see all the life you might have had suddenly snatched away from you. Marriage, children, your career – it's all gone . . ."'

What career? Brendan had asked, when he read that, but I didn't make the same unfeeling remark to Josie. In the middle of all our need to make sense of it, I had to keep reminding myself that her illness might be genuine. I supposed then that that was what Mary Alice had meant by Josie overdoing the acting: she might *really* be dying and no-one believing her.

I went on reading to her. '"You feel cheated. It's so unfair. And in the more destructive moods you look round for someone to blame, and then you think why shouldn't it happen to other people? That's how it all started." Now – this! "Ms Carmody admitted that she had had several relationships before testing HIV positive, and that she had been unsure from whom she had contracted the virus. She had deliberately tried to infect some of her subsequent partners, and was unsure how many men might now be at risk. 'I was mad when I did these things,' she confessed. 'I regret it now, but you can't put the clock back. It's possible – yes – that a percentage of my partners are now HIV positive. I can only say I'm sorry . . .'"'

'So?' she said, defiant. 'You knew I had affairs in England, you knew I'd been out with a lot of people this summer. Why the shock horror?'

'But where *are* all these men? Surely you know there's only one case besides yourself in the whole of Ballycanty!'

'I know there is,' she said. 'Tom Power.'

She was looking at me. It was a look that said something, and the realization grew on me slowly as to what the message was. Something I should have seen earlier. I suppose it was because I had been regarding him as my property in some way: he'd been my schoolfriend and we were the same age.

'You mean – you . . . and Tom?'

'Stranger things have happened,' she said, and gave her attention to the shirt she was folding.

Tom and Josie. Quiet gentle fastidious Tom, and fiery predatory Josie, the scarlet woman of Ballycanty. Tom, walking across the cliffs towards me as I set out from Josie's cottage only a few weeks ago . . . Tom, walking . . . to *Josie*? I couldn't believe it.

'Where . . . ? *When* did all this happen?'

'In England. A year or so ago. We met by accident, and saw each other a few times, and we both felt lonely. It happened.'

194

'But which of you . . . who gave it to . . . ?'

'Maybe I was HIV positive at the time and didn't know. Maybe it was him.'

'But this isn't in the story you told the papers!'

'So what? I wanted to protect Tom.'

'But how could you do it? All this confession stuff! What's the point of all the lies – you don't think the town is just going to let you walk away, do you? They *hate* you, Josie! Even Brendan got hissed at in the street today! It was only some kids, but once there's definite confirmation of an Aids victim, once everybody knows a name for certain, you'll be torn to pieces!' *A nice convenient whore* . . . I'd said those words a lifetime ago. If only it had been so simple! 'If nothing else, didn't you think of Mam and the rest of us, and what it's going to be like for us having to live here?'

Up to that very morning, I don't suppose I'd have spoken those words. They sounded more like Mam than me – Mam, speaking with the voice of Nana – the Ballycanty community voice. Don't let the gossip start about *you*. Now they were my very own words. I couldn't forget Mam's brushed-away tears over the papers, Brendan's anger, Da with that closed, hurt look ruffling my hair and then pressing my face so hard into the shoulder of his jacket. And my walk to work.

Josie was unimpressed. 'Oh, come on, Terry. They were all crying out for the story to be told! And I needed the money. I was already considered beyond redemption round here – what does it matter to me now? They wanted someone to blame, so I obliged. I'm leaving anyway. It doesn't have to affect the rest of you at all.'

I was aghast. 'So are you telling me none of it's true?'

But she appeared not to be listening – she'd already begun on a theme I'd heard before. 'Of course, you're all shining little examples to the rest of us poor sinners. There's not a breath of scandal about any one of you, with Nana Foley as your patron saint! *You'll* be all right. But I'm sick to death with the sanctimoniousness of this place. You do one little thing that somebody disapproves of and you're branded for life. I'm the one who's the black sheep of the family. It's "Hello Josephine – and how are you getting on?" all bright to my face, and "I wonder what *she's* been up to over in England!" behind my back. This won't affect you at all in the long run – but at least a world bigger than Ballycanty will know who I am before I die, which is more than can be said for the rest of you!'

I'd grown a little tired of reminding myself that her illness was affecting her view of things, that she didn't realize what she was saying. Now I was outraged.

'Is that the way you see it – your passport to fame?'

It was then that we heard the car.

'Ssh!' she said suddenly, lifting her head.

We listened to the unmistakable rattle of tyres over the stony track.

'What time did you say Brendan was coming back for you?'

'Not until ten. It isn't nine yet. He must have—'

She had darted to the front door, and opened it. I followed her. Brendan must have changed his plans. I didn't have a chance to peer round her before she was pushing me back in again.

'Quick, inside! Draw the curtains—'

'But—'

'Don't ask, Terry. Just do it!'

She was already bolting the door. I pulled the thin print curtains across the kitchen window that gave the only light into the living-room.

'What about the other rooms?'

'Leave them – there isn't time. Upstairs now!'

I was stopping to protest, but she pushed me in front of her.

'Who is it for heaven's sake? Is it someone from Ballycanty?'

'Reporters. I'm not here.'

We climbed up to the loft. It was still very warm up there.

'But Josie—'

'Ssh. Don't go near a window.'

She stood by the ladder, listening intently. The drawn curtains had reduced the room below to dusk. It was like a scene from a spy movie. More Josie histrionics, I said to myself, though for once there would have been comfort in that thought. Neither of us was looking for genuine action just then.

The car engine had stopped, and we could hear the slam of a door, and footsteps coming nearer on the rolling pebbles of the path.

Silence.

A journalist? I glanced at Josie for a cue, and I thought she almost looked scared.

'D'you think they'll be after scaling the walls with siege ladders?' I whispered, making a joke of it. Would we be having a rerun of the O'Malley blockade?

She put her finger on her lips, warning me.

There was a loud banging, and then a man's voice shouted, 'Josie?'

I looked at her. *Who is it?* I mouthed.

She waited a moment, and there was another shout. 'Josie!' Demanding, this time. 'Josie are you there!'

She took a handful of my hair, and drew my head close to hers. Then she breathed in my ear, 'Oliver. Don't make a sound. He's dangerous.'

I didn't know whether to believe her or not, it sounded so over-dramatic. I remembered Oliver – I'd liked him even less than Gus. A lean, dark man with a hard expression. He sounded angry, and there must be a row in the offing, but did that have to make him dangerous? There was silence for a while, and then the banging started again, but different this time, as though he'd found a metal pole or something, to hit the door with.

At the change of sound Josie looked at me quickly and now there was real fear in her eyes.

'The trapdoor,' she hissed. 'Shut the trapdoor!'

Together we lowered it over the square hole in the floor. Then we lifted a trunk over it. The trunk was heavy and we had to stoop because of the rafters, and it was difficult to move silently, but I relied on the noise from outside to cover the odd sounds we made.

We sat together on the trunk.

'How do you know he's dangerous?' I whispered in her ear.

'I *know*,' she breathed back, and I think, even if we'd been able to talk freely, I probably wouldn't have asked her any more. Then she said into my ear, 'He has a gun.'

'How do you know?'

She just looked at me.

'Why is he here? What does he want?'

'Me. He's seen the paper.'

We were silent after that, too scared to move. We heard more banging, then the smashing of a pane of glass and scattering of pieces falling on the floor, and a wrenching squeak that meant he was forcing open what was left of the kitchen window.

My thoughts were racing, and I felt sweat beginning to trickle down my back. The attic had stored the heat of the day, and I was hot with fear. It was the fear in Josie's eyes that convinced me.

Oliver was one of the 'partners' alluded to in the newspaper. Now he was looking for *his* revenge.

We heard him scramble in through the window. He paced about in the room below, and then, shouting for Josie, opened the door to her bedroom, and then the door to Aggie's, and then the bathroom. He came back into the living-room, cursing. There was a loud crash of fragile things breaking on the stone floor, and heavier objects being flung about with dull thudding noises, and then we heard him on the ladder, his footsteps climbing. He shouted again, his voice booming just below us, and his hands brushed over the wood of the trapdoor underneath the trunk. He grunted as though pushing upwards. Josie's hand felt for mine, and gripped it; her fingers were ice-cold, though when I looked at her I could see a sheen of sweat on her forehead.

My heart was pounding in my ears, and I could hardly breathe, and whether it was from fear or the stifling air I couldn't tell. He was directly below us. If the trap lifted by so much as a quarter of an inch he might deduce that something had been put on it from above to keep it down, and then he would guess . . .

I started to pray. 'Oh God oh God don't let him get in here don't let him—'

He gave the trap a few bangs with the metal object he'd used downstairs, and then we heard him going back down the wooden treads again. He was still swearing and calling Josie a string of filthy names. I didn't dare whisper to her, but I wanted to ask her if he'd ever been inside the house and did he already know that the trapdoor had to have been shut from inside, and that it had no bolt?

There was silence. He couldn't have gone out. I imagined him, standing down there, listening, waiting for sounds from above that would betray us. Perhaps it was better to cling to the hope that he and Josie had spent their time elsewhere, and that he knew nothing of the only way to shut the attic.

We hardly dared breathe in case he should hear us. Our lives ticked by. What was he doing? What would he try next? He might be thinking Josie was out, and decide to wait until she came back, which would trap us there indefinitely. It would be an hour at least before Brendan came to pick me up – and if he was late?

Then I thought – what could a seventeen-year-old boy do against a grown man – with a gun? – if the man wasn't scared off just by the arrival of another car? Suppose Brendan came along early? I was as terrified now for him as for Josie and myself.

Then I realized something else. The front door was bolted from the inside. Though it was possible Josie had left the cottage through the door into the yard, if the key were still in the lock that too could betray us. Seeing it, he would know for certain there was someone hiding in the house.

We none of us ever used the back door. I tried to visualize it – was there a key left in it permanently, or was the key somewhere else? Perhaps Mrs Riordan had it, or Aggie, in case of emergencies? I explored the image of the door in my mind – white-painted panels of wood with two stout crosspieces towards the top and bottom, and a diagonal slanting between them. On the right-hand side was an old-fashioned latch, and a square metal lock screwed to the wood below it. Was there, or was there not, a key in it? In that acute silence, I couldn't ask Josie.

After a long time, we heard Oliver unbolt and open the front door. Did that mean he had realized the significance of the bolt, and, having failed to find us, was pretending to leave so that we would come out of our hiding-place?

My cotton dress was plastered to my body with sweat, and wisps of Josie's hair stuck, damp, to her forehead. She took my hand and pressed it to her chest. I could feel her heart battering against my fingers. I let her feel my heartbeat, which was as quick as her own, and we looked into each other's eyes. She put her finger against her lips again.

I don't know what would have happened if we'd waited for Brendan. He might have assumed, when no-one came out to him, that I'd already left to walk home and so driven away again. Or would he have seen the broken window and investigated, risking a possible attack from Oliver? If he hadn't come at all, Oliver might have waited at the cottage all night . . .

Whether our intense concentration on sounds in the house made us deaf to other noises, or whether there was another reason we had no warning I was never sure afterwards, but after a lifetime of suspense that will surely turn us grey before our time a voice said,

'Glory be to God tonight! What in the name of goodness is going on here?'

I almost gasped aloud, and Josie and I stared at each other, our eyes stretched wide with hope and fear at what might happen, digging our nails into each other's arms. Nana Foley – walking right into it!

'And who might you be?' asked another voice, as unmistakable as Nana's.

A man's voice replied, smooth and normal, 'I'm a friend of Josie Carmody – I came to see her and found the place like this.'

'Oh you did?' said Mary Alice O'Shea, in the mild tone of voice that said *I don't believe a word of it.*

'Somebody must've broken in,' Oliver said. 'This room is a mess. I was just going to search the attic in case they were still here, but the trapdoor doesn't open.'

'No, that's right. It doesn't,' said Nana, telling what I knew to be a barefaced lie. Mrs Riordan had shown Nana and Mam all over the place when she'd first set it up for letting. I nearly laughed out loud with relief. She knew where we were.

'There's no sign of Josie. I hope she's all right.'

Oliver sounded so plausible, so concerned, even the gimlet grannies might be deceived. I prayed that Nana wouldn't give anything away.

'And why wouldn't she be?' she asked.

'You never know what the reporters might be capable of these days!' Oliver said it with a smile in his voice. You could tell he was trying to charm them, lead them away from the idea that he might have had anything to do with it.

'Well, now, you might be right there,' Mary Alice agreed. 'Perhaps you'd like to do something for us?' I could imagine the way she was fixing him with her eye. 'We'd better be staying here, tidying up a bit like in case Josie comes back. There'll be no telephone here. It's your car parked up the lane? That's grand. Then maybe you could telephone the Gardaí in

Ballycanty for us so that we can report the damage? It might have been a couple of tinkers' lads in here after money.'

We heard Oliver take his leave then. You'd never have guessed from the way Nana and Mary Alice spoke to him that they were seeing him complete with horns and a tail – unless you knew them, of course.

We heard Oliver's car all right, starting up, and then the whine of a reverse at speed over the track, a shift of gear, a change of direction, and then the engine sounds dying away.

Silence again.

'Josie – Terry – come out of there!' said Nana, knocking on the wood below us.

We almost fell off the trunk, and dragged it back. Then we lifted the trap together. Nana's head on her thin neck came up like a chicken and I thought she was the most beautiful creature I'd ever seen. And then, squeezing up next to her, there was Mary Alice with her concrete curls, all agog and twice as gorgeous. I nearly strangled them both with love and relief.

'What in the name of St Patrick have you two been up to?' Nana demanded.

'Oh Nana!' wailed Josie, and burst into tears – and really truly for the first time in my life, I was *absolutely convinced* there wasn't one fluid ounce of calculation in them.

TWENTY

The living-room was a domestic Armageddon. Josie's cases were upended and thrown on top of her scattered belongings, and all the crockery on the table had been swept off onto the floor. Only the plastic items weren't broken.

We switched on the lights and made tea – there was no milk, of course – and Josie got a bottle of brandy from under the sink and drank down a glassful straight off, bold as brass in front of Mary Alice and Nana. I suppose she thought that after the revelations in the paper, there wasn't much shock value left in mere alcohol.

'Who was that man, Josephine? Was he a friend of yours?' Nana asked, as we waited for the black tea to cool.

'A journalist,' Josie said, her eyes briefly meeting mine, daring me to contradict.

'And was it him who made the mess?'

'It was three lads, big fellows,' Josie said. 'Terry and I didn't like the look of them when we saw them on the path, so we hid up in the attic. They broke in, and it was Ol – the journalist – who scared them away. I expect they were after money. He arrived only minutes before you, and we were thinking we wouldn't show ourselves to him either, in case he was after another interview.'

It was very plausible, but Nana and Mary Alice exchanged looks openly.

'Had you been up there long?' Nana asked.

I started to say, 'It felt like hours—' but Josie cut across me. 'Oh, no. Only a few minutes. We were grand once the tinkers left. There was no problem after that really.'

It was so dismissive, I knew that Josie throwing away such an opportunity for drama meant Oliver had been a real threat, and she didn't want to be questioned about him.

'So he was the one who wrote this morning's article?'

'No, not him. That was somebody different. I meant he might be looking for an interview for his own paper. He won't be the last of them.'

Mary Alice said nothing all the while, and fanned her tea with her hand. Her eyes were marble-hard with scepticism as she gazed at Josie. I was sure she hadn't missed Josie's warning glance in my direction, nor the fact that her tears of genuine relief on our release from the attic earlier gave the lie to her casual dismissal of any danger.

I was amazed at the quick way Josie had taken up Mary Alice's own suggestion to Oliver that the ransacking was the work of tinkers looking for money, though of course I hadn't expected her to tell either of them the sordid truth about her lethal ex-lover – whatever that was exactly.

But Mary Alice picked that one up too. 'Strange you should have three lads coming down here like that! It's not the kind of place they'd be breaking in to steal annything. The Riordans have never had that sort of thing before. Did you recognize any of them?'

The stony gaze locked with Josie's.

'No,' said my sister.

It was weeks before I worked out what Mary Alice had been asking, and that Josie had understood her.

'What made you both come out here at this time?' I asked innocently, turning to Nana. 'How did you get here? Did you talk to Mam? Did you know I was here?'

'Your Mam said Brendan had given you a lift—' Nana began.

But Mary Alice cut across her. She was not to be

deprived of her moment of glory. 'I'd been thinking of your sister all day. She'd been on my mind, like, and I felt compelled to go to her. I can't explain it, and I can't put it better than that. It was the good Lord who put her into my mind.'

'I'd gone round to Mrs O'Shea's after seeing your Mam to discuss some St Vincent de Paul Society business,' Nana explained.

The substitution of 'gossip about' for 'discuss' was probably automatic on everybody's part.

We drank the tea, more to follow the ritual that restores order after chaos than because we liked it. Josephine had another brandy, and then Nana began dealing with the immediate problems facing us. Nobody mentioned Aids, or asked Josie how she was.

'We can't sit here all night with the window broken and all your clothes scattered over the floor, Josephine. It looks as though you were packing to go somewhere?'

'Well I was,' Josie said. 'I can't stay here until the papers finally decide to give up on the story, so I'm going back to England. I thought I'd stay with Denise for a while.'

'You were going to England *tonight*?'

Though it was all over in a split second, I could see Josie toying with the answer 'yes', seeing no great advantage in it, then shaking her head. 'Tomorrow. Aggie was coming to pick me up really early, and then I was going to Cork or Waterford, to wait to catch the London bus back. It goes on the Rosslare ferry to Fishguard and calls at Bristol. I could get to Denise from there.'

'You shouldn't be stopping here on your own tonight. You should come home to your Mam, or me,' Nana said.

I wondered if Josie being ill and faced with the hostility of the whole town was in her mind, or if it was just the broken window. There was no missing the fact that the O'Shea chill seemed to have affected Nana too, and her remarks lacked any trace of familial warmth.

'There'll be a press siege on your doorstep tomorrow if I do. Once one journalist has got the story, the rest all pile in behind in the hopes of more information.'

Nana gave her one of her looks. 'And *is* there more information?'

Josie's smile was wry. 'Haven't I said enough?'

Nana and Mary Alice both breathed in sharply at the same time.

'Who was it,' I asked, 'who wrote the story?'

The paper was lying in the wreckage on the floor. I salvaged it and looked at the front page. I should have known. It must have been the headlines, and the shock of seeing Josie's picture and everything that had blanked out the name.

'Sean . . . !' I said. 'How on earth did he get to you?'

Josie shrugged. 'Asking questions I suppose. I thought the man who came here must have asked *you* a few – he was tall, dark – he said he knew you. That's why I talked to him in the first place. I didn't realize he'd come from the papers until later.'

After all that swearing the family to secrecy! I felt just a bit outraged. 'You told a complete stranger you were *ill*?'

'Of course not! We were just passing the time of day to begin with.'

'Sean Butler usually writes for the *Irish Times*—'

'So what? If he's freelance he can sell his stuff to anyone. He must have thought he could make more money out of the English papers.'

'And what about you – you told me they'd paid you?'

I could see Nana and Mary Alice were intent, and their speechless disapproval bristling with static.

'Everything was arranged through him – Sean Butler. That's all I know.'

Josie was beginning to sound impatient. She hated open question-and-answer sessions, especially when she hadn't had time to think out a story that would satisfy me as well as the Foley/O'Shea party.

Sean Butler . . . He had claimed he knew the identity of the Angel. But how had he tracked down Josie – unless the people at the wild parties she'd been going to all summer knew a great deal more about her than any of us might guess, and had dropped a few heavy hints? So much for her so-called friends!

Nana dragged us back to the problem of the broken window, and what arrangements we were going to make for Josie for the night. We started by clearing up the destruction in the living-room – Nana and Mary Alice sweeping the debris from the table and tut-tutting the while, and Josie and I repacking her cases. Josie chose to stay in the bedroom, to avoid the Inquisition.

'I can't have them grilling me over every little detail!' she told me in a hiss, as I tipped her scrambled clothes onto the bed. 'Old cats!'

The apocalyptic scene had galvanized Mary Alice, and she set to work with a will. Both Inquisitors oper-ated in the ambience of disapproval contrived only by the virtuous in the presence of the fallen, confining themselves to the kitchen and living-room areas, exchanging remarks meant for each other in low voices loud enough for us to hear, all of which had a bearing on the general slovenliness of household practices at the cottage, and none of which could be challenged openly. The subtext, I supposed, was a commentary on Josie as a liar and a whore.

'Just listen to them!' Josie exploded under her breath. 'The old b's! It makes me glad to be branded as the Disgrace of the Nation when I think how I've been saved from ending up like them!'

I thought of what Declan had said of Oonagh, Rose and myself, and was lost for a reply.

Josie soon grew tired of giving me orders, and I was forced to switch camps or sit and watch her, which would have drawn the remarks from the kitchen my way. There were still lots of questions I wanted to ask my sister, but it would have been unwise to attempt any of them in the circumstances.

It was when we were about halfway through with the kitchen floor that Mary Alice said in a quick low tone, 'Now Teresa, mind what I say! Your Nana knows what I think, and she's inclined to agree. Josephine no more has Aids than I have, and if she stays around here she'll be in more trouble than she's ever seen in her life. Whatever the truth of her situation, she'll be better off over in England!'

I glanced over at Nana, on her knees, brushing.

'That's right,' she said.

'Listen to me now,' went on Mary Alice. 'It'll be nothing but a mistaken sense of loyalty or kindness or whatnot that wants to keep her here. She says she's made arrangements to leave – it's the only bit of sense she's shown so far. You see to it that she goes! Don't let your Mam be persuaded into letting her stay!' The three of us, on all fours, exchanged conspiratorial looks. I got the message that we weren't to discuss it any more just then.

So this was the fulfilment of the O'Shea prophecy made to me on that day Josie had raided the fridge. Josephine Carmody had finally overstepped the mark.

On the side of the sceptics with Brendan were now Mary Alice and Nana, the real heavyweights. In the 'Don't knows' camp were Mam, myself and Father. Grace couldn't believe her sister would lie over such a terrible thing, and Denise, given Josie's lifestyle, thought the Aids story far more likely than the vague 'blood disease'. With no medical evidence to go on, the more charitable – or gullible – amongst us would be obliged to continue to give her the benefit of the doubt, while the sceptics attacked us for pandering to her pathological need for attention and making her worse. She was effectively dividing the family.

After a while, I thought to ask the question that had

got lost some way back. 'How did you and Mrs O'Shea get here, Nana? Did you have a lift – you never drove Mrs O'Shea's car?'

Mary Alice's car has been sitting in the garage ever since her husband died ten years ago. She has a nephew of hers look it over once in a while, and take it out for a spin, but she's never been known to start it up herself though it's rumoured that she knows the trick of it.

'*We* didn't drive it—' said Nana.

Mary Alice clapped a hand to her false teeth, and spoke through her fingers. 'I forgot all about her! She'll have been sitting up there waiting for us to come out, and she'll have seen that tall fellah leaving and be thinking the worst has happened to us!'

With surprising agility she and Nana leapt up from their knees, abandoning dustpan and brush, and crowded out of the door. Then all three of us stood squinting up the track to where the ageing Cortina might have been. It was a light colour, and we'd have been able to see it clearly in the dusk if it had been there.

'She's gone to the Gardaí!' Nana said. 'She must have thought he'd murdered us in there!'

'She's a good girl. It's what I told her to do if we didn't come out like we said we would,' Mary Alice explained. 'And now we've got something to report, it'll save having to get a man out here in the morning. You can be sure that *so-called* journalist won't have rung the station. What's going to happen about the broken window? You can't leave the Riordans' place open like this.'

'Who's gone for the Gardaí?' I asked. 'Who drove you down here?'

'It was my granddaughter, Rita.'

We'd scrubbed up everything there was, and tidied down all the surfaces, before there was the sound of a car on the track again. If there's one thing Nana's generation really knows about, it's cleaning. Even Mam's contemporaries don't measure up, and the rest of us are nowhere.

We'd been wondering what to expect – two cars crammed with guards screaming down to our rescue? Or Rita nervously sneaking back with her father, having failed to find anyone on duty? The local guards' uniforms have a way of slipping off them when they think it's going to be a quiet night.

The car was the wrong colour and shape for the O'Shea vehicle, nor did it belong to the O'Malleys. A man and a woman got out and came down the track towards us. When they reached the cottage path, I recognized Rita with Joe Daly, one of the Ballycanty Gardaí. He wasn't in uniform, and the car was his own.

I've heard since that Joe has a soft spot for Rita. He's a young man, easy-going with a good sense of humour, and he'll generally go miles out of his way for you. It was the first time I'd ever seen him without a grin on his face. He managed a tight smile when he saw Nana and Mary Alice.

'Rita was afraid there might be some trouble here – glad to see you're all right, Mrs O'Shea – Mrs Foley. Hello Terry. Is it trouble with the journalists you've been having?'

He pointedly failed to address Josie, who had joined us on the doorstep. Only the day before he'd have been laughing and joking with her. Instead, he gave her one penetrating glare, and I knew he was seeing her with black wings and a reaping hook.

Rita said nothing, while Joe turned his attention to the broken window at Mary Alice's invitation. All other evidence of criminal damage had been so tampered with by the clean-up team as to have been totally obliterated. The cottage was tidier than ever before, and there was only the broken crockery in the bin for the guard to inspect.

'I'm off duty now,' he explained, 'but we're a bit short-handed at the station, and I happened to meet

Rita as I was passing so I thought I'd look into it for you.' I wondered what he'd have done if Rita's fears had proved true, and Oliver had been holding us all at gunpoint inside the cottage.

He took down a reluctant shadow of a statement with a pencil on the back of a paper bag we found in a drawer, but I'm sure it couldn't hold its head up as official. In outline it followed the version of the story Josie had given Nana, the blame firmly laid on the three mythical tinkers.

'Don't you worry about the window now, Mrs Foley,' Joe said as he pocketed the paper bag. 'I'm on my way to John Dooley's and I'll bring back a couple of lads after I've run you home. We'll fix something up for you until Mrs Riordan can get it seen to. I wouldn't think there'd be anyone coming back here tonight. Will anyone be staying here at all?'

That of course meant Josie.

'Not tonight,' said Nana firmly. 'My granddaughters will be coming back with me.'

There was some discussion as to how six of us were going to return to Ballycanty with Josie's luggage which she refused to leave on account of the designer labels. Perhaps she suspected Oliver might creep back in the dead of night and take his revenge by snipping them all out.

I was asking myself how the rival Angels of Death – the innocent and the not-so-innocent – would get on squeezed in the back seat shoulder to shoulder, when the lights of a second car appeared up by the gateposts at the top of the track. In all the excitement I'd completely forgotten Brendan. When I glanced at my watch it was after half ten, and I was glad we hadn't had to rely on him to rescue us from Oliver.

Joe failed to see Brendan in charge of a moving vehicle, so nothing was said about licences, and while we were deciding who was to go in which car, the two Angels of Death faced each other in the kitchen – the pale fair one you could see through with the wispy hair and shining contact lenses, and the pale dark one with eyes opaque as hell.

'Hello, Josephine,' said Rita, in her soft clear voice.

'Hello Rita,' Josephine said, in her smoky actressy tones.

Rita seemed to think she should say something more. In the whole of the world there probably was only one common piece of ground between them, and Rita knew it even if Josie didn't. She gave a quiet nervous giggle. 'I hear you've been having a bit of trouble with the press . . . I know what it's like!'

'I've heard you do. It's the price of fame, I suppose.'

Rita's faint smile faded, and she looked at Josie steadily. 'Oh, no!' she said. '*I* never wanted it!'

I'd say the score was one-nil – to Rita.

It was decided Josie, Nana, the luggage and I would go back with Brendan, and Joe would take Rita and Mary Alice back to the Gardaí station where Rita had left the car.

Before they set off, Mary Alice couldn't resist one parting shot in Josie's direction.

'I'd steer clear of that journalist type in the future if I were you, Josephine. I didn't like the look of him at all, and neither did your grandmother. I wouldn't put it past him to have done all the damage himself.'

'Oh no, Mrs O'Shea,' said Josie firmly. 'It was the tinkers.'

Their eyes met. I could see Josie in the light from the cottage doorway, challenging Mary Alice to call her a liar. It was as compelling an example of the irresistible force and the immovable object as you'd ever come across.

Without a Revelation straight from heaven beamed down direct on 36 Dunmore Road to short-circuit Josie's deviousness, Mary Alice is never quite going to know the truth.

* * *

We turned off the lights and locked the door. Nana gave the key to Joe Daly so that he could cope with the window repairs more easily when he returned later, with whoever he had found to volunteer for the job. Then the O'Shea party left, while we stood about waiting for Brendan with his brilliant mathematical mind to solve the problem of Josie's baggage and the space available. Behind us the edge of the cliff drew a dark line along the brighter sea. There was a moon, and stars, and the air was fresh and cool. Of the cottage, tucked down to our right in the folds of the cliff, we could see only the roof. The slates shone under the moon.

I had plenty to occupy my mind and while away the minutes – Josie, Oliver, what might have happened . . . Sean Butler's role in the newspaper story that had been the catalyst to the evening's events . . . Then I thought about Mary Alice. I didn't care if she was a visionary, clairvoyant or what. If it hadn't been for Mrs O'Shea and the Lord's inspirations, I didn't like to think what might have happened at the Riordans' cottage that night.

'Wasn't it extraordinary the way Mary Alice turned up with Nana in the nick of time?' I commented to Josie as we waited for Brendan. 'You being on her mind all day, and that!'

'Extraordinary my arse,' said Josie. 'She's just a mean-minded busybody spoiling to give me another lecture.'

TWENTY-ONE

Of course, like the O'Malleys, we had our press siege,
only this time it was less than no fun at all, and twice
the length. I have no comprehension how anybody can
want to be famous. Even with the doors locked and the
curtains drawn, our most trivial actions were up for
public scrutiny as though by right. Jacky Dooley continued to deliver the papers, but we could none of us
bring ourselves to open them when every fleeting
facial expression, every chance word would be
snapped up, chewed over and then spat out, labelled
'Caring' or 'Uncaring', 'Guilty' or 'Not Guilty', depending on the angle and the popular demand of the
moment. The whole family was on trial, not just Josie,
and what the reporters couldn't find out they invented.

On sheer numbers, I have to give it to Rita: she'd
attracted the greater crowds. But Josie had a higher
proportion of photographers and TV cameramen in her
entourage. They began to arrive the night she returned
home from the cottage.

We spent much of that night debating the best time
for Josie to leave. Mam of course was for keeping her
indefinitely, and warning Brendan with her eyes not to
issue any open challenges. Josie herself was keen to go,
but Father forbade her to set foot outside the house
while there was any chance of being mobbed by the
press. Only if there were no sign of reporters the following day could she make a bolt for it, in the hopes
that it would take them some time to catch up with her.
She could lose herself more easily in England. But if
too many advance members of the pack had already
turned up, she would be better hiding at home.

I'd never seen Father so stern. 'There are to be no more interviews while you're under our roof, Josie! It'll be old news in a couple of days, and then they'll leave us alone for a bit. So there's to be no stirring it up, do you hear? What you do when you go to England is your own business, but you're not going to be talking to any of them while you're here.'

Brendan, avoiding Mam's glare, suggested she might find sanctuary with Mary Alice. 'It'd be the last place they'd think of looking. You'd be fine holed up there in Mrs O'Shea's back bedroom! She'd be only too pleased to have you. Will I give her a ring for you?'

To Josie, the suggestion wasn't even mildly humorous. She had no choice but to stay at home (my bedroom again) until such time as the reporters left, or in defiance of Da she succumbed to an interview.

Since Father, Brendan and I had to leave the house for work and educational purposes, like Father Jim and the O'Malleys we lived a cat and mouse life with the press. When caught, the official line to all enquirers was that Josie had already left for England, and no, we didn't know her whereabouts just at present.

We warned Grace to stay away. There was no point in exposing her and the children to the newsfiends outside. We even cut down on the telephone calls, and were careful what information we exchanged in case the line was tapped.

Keeping Josie cooped inside the house wore everyone out – the cameras exerted an evil magnetic pull on her. Although she spent most of her time in our darkened living-room sulking in front of the television with either Mam or Nana on guard, watching pictures of the outside of our house in the news bulletins, she did manage to slip out once – so heavily scarfed and shaded that the reporters were onto her in the flash of a bulb. We only found out about it the next morning, when, after a four-day siege, they started to leave.

The press exodus seemed like a miracle until we

discovered Josie's picture in the paper again, an Irish one this time. There were no further shocking revelations; just speculation about her story, her plans for the future, the effect she'd had on the entire population of Ballycanty – *and the promise of a further in-depth interview once she got back to England.*

Any lingering patience (mine and Mam's) with her and her illness was stretched thin. Father had transferred himself to Brendan's camp the night she flatly refused to have a doctor visit her to take a blood test. Now he told her that since she couldn't resist the lure of the press, she was free to follow them.

Mrs Power opened the door when I rang.

She was surprised. 'Hello Terry!' Then she looked at the flowers I was carrying.

'I'm sorry to bother you, Mrs Power, but I had a few things for Tom. I heard that he wasn't seeing any visitors at the moment, and I wondered if you'd take them along when you thought it was a good time. I brought him a book, but perhaps he isn't well enough to look at it just now.'

She smiled, but not with her eyes. 'That's kind of you. Come in for a minute.'

I didn't want to go in. I wasn't sure whether Tom wanted his family to know that he had told me the truth about himself. Perhaps they blamed me for being part of the Carmody clan that had bred Josie, the destroyer of their son – or had he kept her name from them?

We went into the living-room and sat down.

'I've brought him this,' I said for something to fill the silence. 'He used to like cartoons.'

'I think you should take them round yourself,' she said. 'He was asking for you. He'd like to see you.'

'Me?' I was surprised he had expressed a particular desire to see me. I'd visited him briefly once since the revelations about Josie. We hadn't spoken directly of his relationship with her – I'd only made one oblique reference – and I wondered if he now wanted to talk about it.

'You know what's the matter with him, don't you?'

'Yes, Mrs Power. But I won't tell anyone. He told me in confidence.' It was a relief that there was no necessity to pick my way through that particular minefield any longer.

'How's your sister?'

Perhaps she saw us as companions in misfortune, and that was why she had asked me in. 'She's going back to England. She's to have some sort of treatment from a clinic there.'

She nodded. 'They say there's hope of controlling it at least with new drugs. I hear they're even trying thalidomide.'

'And Tom – what are they trying with Tom?'

She didn't say anything. She just smiled with her mouth. Her eyes said: it's too late for Tom now.

I had some trouble getting in to see Tom, though it was my third visit. The nurse on duty told me first that he wasn't having any visitors, only family. I almost gave up, but when she heard his mother had asked me to come, she went to see if he was awake and let me have five minutes.

He looked much worse, if that were possible, than the last time I had seen him – gaunt, his eyes huge, and very weak. The unshaven stubble round his jaw made his whole face look grey.

'Thanks,' he said, when he saw me. 'Did my mother ask you to come?'

His voice was like a whisper through dead summer grass.

'I would have dropped these in for you anyway,' I said. 'I just wanted to check with her that you were seeing visitors. They nearly wouldn't let me in.' I showed him the cartoon book, opening the pages for him. They were offbeat, showing up the oddity of human attitudes rather than making any topical comment. They seemed to appeal to him, and he smiled a couple of times. I felt a desperate gratitude – to the artist, I suppose – that they could be counted a success.

'You look a bit of a ruffian, Tom,' I said, hoping to amuse him a bit more. 'Is this the Power version of designer stubble?'

'Disguise,' he said. 'Terry, you said something last time you came, and I've been trying to make sense of it. About Josie and you.'

'Yes?' I wasn't sure which aspect of the matter he meant.

'That you felt guilty because of her. Why?'

His voice was so weak, it took a long time to roll out the words.

I'd thought it was obvious. 'Because of Josie. Because it must be her fault.'

The eyebrows drew together, and he looked at me. His eyes were like his mother's. He said, 'It wasn't your sister, Terry. I've never had sex with a woman.'

Stupidly, I didn't take in what he was telling me.

I suppose it should have been obvious, but my mind flittered back to a silly conversation in Whelan's, when we'd first heard the rumour. 'Was it drugs then, Tom?'

He really did smile at that, the first fleeting amusement I'd seen in his face.

'Dear Terry!' he said. 'I'm gay. Surely you're the one person in Ballycanty not to know it?'

I stared at him. First because I had to readjust to what he was telling me, and to fit it into the context of the Tom I knew, and second because no-one, not one single person had so much as hinted homosexuality. Even Father Lafferty in the famous sermon hadn't stirred up any gossip about it. I could only suppose it had something to do with the fact that Tom had spent much of his time for the last two or three years studying out of Ireland.

'But Tom – no-one's said that – no-one has any idea! Most of them don't know anything about you – they think you've got – you've got summer flu or something!'

'Rumour flies,' he said bitterly. 'How can they not know?'

It would be the final irony if the whole town had been talking about it, and Teresa Carmody, one of the first incubators of the egg that hatched so many rumours, hadn't heard. As one of the now infamous Carmody family, had I been relegated to an outer circle? I couldn't believe so. Oonagh, or Rose, would have passed on everything.

'I promise you, I haven't heard one single whisper about it.'

I couldn't tell what he was thinking; his eyes were blank. 'Well, how's that now. Wouldn't you just know it? Me one claim to fame and notoriety and they all ignorant of it!'

'What about your parents – do they know?'

'Mam does. I haven't told my father. I let him think it was an infected needle.'

'You told him you took drugs? *Did* you?'

'No. But I thought he could handle that better. I told him it was only once, as an experiment like, and I must have been unlucky.'

'Perhaps he doesn't believe you.'

'I don't know. He might suspect it was some girl, but he wouldn't want to find out. You don't go to hell for taking drugs. Not yet, anyway.' He turned towards me with an effort, his eyes now pleading. 'You won't say anything, Terry, will you? I don't want it to get out so that my father might know. He couldn't bear it.'

'Of course I won't tell.'

No. I wouldn't tell a soul. It was Tom's secret, not mine. I was shocked; I still couldn't adjust to it.

When I left, my mind was full of questions – had he had only one partner – or many? Had he been to the gay clubs in England – was it in one of those he met the man who had infected him – did he know who had given him Aids? Lots of questions, but I could never ask them.

Josie was getting ready to leave for England, painting again. I watched her spread her left hand, fingers splayed on the dressing-table in my bedroom, carefully transferring the pearl gloss from the brush to each nail.

Press activity had died down very quickly, only the occasional reporter still turning up on the doorstep. Following Father's curt outburst regarding Josie's departure, her decision to leave had been immediate. She would catch the night ferry to England, stay with Denise, or some friends in Oxford, and visit a local clinic. Still no-one had challenged her openly over the Aids story, and she had given nothing away despite the climate of scepticism in which she had been forced to exist.

I remained an agnostic, resigned to letting Time Reveal All. Except for one thing I had to have out with her before she left.

'I saw Tom Power in hospital last evening.'

'How is he?'

'Not good. I didn't stay long.'

She held up her hand, scrutinizing it, and then put it down on the table again.

'He told me something very odd,' I said.

'Oh?'

I could see her attention was absorbed by what she was doing, and by whatever it is that continually goes on in her head.

'He told me he'd never slept with you. He even laughed, it seemed so peculiar to him.' I'd promised not to say why.

'He's lying.' She kept painting, the long shining stripes of pink covering each nail.

'No, Josie. You're lying. I believe Tom. If you've got Aids you can't have got it from him, and he can't have got it from you. He told me it's been two years now since he tested HIV positive—'

She didn't let me finish. 'So? Why do you believe him and not me?' She was instantly on the defensive, angry and challenging.

'He has no reason to lie. Why should he? If he's this bad, he really must have had it for some time. And Tom's no Angel of Death. He'd never risk infecting someone else once he knew. You don't suddenly get ill with Aids – although lots of people walk round with it for a while without even knowing they have it. Then they get one infection after another, and they begin to suspect. Some of them can go on for a long time after that.'

'So what are you saying?'

It was difficult to be clear when I couldn't give her the true reason I was so certain her story about Tom was nonsense. 'That whoever else you might have slept with, you haven't had anything to do with Tom Power. Among other things, I don't think you're ill enough – your relationship with him would have to have happened over two years ago. But why lie about him?'

She was fiddling with the pot now, ducking the brush in and out. 'The fact that he might have had Aids longer than me doesn't prove anything – except that he gave it to me and not the other way round.'

'He told me he had never slept with you, and he got it in the first place from an infected needle – you're a liar, Josie, and I'm beginning to agree with a lot of other people round here after the way you've behaved. You haven't got Aids at all!'

'You have no proof of what he says.'

An accusation like mine isn't the sort of thing over which you can afford to make a mistake. But I was sick of her lies and evasions. We were both dealing in lies, of course, but mine were to protect Tom's secret. My last stinging shot was meant to be my exit, but she stopped me.

'Don't go. All right, perhaps it wasn't Tom—'

'You mean you couldn't see who he was in the dark?

Come on, Josie, pull the other one! You'll be telling me next you've caught Alzheimer's from sitting next to some old fellow at a bus stop. Don't take me for a *complete* eejit, Josephine Carmody!'

She sank back in her chair, dropping her head between her hands. I couldn't see her face; her hair fell forward like a curtain. 'It was easier to explain that way. I don't know who I got it from—'

'You mean – you can't even remember the men you've slept with? I'm not surprised, after—' I was going to say after leading the sort of life the photographs revealed, but thought better of it. 'Why on earth involve Tom?'

'I haven't involved Tom. You're the only person who knows besides Aggie – unless you've spread it around!'

She's too good at putting you on the defensive. I was growing really angry now.

'Of course I haven't – I didn't even discuss it with Tom until he guessed from something else I said! Doesn't he of all people have a right to know if lies are being told about him?'

Lies. Could anyone ever tell the whole truth about it? There was a lie in what I'd just told her about Tom and the drugs. There were lies in what she'd told me – no end to them.

'You're actually saying,' I went on, 'that you gave a quick explanation, which wasn't the truth though it reflected directly on somebody else, because it was easier than the details of your sordid love life in England?'

She began to shout. 'Yes I am! Who are you to judge me? How do you know what it's like to wake up every morning and know that you're alive but it's only a kind of stay of execution? I could have slept with only one man in my life, and I could still have caught it! You're in no position to play the spotless virgin, Terry. How many men have you slept with and you're only twenty-one? It could have been any one of them for you too!'

She began to cry, long racking sobs, that turned the

scene from a sisters' quarrel into a confrontation with death that tore at me too. And she was right. I couldn't cast any stones.

I came back into the room, and knelt down at the corner of the dressing-table beside her. I put my fingers round her wrist, to let her know I was still there. She had her hands over her face, and wouldn't take them away.

'Josie, I'm not trying to condemn you. I only want to understand. Why involve Tom?'

'I didn't think it would make any difference to him. And I told you, it seemed like a quick way to explain it. I wasn't thinking straight after all that press harassment. I just didn't want you, my sister, to believe I was leading a bad life in England—'

Her voice tailed off, like a little girl's, and I saw it for the childish excuse it was.

'I already knew about the photographs – or have you forgotten?'

She sniffed, and drew the back of one hand across her eyes. 'Oh that. Well, there was that, but I only did it once. I needed the money. There were other men I went out with.'

'And what about this summer, since you've come home? The place has been buzzing with talk about you – all the men you see.'

'Oh the Ballycanty gossips!' She was full of contempt. 'Don't they just love to find a wicked woman to persecute with their stories? It'll never change. All the hypocrisy in this town'd whitewash the world's sepulchres!'

'Why have you given them so much to talk about then? What about Gus, and Oliver, and the others?'

'I just wanted a bit of fun. I have no money, no job, and no car. What else am I supposed to do?'

I could see that from Josie's point of view I was making judgements about her, and that in the circumstances it was no help to anyone. The fact was she had led an awful life, wandering on the borders of kinky

223

sex and prostitution, going with any men who would pay for her one way or another. What was the point of condemning her now? The only useful line of argument would be to make her see that she shouldn't put anyone else at risk by sleeping around – if she *did* have Aids, and I was still none the wiser about that – no matter what her financial predicament.

'How did you pay for the cottage, if you hadn't any money?'

'I didn't. Aggie paid.'

'For you to stay here, on your own?'

'I hadn't anywhere else to go.' She began to cry again.

'But Josie, you could have come home any time.'

'I didn't want Mam to know.'

'You could have told her some other reason. You're good at thinking up—' I was going to say excuses, and the real word at the back of my head was lies, but I changed it. 'You're very imaginative.'

'I want to be independent as long as I can . . .'

'How can you call yourself independent when you were relying so much on Aggie?'

The discussion, full of inconsistencies and the usual evasions, went round in circles. Again I struggled to put it down to the way in which worry about her illness must have affected her brain, and again doubt nagged at me. I wished there was someone who could settle the whole thing for me one way or the other.

The only people who knew most of the story, as I did, were Denise and Aggie. I had the feeling Denise wanted to distance herself as much as possible from the responsibility of Josie, who could at any hour turn up on her doorstep. Which left Aggie – or, as a last resort, Great-Uncle Danny. But Danny was back with his nuns, and Aggie into her autumn school term.

TWENTY-TWO

It rained on the day of Tom Power's funeral.

There was a Requiem Mass in St Dominic's, on the hill a couple of miles outside Ballycanty, where the Power family graves are. The church was full of live bodies, packed shoulder to shoulder, steaming slightly and smelling of damp wool, moving only to stand, or sit, or kneel, and I couldn't believe Tom's dead body was lying cold in the middle of the aisle. I had a horrible fantasy of opening the coffin to make sure – of squeezing out of the bench across everyone's knees and prising up the wooden lid.

My imagination stuck there. I couldn't visualize what Tom would look like; very pale perhaps – with the black shadows of that last hospital visit under his eyes – but asleep? I had read a story once of Padre Pio: how the marks of the stigmata he had borne most of his life disappeared from his body within half an hour of his death. Would Tom too be changed by death, the lines of his suffering fading away until he became again the person I had met striding across the clifftop near Josie's cottage, thinner but recognizably himself? Or would he revert further, to someone like the bright-eyed fourteen-year-old who had spent his time crouching among the gorse prickles with his father's binoculars?

Tom's eyes were shut under the lid of the wooden box; that I could know for certain. I had heard once that in laying out a body they stuff cotton wool up the corpse's nose. Would they have done that to him, and you able to see it? I didn't want to look at him like that. In my mind I pressed the 'pause' button on my fantasy,

225

and I saw myself quite clearly – a fair-haired young woman in a dark coat – frozen with my crowbar before the altar, and the pale wood of the coffin just splintering upwards, to open a narrow dark gap between the box and the lid.

Tom's is the first funeral I have ever been to where the dead person was one of my own friends. Nana Foley spends most of her time going to funerals. She says she knows more people in the churchyard now than she does in the streets of the town, and her conversation with her living contemporaries is all of deaths and wakes and funerals. There was no wake for Tom.

There are not so many wakes now, not the real old sort that Nana told me about. They had the best ones out in the country, where the wildest things used to happen. Nana told me about how a man she knew died sitting up. She was a girl then, and her brother Albert was alive. Albert loved the obsequies – plumes, horses, glass-sided hearses and all – and he'd go along whether he was personally known to the corpse or not, following the whole thing through to the last shovel.

In Nana Foley's words, 'Albert and a friend of his went along to the wake of a man who died sitting up in bed. I can't tell you his name for the life of me, but he was a cousin of Queenie Riordan's. Well now, there was the body stretched out on the bed as though he'd just had a flat-iron over him. Albert and his friend were surprised. They'd heard about the sitting up, and they knew about the rigor mortis and that, and they'd fully expected to see your man holding court with the family gathered round.

'Now there were quite a few people in the room, come to pay their respects. Some of them were kneeling by the bed, saying a prayer, and Albert and his friend had to wait a bit to get a look in. Some people like to stay a while, to impress the world with their piety and that, and it was late in the afternoon when Albert had gone there. So it was dusk when they finally got near the bed. Now the boys had a look at the body – eyes closed, hands jined. Then they saw a piece of string. Don't ask me where this piece of string went, but Albert saw it was tied to the bedpost and for a bit of divilry, just to see what would happen like, he cut it with his penknife. Then there was a wake all right – your man sat up!

'Consternation!' (Nana at this point would raise her eyes for emphasis and tip back in her chair) 'I don't know if it was the candlelight in the place or what, but they all thought he'd opened his eyes. There was screams and people jumping and falling over each other in their haste and fighting to get out of the door. Albert was after giving himself a bit of a fright as well as the rest of them, and it was all round as far as Cork in a couple of days. That was a wake, all right!'

I wore an old blouse to Tom's funeral, under my black coat. It was too tight, but I wore it because I'd had it when I was fifteen and Tom and I were still knocking around together, on the cliffs, and doing each other's homework. I hadn't worn it for years, but it brought the Tom I had known closer. I shut my mind on the fantasy of the dark box and tried not to think of him as I'd last seen him, gaunt, an old young man with his eyes full of fever and looking at me. Looking. Looking.

You know that no-one goes lightly out of this world, and that at the Requiem Mass the words you're saying should be rooted in the belief that the dead go on to a further existence with God, where they have a future which is dark to you but clear at last to them. You know this, if for no other reason than it's the promise Christ made on the cross to the dying thief. This is what Uncle Danny said to me some time afterwards. I'm not sure how many of us in the church believed all that any more.

The priest at St Dominic's is in his seventies, and not one to let a man go straight to heaven. He keeps to the old-fashioned view, like Father Jim, and unlike Father

Aidan who has ditched Purgatory along with Limbo and the miraculous Feeding of the Five Thousand. So poor Tom was destined for the Halfway Fires, according to Father Haggerty. I wondered what he'd have said if he'd known what Tom really died of. Or perhaps it didn't matter because Tom confessed it all in the hopes of a glimpse of the harps and the crowns. I've yet to meet one person who'd be satisfied with such unfashionably élitist headgear and a musical instrument they couldn't play, even if it is one of the national symbols.

Oonagh believes in reincarnation, though that's probably because she fancies she's been Queen Maeve of Connaught, rather than some insignificant Kathleen or Katie who died of starvation during the potato famine. I'm not sure about reincarnation. It sounds too good to be true, getting extra lives like that. I'd prefer to think that you just flick out, like a switch. Anyway, how do we know what Tom really believed in, apart from fear, at the end?

It's music at funerals that makes you cry. When there's no music, you can keep going. You can make yourself think in certain ways – cynical, if you don't like the priest, or comic if you describe to yourself the thoughts and motives of the other mourners. You can even imagine discussing some unsuitable hat with a friend afterwards, or you can look for cracks in the church roof and guess at the next sum they'll be appealing for. But the music doesn't let you off lightly. If it was the favourite tune of the deceased – even if it's Enya singing to herself in some multi-layered cloud land miles away from the harsher realities – it sets you off.

The Irish are bad church singers, as I've said before. We had a hymn, and a local choir to sing it, so there was no need to join in. And sure enough before they got to the second verse the tears were streaming down my face.

*   *   *

It was Brendan who took me out of church. I was glad we weren't too near the front; it was a long walk down the side aisle to the door, with everyone looking.

Brendan said outside, 'Look at you, disgracing the family like this. You know even his sisters aren't crying? What do you have to make an exhibition for?' He kept his arm round me.

There was such a catch in his voice, I knew we'd both be crying if I didn't pull myself together.

'At least it shows I care, Brendan Carmody. Aren't you the stony-hearted one!'

He blew his nose after that, but neither of us said anything about colds.

We walked over to the church wall. St Dominic's overlooks the town from its hill. I wondered if all the houses were empty that day, so many people had turned out for the funeral. There were cars parked at angles all the way down the hill road, like a child's multicoloured toy snake.

Rough heathland rolls down over the rocks to where the first houses begin. It was all grey – grey walls, grey roofs, grey veils of water – but for a few gorse flowers, yellow in the rain. The air was too damp and cold to carry their waxy sweetness.

'You know what I was thinking in there?' Brendan asked, after a silence while the drizzle wetted our hair and our dark coats. 'The words of that hymn . . . that the day was very short for Tom, and it could be short for any of us, but we never somehow believe it will be until it happens. You saw Tom last of any of us – did he believe it was the end or was he still hoping?'

'Don't, Brendan. You'll start me off again.'

'But Terry, if you don't face the serious things at times like now, when will you face them?'

Brendan has a kind of ruthless courage in him. I don't know whether it's because he's still very young in himself and there are no softer edges yet, or it's because he's Brendan. For myself, I don't know when

I'll be ready to face questions like that. God, if he ever existed, has become even more inscrutable. I thought of Father Haggerty's voice saying, 'God's ways are not our ways. His thoughts are above our thoughts.' That always sounded like a nun's cop-out to me: you ask about God, and Sister Mary-Whoever says, 'God is a Mystery, dear,' and that is the end of the discussion as far as she's concerned. I was feeling bitter with the Mystery called God. Why did he take one of the nicest people in the whole town and leave all the rest of us, malicious little troublemakers, to stew in the nasty juice we'd made of it? Why didn't he punish us with medieval pitchforks for all the calumny and detraction that had been going on, and leave Tom alone?

'I'm ashamed of this summer,' I said. 'It's been the worst summer of my life.' I don't know if that was an answer to his question, but he didn't say anything.

'You know what?' I said then. 'Oonagh and I started the whole rumour about the sports team and the trip to England.'

'You did?' He was surprised out of his grief.

'I'm so sorry, Brendan. I felt so guilty afterwards. We'd no idea it was all going to get out of hand like that.' It'd been weighing on me more and more heavily since the trip had been cancelled.

'It isn't me you should be confessing to.'

I had to go on about it, get it all off my chest, as though telling someone else would make it all right again. 'We took it all so lightly at first – it was a joke. We were playing with death . . .' And then I was caught out again. 'Tom is so *young* – it isn't fair!'

'Don't.'

We stood, looking out across the dips and rises of the gorse through the rain to the hills beyond, and the waterpainted clouds above them. We didn't go back into the church.

We stood by the wall while they carried the coffin out of the double church doors and round out of sight to the plot they'd opened, next to the other deceased members of the Power family. I saw Declan in the file of mourners that were walking to the graveside. He was studying in Cork again for the autumn, and he must have come home specially.

I didn't want to see Declan. He belonged to the part of the summer of which I was most ashamed. I thought he would follow the coffin with the rest of them, but he came straight towards me. It was too late to hurry away.

He looked tall and serious in his black raincoat, with the collar turned up to his ears and a sheen of rain on his hair. He had his hands thrust into his pockets, and he walked with his eyes cast down looking out for the uneven ground. He could have been a businessman visiting from the city, or a dark-haired foreign tourist. A stranger.

He and Brendan shook hands. I didn't even hear what they said, for thinking how I should escape.

'Terry—' He was holding out a hand to me, formal and polite.

I put my own into it mechanically. I felt nothing but embarrassment, and the vehement wish *I don't want to be here*, as though the sheer intensity of my desire could whisk me away from the consequences of everything that had ever passed between Declan and myself.

'Declan.'

'I was hoping to see you.'

'Oh.'

I looked around for Brendan, but he was already marching away with blatant tact towards the tail-end of the mourners.

'Oh,' I said again, to fill in the gap and feeling un-utterably foolish. 'Not the best time to meet, is it?'

'Why haven't I seen you?'

With the pain of Tom's death still inside me, it didn't seem the right time to discuss my relationship with Declan. I was on the point of giving a flippant reply as a defence against anything like seriousness with him, when I heard Brendan's words in my head – *if you don't face the serious things at times like now, when will you face them*? Death and Love. The big ones.

'We'd better not stay here – we'd better go nearer the rest of them. We don't want any more gossip just yet . . .' I started to walk in the opposite direction to the one Brendan had taken, to come round the church the other way and join the mourners by the grave.

Declan walked beside me, both of us with our attention on the tussocks of graveyard grass and avoiding the drunken Celtic crosses and snags of rusted iron railing that marked out some of the plots.

'Why haven't you rung me?' he asked. 'I've left you phone messages.'

I could lie and get myself out of it. I could make a joke of it and build another barrier. I could tell the truth and deal with the consequences.

I found a path between the rows of marble chips and plastic flowers, and followed it, Declan behind me. When I saw it led to the far boundary of the churchyard, I stopped again. It ended abruptly at the stone wall that separates sanctified ground from the rough pagan heath of the old Celts and the Fairies. The heath is wild and unproductive, and full of life – gorse and birds and rabbits – but there are no paths over it.

'This is the wrong way,' I said foolishly. The other mourners were over to our left and behind us now. No doubt, separated from them and in full view, we were making targets of ourselves. Turning to go back, I caught sight of one smart hat already angled in our direction. Then I found myself facing Declan.

'Why didn't you answer my messages?'

'I don't know – I – we can't talk now—'

'Don't you want to see me again? You really don't want us to go on, is that it?'

With the hats (two of them now) and the rain, and the way I was feeling, I didn't want him to sound so urgent about it, or hurt. If only it could all go away, and

Declan and I could meet again for the first time at some vague date in the future, and it could all be different!

'It was going so wrong,' I said, when he waited for an answer. 'I don't know what I wanted, but it wasn't that—'

He tried to put his arm round me and draw me against his coat. 'I'll do whatever you want, Terry. I want us to begin again. Can't we try?'

I pushed him away. 'How? We started at the wrong end of everything.' And then I said, 'I don't even know you!'

He looked as though I'd suddenly scratched his face, or screamed abuse at him in an alien language, but even as the words came out I realized it was the truth.

I *didn't* know Declan the real person. I knew Declan the desirable disco partner, sexy Declan, Declan with whom to make jokes about other people, but I hadn't cared about any of his ideas, or his beliefs, or his feelings in all the time I'd been going out with him. Asked what he believed about abortion, or child labour, or cutting down Amazonian rain forests or the EC, I could only make a wild guess. I hadn't been interested in finding out about anything but his body.

It was at exactly that moment I had another of those fantasies – unexpected – just a flash this time. I was looking down into the open grave. The coffin was resting on the bare earth, and the lid was off. The sides were fluted with white silk like a lampshade, and Tom was stretched out in the middle of it in a white First Communion shirt and dark trousers, with his hands crossed on his chest. His face was white but he looked about seventeen.

Then I saw myself from above, still from a viewpoint at the very edge of the grave among the other mourners, all of whom were looking down, watching – watching *me* lying on top of Tom's dead body. I too looked on as though at a stranger on a television screen. The woman that was me touched the face and the lips with her mouth and slid her tongue along the jawline, and then opened the shirt running her hands over the chest and down over the small horizontal furrows of the ribcage and the cold flesh of the stomach, unfastening the waist of the trousers, and then the zip, and all the while the smell of cold earth in her nostrils. I could sense the disapproval all round me – but that was all it was – disapproval. No-one made a move to stop what was going on, though they were all tut-tutting in their heads.

'Terry?'

I was so shocked at myself that for a moment I couldn't speak. Me – with Tom! Wherever did *that* weird necrophiliac fantasy come from? A voice in my mind asked the question. It was my own voice, and Oonagh's and Rose's, all mixed up with the intonations borrowed from some cartoon character. Behind it, I wasn't asking myself that question at all, but wondering what such a kink in the imagination could actually mean. Was it something merely fed in by a film I'd seen and long forgotten – a blip in the memory files? Or an unexpected hint from my most deeply buried self about my true feelings for Tom . . . I couldn't believe that. Perhaps then in my subconscious I was trying to claim him back from the sexual orientation that had cut him off from women and children of his own. Or – even less acceptably – receiving a stark message about my real feelings for corpses. Making love to Tom's dead body! After all I knew about him, and after all the pain and waste of his death! I began to ask myself if I was no better than Josie. At least her sexual fantasies had been acted out with the living.

My expression must have been strange, or perhaps Declan was reacting to my last remark, but he was looking at me intently. I could see beyond him to the mourners.

'Turn round, will you?' I said, giving him a push in the chest. 'Start walking back – we're being looked at.'

He did turn round then, and I walked behind trying to dismiss the image of myself in the coffin with Tom, until, at a fork in the path which would have led us to the graveside, he continued the way we had come.

'It's this way!' I called after him, not too loudly. But he continued walking.

In the end, I followed him.

We sat in Declan's dark blue car, out of the drizzle. 'They'll gossip whatever we do. Why did you say that – about not knowing me?'

It was pointless to evade him again. 'Can't you see it's all sex?' I said. 'And we've spoilt that.' I watched the tiny dots of moisture gather together on the windscreen to form big drops and run down the glass. 'And now how can it be the same for any of us any more?'

'You mean . . . because of Tom's death?'

'It's not just Tom. It's all of us. I can't really explain, but it's to do with *our* world, the world we're making to live in.'

That image of myself in the grave was still there, flashing up like a slide picture that cast its own tainted light over all my thoughts. I was tempted to tell Declan about it; but it would be the first time I had ever let him into a part of my mind that even I didn't understand, and I didn't want to open myself to his judgement. It was hard to lose what might remain of his good opinion. I couldn't bring myself to describe my own necrophiliac fantasy, so instead I told him about Josie and the pornographic photos, and what remained of the life she led that hadn't hit the papers, since the topic was related to what I wanted to say and shed no lurid light on me personally. That was of course cowardly, but even so it was the first time I'd talked to him about any subject that deeply mattered to me.

He didn't comment, merely receiving the facts as I related them. I felt suddenly that I could trust him. He wouldn't be telling anyone else about Josie.

We sat there in an awkward silence for a while. I

watched the rain and Declan looked in the driving mirror at the long trail of cars down the hill behind him.

Perhaps he was deciding he had had enough of the Carmodys – of Terry who had been out merely for a one-night stand, and her degenerate sister who had been, notoriously now, into a whole series of them. I felt obliged to defend us both, to sum up what I'd thought I wanted to say. The mourners would surely be coming away from the grave soon; it doesn't take so long to recite the prayers and lower the coffin in. I didn't want anybody wondering what was going on, seeing me in Declan's car when my family had all been at the grave.

'I don't know how to explain this, Declan, but . . . well, I feel the whole of our world is wrong. We're all going in the wrong direction . . . I think I want to stop now, and face the other way even if no-one else does, because ahead of us is only a kind of ugliness, and destruction.' I stared fixedly at the sliding drops on the windscreen. It was easier not to see his expression. 'Josie with her pornography and her awful men, Tom with Aids, the rest of us dancing round changing partners for sex as though we were all at some demonic *ceilidh* . . . Does any of this make any sense to you?'

'Maybe it does.'

'You'd better keep your girl in Cork,' I said. 'She's probably more what you want.' I felt a pang as I said it, remembering all that agonizing over the *other woman* in the long discussions with Oonagh.

'There isn't a girl in Cork any more. That finished before the summer. I'd rather be with you.'

I remembered the words I'd said to Oonagh in Whelan's. About rejecting someone you didn't want to have sex with any longer and how hard it was to hurt them, and I think at that moment I moved one inch closer to knowing what real love for Declan might be like.

'I don't want a lover,' I said, hoping he would understand exactly what I meant by that, and not wanting to spell it out because there were no words that were wound-free. 'I would like . . . someone to talk to!' I almost laughed as I said it. *As if*, I thought to myself, *I hadn't been talking all summer*!

He gave a wry smile. 'You mean drawn swords down the middle of the bed – that kind of thing?'

'I mean no beds. No sex.'

'You know James Joyce wrote somewhere that love between man and man was impossible because there must not be sexual intercourse, and friendship between man and woman was impossible because there must be sexual intercourse.'

He said it half as a joke, but he was looking at me. I had hurt him, I could see it in his eyes. Perhaps it wasn't the sex itself he minded about, but the implied rejection of *him* – everything that he was summed up in that one act. I couldn't soften it; he must know now that I had rejected him from the start – I'd never bothered to see him as another being. I'd treated him as though he were just a body – a body as Tom's now was, with no living thoughts, or feelings, or hopes, or beliefs.

As I looked at him, I saw in his eyes some of those thoughts, and feelings, though I couldn't interpret them. I discovered then that I did want to know what they were – and that, in spite of the waste of the summer, there was one positive thing I could salvage from the wreck of my relationship with Declan O'Connor: the fact that I really liked him.

'I want a good friend I can talk to,' I repeated.

'Try again?'

Brendan rapped on Declan's side window. 'Are you coming home with us, Terry, or will Declan bring you?'

'I'm coming with you!' I was already opening my door, but I couldn't leave in quite such indecent haste without a word to Declan, though I needed time to think about my reply.

He wound the window down, and I went round to say goodbye.

'Is it the gossips or me you're so keen to avoid?'

I tried to laugh. 'I'd like notice of that question!'

'I'll ring you.'

'Yes.'

'And this time, answer! Even if it's to tell me to go to hell.'

TWENTY-THREE

It was tipping down with rain. Again. The earth and the plants that had been brown turned green, the rivers and sea that were blue turned brown and grey, and the streets shone and trickled and splashed with water. Ireland was herself.

I had my umbrella up, and a severely limited view of the pavement. A car drew up with careful slowness along the kerb beside me so as to minimize the tidal wave from the gutter, and the horn tooted. I peered out from under the umbrella. It was Aggie. She leaned across the passenger seat and wound down the window.

'Terry – hop in a minute! You're just the person I wanted to see!'

I got in backwards, shaking my umbrella, and slammed the door.

Aggie's summer freckles had already faded. Her cheeks were pink, and there were drops of rain caught in her loose curls of red hair. I was pleased to see her – Aggie is always so uncomplicated and cheerful. 'How are you, Aggie? We haven't seen you since Josie left!'

'Well, that's it. It's about Josie—'

'We haven't heard from her since she left for England. We keep ringing Denise, but there's been no contact there either. I just hope to God she's all right – we're so worried about her! Is she ill? Isn't she ill? What's happening?'

'Will you let me get a word in, girl? It's about Josie – I've had a letter from her.'

I stared at her. 'When? Why didn't you tell us?'

'Will you listen? I've only just got it. She isn't in England at all. She's gone to America!'

'Well Mam,' I said when I got home. 'You'll never believe it. THERE'S BEEN A MIRACLE IN BALLY-CANTY AT LAST.'

Mam, taking her cue from my sceptical tone, was prepared to be quietly amused.

'Ah, what rubbish. You've been seeing too much of Mary Alice.' She was scrubbing the potatoes for dinner, and didn't even look up.

'No. Only Aggie Riordan, and she doesn't joke. I mean it. Josie's *miraculously* well. There's nothing wrong with her.'

Mam did glance at me then, but I couldn't read her expression. 'Is this Aggie's view of the situation, or has Josie finally come out with the truth?'

'Josie? Tell the truth? Well now, Mam, that just might be a real miracle. But she's come as near to it as she ever will. She's as good as admitted she never had Aids at all. She says the doctors got it wrong when she was first tested. It was a mis-diagnosis.'

Brendan, predictably, was the first to react.

'Didn't I tell you it was all a pack of lies?' he crowed triumphantly. 'First it was skin cancer, then it was her leukaemia, then it was Aids and she was the Angel of Death with her face all over the national papers. Did anyone think to ask how she could have had all those men at death's door so quickly when none of us had seen her in Ballycanty for years?'

'She never said she had skin cancer. That was your idea.'

'No she didn't, but it just shows how gullible you are, Terry, if you believe she wasn't toying with the notion before she thought of something with a bit more drama to it. *Mis-diagnosis*! What does she take us all for – eejits like Terry?'

'Well Brendan, I have to admit it too,' Mam finally got out. 'It's true Terry and I were the only ones who were still prepared to give her the benefit of the doubt after all that flirting with the media while she was staying here. But it shows what kind and charitable people we are, even if we have been proved wrong in the end!'

No, I thought. *Not kind – or charitable – not me. I just knew something that you didn't, and the reasons for my belief were different from yours.*

From the sudden relief in Mam's voice, I knew a great darkness had been lifted from her.

'You'll never guess what she says she's doing now!' I said.

'Would it be wise to sit down for this, do you think?' Mam asked.

'Helping Mother Teresa's nuns.' That was Brendan.

'Not yet.'

'Then she's holed up with the Carmelites somewhere. I'll put any money on it – her next stunt will be religious.'

'That's just where you're wrong, Mr Knowall Carmody. Wait for it – she's in Hollywood, and she's got a part in a film!'

Brendan made a noise, loud and rude. 'Didn't I tell you? She's a screen goddess – now isn't that about as religious as you can get?'

Mam, arrested at the sink, just stared at me. I could tell she was still somewhere back in the Aids story.

'Aggie says Josie says some casting director met her with some friends in a restaurant, and he was *so* impressed by her he offered her a part.'

There was the loud tumbling noise of potatoes hitting the sink in a heap. Mam had given up. 'Wait a minute! Do we believe this? I think I'll have to have a drink!'

We sat at the kitchen table, Mam and I with our gin and tonics and Brendan with a glass of Murphy's.

'Now start at the beginning,' Mam directed. 'There's a lot of this that's still a mystery. What about poor Tom Power? I thought Josie told me he and she were supposed to have—'

So Mam had known that from Josie! 'No Mam. I found out all about that from Tom. He got Aids from injecting himself with drugs with an infected needle, the silly boy. He only did it the once.'

'Was that it?' said Brendan. 'I must say I thought it was something else. I heard a few rumours—'

I'd promised myself solemnly that I'd never listen to, or pass on, gossip again. I looked him firmly in the eye. 'Forget them. They're just talk. I had it from Tom himself before he died. So there never was an Angel of Death. Josie just hopped on to the bandwagon for the money they paid her.'

'Are you *sure* all this is true, Terry?' Mam said. 'Aggie obviously believes it, but is it Josie just putting a brave face on things after leaving here the way she did? It's a lot to live down – perhaps she is ill, though she hasn't got Aids!'

'Well, Aggie showed me the letter Josie wrote. It's her handwriting and it was posted in the right place. We won't know the truth until the film is on general release.'

Brendan looked at me across his glass. 'She won't be in it. You can bet your last Irish pound on that. Then she'll say they left her bit on the cutting-room floor.'

'But why did she do it to us – having us all running round her worried out of our minds?'

'That's *exactly* why she did it, Mam. Anything to be the centre of attention.'

'Ah no, Terry. She'd never be so callous as that—'

'Perhaps she *is* sick,' Brendan cut in again. 'Sick in the head.'

'You don't know what Josie's capable of, Mam,' I said. But I couldn't tell her what I'd been thinking of.

I wouldn't have guessed the depths of my sister's capabilities myself – but hadn't I seen the proof of it with my own two eyes in half a dozen photographs pushed to the back of a drawer? And hadn't I seen the real fear in *her* eyes when we'd been hiding up in the loft in the Riordans' cottage? Josie's capable of almost anything. She craves limelight the way a plant looks for sun, she has no scruples, and she can even persuade herself for a while that the lies she's telling are the truth.

Until, that is, she's found out. Or thinks, as Brendan said, of something more dramatic. She's a born actress. But Hollywood? We could none of us bring ourselves to believe it.

'She'll be leader of some crazy cult next, you mark my words!'

Brendan Carmody. Deputy prophet. No appointment needed.

Now there's one other interesting little story I have to tell you – but maybe it's something you've guessed already. I learned half of it from Rose, and the answer to the last bit of the puzzle from the culprit herself.

Rose and I met for our usual coffee in Whelan's one Saturday, not long after Tom's funeral. The three witches had been down to two for the weekend covens for some time, and this was because we knew Oonagh had reasons more compelling than shopping to be going to Dublin so many Friday nights. You'll have heard Dublin called a 'vibrant' city. What is really meant is sex. Oonagh had a man in Dublin.

'Oonagh told me something and she swore me to secrecy,' Rose said, leaning forward over the table. 'I've been dying to tell you!'

Irrepressible, unregenerate Rose! Nothing will ever make her serious. But I remembered my resolution. 'Perhaps you shouldn't when you promised her, Rose.'

'But it's something I think you ought to know. She'd have told you herself if she hadn't been such a coward.'

'If she swore you to secrecy, she obviously had no intention of telling me.'

'Well will I tell you, or won't I?' Rose asked herself, deliberating.

'I don't think you should.'

'Well I will. It's this. I know who Oonagh's man is!'

Oonagh had kept her new man a dark – and presumably handsome – secret. Beyond admitting to his existence, she'd refused to discuss him. Now I couldn't see why I shouldn't know as well as Rose. Surely just his *name* couldn't be the secret? I gave in to temptation. 'Who?'

'Someone we both know!' Rose was gleeful, dragging it out.

My mind went blank. I couldn't think of a single likely person. 'Who?'

'Sean – Sean Butler!'

I thought my eyes must be popping out on stalks. '*Sean*!' I shouted. 'Since when?'

We gave the usual squint round to see who was listening, and then leaned closer. 'Remember that weekend she went to stay with some cousin and was off work sick the Monday and Tuesday? She was in Dublin with Sean. And all those shopping sprees? She was in Dublin with Sean. And all these coffees just between the two of us?'

'*She was in Dublin with Sean.*' Chorus.

'*And*—' said Rose. '*And* – there's more!'

'Well you can't stop now,' I told her. 'I won't sleep for imagining what you might have said!'

'You know who got the story about your sister?'

'I do,' I told her, with some satisfaction. 'His name was in the paper and Josie herself told me – it was Sean.'

'And you know how he got onto her? Oonagh!'

I'd been slipping back into our old enjoyable ways until that point – the thrill of gossip, new titbits to feed on.

Then it changed.

Oonagh. I remembered how I had told Oonagh of Josie's 'illness'. I had told her what we all thought at the time – that it was some blood disease – and I had sworn her to secrecy.

Oonagh. I'd believed in her as my best friend. I'd

told her things I hadn't told Rose. I'd relied on her being older and wiser than me; relied on her sophistication, her judgement. You could say that while Rose and I confined ourselves childishly to egging each other on, Oonagh had been a leader, and I'd willingly followed.

I stared at Rose, tasting the bitter metallic tang of betrayal in the coffee I'd just sipped. Josie all over the papers. The skin-searing shame of her stories. The violent and very probably criminal Oliver trying to get at us in the attic. The press siege outside our home. All those had been the direct result of Oonagh telling her new boyfriend what she'd promised me she'd reveal to no-one. She must have suspected Aids – or perhaps – to give her the benefit of a pallid doubt – she just mentioned she knew someone with a blood disease in Ballycanty. To a journalist like Sean, a hint would be enough, and he'd already dropped heavy ones he was onto the identity of the Angel. Those had probably been bluff, of course, but there could be no doubting the consequences of Oonagh's revelation.

'Terry?' Rose examined me across the table. 'Say something.'

'I'm not surprised Oonagh doesn't want to tell me herself,' I said.

And it struck me again how Rose had just betrayed Oonagh's confidence.

I wasn't in a position to blame either of them. I hadn't been too good at keeping secrets either, but between Rose, Oonagh and me, bound into our little trinity, that hadn't been important. I believed we shared almost everything, living out our emotional lives in common like adolescents, testing everything against each other's experience, seeking each other's approval for our actions and reactions. Over the years we had become a single living entity, or so I had thought. Now I discovered that those old careless assumptions had already vanished with the summer, and I hadn't known it. I could see suddenly that

Oonagh had been living her life apart from us. I could see that I too now had my own secrets I wouldn't share. And Rose? Perhaps Rose was keeping her life to herself – perhaps she also had had a secret lover all through those long hot months when a madness seemed to have come to Ballycanty.

They say if you have a limb cut off there's no pain at first. I felt like that: aware that something was missing – there was a space where there had once been a vital part of my life – and sure it must hurt when I had recovered from the shock enough to feel it. I didn't know how I would face Oonagh again at work.

TWENTY-FOUR

Well, the gossip's faded away now – the old bird and its many offspring got terrible thin and died. Bits of the truth have come out, but no-one knows all of it, except perhaps Treesa Carmody Herself – and she wouldn't want to be boasting about it. There are things I can never tell anyone, though I share all the secrets with at least one other person. The real reason Tom got Aids only his mother and I know now; I know *she* knows, but she doesn't know *I* know. It's like a black joke.

Josie told Aggie of her sordid past, and I told Uncle Danny, and then Declan, so the four of us share that with my sister, except that only Declan knows I told Uncle Danny, and nobody knows I told Declan.

The frightening evening at Aggie's cottage with Josie and me clinging to each other and Oliver raging outside the door – I never told anyone about that, even Declan. Only Josie and I share it, though Nana Foley and Mary Alice – the latter in her unofficial role as Seer and Prophet, and official one as Town Busybody – might have their suspicions.

I had my scene with Oonagh in Our Ladies' Boxroom. Where else? I just came straight out with it.

'Why did you tell Sean Butler about Josie?'

She was standing directly in front of me at the mirror over the basin, and in the reflection her eyes met mine. She had a lipstick in one hand, halfway to her mouth, and her hand was still. She guessed at once how I had found out – there was no point discussing it. Her eyes were startled.

'I didn't tell him about Aids, Terry, I swear to you! I

didn't know until it all came out in the paper. I only mentioned about Josie twice – two completely different things, different times! He was asking a bit about you, and I mentioned your sister, and England and the parties and that. And then, another time it was, I told him she was ill, and they thought it might be leukaemia. He was the one put two and two together!'

'You promised me you wouldn't say anything!'

'Ah Terry, I know! It's that – well – I thought it was safe, just to mention it. I never thought he'd use it like that. I never knew it was supposed to be Aids.'

'You thought it was safe to mention it to a *journalist*?'

Oonagh – naïve?

She looked stricken. 'Terry, I know – I know what you're thinking! But Sean and me – well – Rose must have told you I've been seeing a lot of him?'

'You told us yourself there was a new man.'

'Well, I thought it might be different if we were – well, you know. You exchange confidences with people you're close to. He told me lots of things. I told him lots of things. It's really serious – as serious as me and Dan. He's the first man I've felt interested in since I broke up with Dan.'

And then she told me about her affair with Sean.

'I suppose he made quite a bit of money out of that report?' I said when she'd finished.

'I didn't ask,' she said.

I believed that.

'He thought the story would make a bigger splash in the English papers, and he was concerned that Josie should make something out of it one way or another. Any road, he probably won't be showing his face down here again, so you won't have to worry. You know what the gossips here would all be saying about him . . .'

'Yes, Oonagh,' I said. 'I know.'

We're still friends of course, and of course I've forgiven her. She was so anxious to explain it all, so anxious for the first time for my approval. It used to be the other way round.

We still see each other, we three witches – Rose, Oonagh and Terry – but not so often. Oonagh goes up to Dublin every weekend, and I – well, I have lots of other things to do now. I'd feel sorry for Rose, stuck in the old life more firmly than either of us, only she's the kind of person who'd make a party out of a week in Lough Derg in the middle of Lent, and the sympathy would be wasted on her.

I went up to Tom's grave again, at the end of October. I wanted to be there by myself, to say goodbye in a way that wasn't possible at a public funeral.

It was a long climb up to the churchyard on foot. The last time I'd made it with Brendan. We'd walked slowly, following the hearse, and the other cars, and the mourners who walked though the rest of the Carmody family had driven up. I wanted to walk it again. It was my pilgrimage, though I'd arranged to be picked up at the church afterwards.

The stone walls each side of the road are partly turfed over, and sprouting with brambles and bits of thorn bush. The blackberries tasted of rainwater, and fell apart in your fingers, staining them purple. Water was running down the tarmac under my feet, and the shower only eased off when I reached the churchyard.

It wasn't difficult to find Tom's grave. The old flowers are usually cleared away, but Tom's family had asked for them to be left so no-one had touched them since the funeral. There was no headstone yet, no green turf, only crumbled earth and flowers, dead in their rainspotted cellophane and spoilt ribbons.

Tom. Very dear Tom. A nice Irish boy. Twenty years ago, he would have been exactly that and no more – what he seemed. And he wouldn't have died – not of Aids, anyhow. Do all nice Irish boys have secrets these last days of the old millennium?

It seems to me that Ireland herself has become a

façade; behind all of us now there's a secret, and our lives don't stand up to examination in the way they might have done in Nana Foley's time. I'm not saying that Nana's generation were saints – there was plenty going on then, just as now – but they were different. Once there was Haunted Ireland, with its Ghosts and its Fairies; Holy Ireland, with its priests and saints and apparitions; Historic Ireland of the kings, and the brave rebels; Tourist Ireland with its crack, its harps and shamrock and its honesty and its easy-going ways. Nana's generation, in their lives and in their beliefs, kept in touch with those Irelands. Now they have gone. Our new rebels are thugs, or empty boys looking for a reason to live and a desperate fame. We none of us believe in the Church any more – either her teachings or her prelates – and the fairies have left in droves. The tourists are in for a shock too: we boast the best politicians money can buy, and their noble sentiments are filtering down to us bog peasants by the minute. We'll give you the harps and the shamrocks, but at a ruinous price and possibly imported from the Far East.

Today we have modern Ireland, Great New Eire, that has signed away fishing rights the richest in Europe for a mess of EU pottage – grants, directives, and divorce and abortion on demand. We don't have the last one quite yet, but we will.

Now you might wonder, is this Terry Carmody speaking, this Terry that we have come to know and love in the course of her book? No, of course it isn't. It's Nana Foley, with a not inconsiderable dose of Mary Alice O'Shea. But I'm thinking there might be a bit of sense in a few of the things they have to say, after all. And before I forget to tell you – I'm going back to college and after that I'll be applying for a university place to read history.

'Pigs might fly,' said my admiring brother when I told him. 'What do you want to do that for?'

I blamed Uncle Danny.

The sun has gone for a while. The dried-up grass is

green again, and we have as much Irish rain as we might wish to see. Mary Alice says the drought was a warning and there'll be worse to come if we don't heed it, but then she's settling back into her comfortable old role as Jeremiah after the shocking events of the summer. The rain has drowned our flying rumours – the whole black flock of them. We're none of us keen to talk about Aids any more, and it's hard to look poor Rita O'Malley in the eye (though she hasn't the squint). The Carmodys have been exposed to enough publicity to see them through future generations, and we've all got identity tags that'll outlast our gravestones.

I found I was saying all this aloud, to Tom. The rain had started again, finer this time, and was dripping off my umbrella. I gave him the sprays of late fuchsia I'd picked from the hedge. They grow wild in our part of Ireland. Then, I don't know why because I'm still not sure what I really believe, I said the prayer for the dead. Rest. Eternal rest, peace, perpetual light. No mention of harps and crowns. Light and peace. Isn't that what we all want? I could wish it with my whole heart for Tom.

I turned back towards the road. I could see a dark blue car starting up from the bottom of the long hill – Declan, coming to fetch me. I stood waiting for him, looking down on Ballycanty. Báile Cainte it is in the Gaelic. The Town of Talk.

THE END

KISS AND KIN

Angela Lambert

'A HIGHLY READABLE NOVEL ABOUT LOVE AND
LOSS'
Express on Sunday

Life for the newly widowed Harriet Capel is not
expected to hold any surprises. It will be spent
watching over the vicissitudes of her children's
marriages and relationships, and looking after the
grandchildren. That is, until she sees Oliver Gaunt
again. He is her daughter-in-law's father. The
relationship between the parents-in-law has always
been difficult since their children's wedding day
and few words have been spoken. When they meet,
they do not at first recognize one another, but the
physical attraction between them is powerful and
instantaneous. As their love affair gathers intensity
and pace, so do its consequences for the family as a
whole.

In *Kiss and Kin*, two generations walk a dangerous
tightrope between fidelity and parenthood, each
guarding past and present secrets, the revelation of
which, in the white heat of passion, may destroy
the carefully erected boundaries of tradition and
propriety.

'A WRY LOOK AT LOVE AFTER THE MENOPAUSE . . .
CANDID AND ENTERTAINING'
Mail on Sunday

'SPIRITED, SHREWD AND STYLISH'
The Scotsman

0 552 99736 6

BLACK SWAN

THE CUCKOO'S PARTING CRY

Anthea Halliwell

For Fidgie, a child of the pre-war years, the long school holiday stretched blissfully ahead. With her new friend Chaz as companion for idyllic summer days by the sea, she was able frequently to escape her edgy mother and her malicious older sister, Cly. Her father, mercifully, was away from home . . .

Through Fidgie's clear eyes the events of a brief hot spell in August unfold: her family and neighbours become involved in adultery, deception, and other, darker, misdemeanours. The eight-year-old is an engaging and lively narrator; swept along in her extraordinarily compelling tale, the reader will realize that underlying Fidgie's innocent accounts of family meals, fishing trips round the bay, tree-climbing and playing at May Queens, a very adult sub-text is developing. Its conclusion is both tragic and inevitable.

Anthea Halliwell's novel marks the emergence of a delightfully individual voice and a most original storytelling talent.

0 552 99774 9

BLACK SWAN

WRITING ON THE WATER

Jane Slavin

'BRILLIANT ON THE THEME OF OBSESSIONAL LOVE; FUNNY, SEXY, PAINFUL AND TOTALLY READABLE'
Fay Weldon

Ellen Millar is an independent soul. An actress whose star is in the ascendant, she also has a partially decorated flat, a mountain of debt and some very good friends to sustain her. Into the equation of her life comes Aedan, an Irishman some twelve years Ellie's senior. Their attraction is instant; their affair intense and all-consuming. This five-day courtship is the prelude to a life together, until Aedan returns to Belfast and realizes that some emotional entanglements are impossible to untie.

Jane Slavin conveys the agony of a broken heart and a restless mind with shocking clarity. In Ellen Millar, she has created a candid, witty and uncompromising narrator whose addiction to one man takes her close to madness.

0 552 99781 1

BLACK SWAN

A MISLAID MAGIC

Joyce Windsor

'I LOVED IT. I THOUGHT IT FRESH AND SHARP AND
FUNNY, WITH A MOST WONDERFULLY ECCENTRIC CHARM'
Joanna Trollope

All the beguiling charm of Dodie Smith's *I Capture the Castle*
combined with the witty view of Britain's upper classes
portrayed in Nancy Mitford's *Love in a Cold Climate*. A totally
compelling first novel which is funny, sad, and utterly
delightful.

Lady Amity Savernake, neglected, rather plain, and youngest
daughter of the Earl of Osmington, was seven years old when
her stepmother (disparagingly referred to within the family as
Soapy Sonia) took her to London, bought her a fitted vicuna
coat with a velvet collar, and introduced her (at the Ritz) to
Rudi Longmire, the genie who was to change their lives.

It was Rudi's idea that there should be a midsummer Festival of
Arts at Gunville Place. The ugly Dorset pile, seat of the
Savernakes, would be transformed into a pastoral paradise;
singers, actors, musicians and exotic visitors – as well as the
family – would bring enchantment into their world. As Rudi,
Master of Revels and Lord of Misrule, drew each and every one
of them into his exotic plans, so excitement spilled out into the
countryside. A dead may tree threw out leaves and blossomed.
The local white witch absentmindedly gave her pig a love
potion, and two village maidens were accosted in the woods by
a genuine Dorset Ooser.

And within the family it seemed the enchantment would solve
their various discontents. Soapy Sonia, Grandmother
Mottesfont, even Claudia, Amy's corrosive and rebellious sister,
bloomed in the midsummer revels. And young Amy watched
and listened and for a brief childhood span was given the magic
of complete happiness – a happiness she never forgot – not even
in the disruptive aftermath of that heady summer, or in the
years that followed.

'IT HAS ALL THE INGREDIENTS OF A FAIRY TALE . . .
WHIMSICAL . . . SHARPLY FUNNY IN PARTS'
The Times

0 552 99591 6

BLACK SWAN

A SELECTED LIST OF FINE WRITING
AVAILABLE FROM BLACK SWAN

THE PRICES SHOWN BELOW WERE CORRECT AT THE TIME OF GOING TO PRESS. HOWEVER
TRANSWORLD PUBLISHERS RESERVE THE RIGHT TO SHOW NEW RETAIL PRICES ON
COVERS WHICH MAY DIFFER FROM THOSE PREVIOUSLY ADVERTISED IN THE TEXT OR
ELSEWHERE.

R⋯⋯⋯⋯⋯⋯⋯⋯⋯⋯⋯⋯⋯⋯⋯⋯⋯⋯⋯ ublin,
I⋯⋯⋯⋯⋯ ⋯n usually ⋯⋯⋯⋯⋯⋯⋯ in coffee
sho⋯⋯, hanging around libraries, or walking the
streets of Dublin, making up stories.

Hidden Lies is her first novel and is an *Irish Times*
Top Ten bestseller.